TheChristmasBooksofMr   .M.A. Titmarsh

By
William Makepeace Thackeray

THE MULLIGAN (OF BALLYMULLIGAN), AND HOW WE WENT TO MRS. PERKINS'S BALL.

I do not know where Ballymulligan is, and never knew anybody who did. Once I asked the Mulligan the question, when that chieftain assumed a look of dignity so ferocious, and spoke of "Saxon curiawsitee" in a tone of such evident displeasure, that, as after all it can matter very little to me whereabouts lies the Celtic principality in question, I have never pressed the inquiry any farther.

I don't know even the Mulligan's town residence. One night, as he bade us adieu in Oxford Street,—"I live THERE," says he, pointing down towards Oxbridge, with the big stick he carries—so his abode is in that direction at any rate. He has his letters addressed to several of his friends' houses, and his parcels, are left for him at various taverns which he frequents. That pair of checked trousers, in which you see him attired, he did me the favor of ordering from my own tailor, who is quite as anxious as anybody to know the address of the wearer. In like manner my hatter asked me, "Oo was the Hirish gent as 'ad ordered four 'ats and a sable boar to be sent to my lodgings?" As I did not know (however I might guess) the articles have never been sent, and the Mulligan has withdrawn his custom from the "infernal four-and-nine-penny scoundthrel," as he calls him. The hatter has not shut up shop in consequence.

I became acquainted with the Mulligan through a distinguished countryman of his, who, strange to say, did not know the chieftain himself. But dining with my friend Fred Clancy, of the Irish bar, at Greenwich, the Mulligan came up, "inthrojuiced" himself to Clancy as he said, claimed relationship with him on the side of Brian Boroo, and drawing his chair to our table, quickly became intimate with us. He took a great liking to me, was good enough to find out my address and pay me a visit: since which period often and often on coming to breakfast in the morning I have found him in my sitting-room on the sofa engaged with the rolls and morning papers: and many a time, on returning home at night for an evening's quiet reading, I have discovered this honest fellow in the arm-chair before the fire, perfuming the apartment with my cigars and trying the quality of such liquors as might be found on the sideboard. The way in which he pokes fun at Betsy, the maid of the lodgings, is prodigious. She begins to laugh whenever he comes; if he calls her a duck, a divvle, a darlin', it is all one. He is just as much a master of the premises as the individual who rents them at fifteen shillings a week; and as for handkerchiefs, shirt-collars, and the like articles of fugitive haberdashery, the loss since I have known him is unaccountable. I suspect he is like the cat in some houses: for, suppose the whiskey, the cigars, the sugar, the tea-caddy, the pickles, and other groceries disappear, all is laid upon that edax-rerum of a Mulligan.

The greatest offence that can be offered to him is to call him MR. Mulligan. "Would you deprive me, sir," says he, "of the title which was bawrun be me princelee ancestors in a hundred thousand battles? In our own green valleys and fawrests, in the American savannahs, in the sierras of Speen and the flats of Flandthers, the Saxon has quailed before me war-cry of MULLIGAN ABOO! MR. Mulligan! I'll pitch anybody out of the window who calls me MR. Mulligan." He said this, and uttered the slogan of the Mulligans with a shriek so terrific, that my uncle (the Rev. W. Gruels, of the Independent Congregation, Bungay), who had happened to address him in the above obnoxious manner, while sitting at my apartments drinking tea after the May meetings, instantly quitted the room, and has never taken the least notice of me since, except to state to the rest of the family that I am doomed irrevocably to perdition.

Well, one day last season, I had received from my kind and most estimable friend, MRS. PERKINS OF POCKLINGTON SQUARE (to whose amiable family I have had the honor of giving lessons in drawing, French, and the German flute), an invitation couched in the usual terms, on satin gilt-edged note-paper, to her evening-party; or, as I call it, "Ball."

Besides the engraved note sent to all her friends, my kind patroness had addressed me privately as follows:—

MY DEAR MR. TITMARSH,—If you know any VERY eligible young man, we give you leave to bring him. You GENTLEMEN love your CLUBS so much now, and care so little for DANCING, that it is really quite A SCANDAL. Come early, and before EVERYBODY, and give us the benefit of all your taste and CONTINENTAL SKILL.

"Your sincere

"EMILY PERKINS."

"Whom shall I bring?" mused I, highly flattered by this mark of confidence; and I thought of Bob Trippett; and little Fred Spring, of the

Navy Pay Office; Hulker, who is rich, and I knew took lessons in Paris; and a half-score of other bachelor friends, who might be considered as VERY ELIGIBLE—when I was roused from my meditation by the slap of a hand on my shoulder; and looking up, there was the Mulligan, who began, as usual, reading the papers on my desk.

"Hwhat's this?" says he. "Who's Perkins? Is it a supper-ball, or only a tay-ball?"

"The Perkinses of Pocklington Square, Mulligan, are tiptop people," says I, with a tone of dignity. "Mr. Perkins's sister is married to a baronet, Sir Giles Bacon, of Hogwash, Norfolk. Mr. Perkins's uncle was Lord Mayor of London; and he was himself in Parliament, and MAY BE again any day. The family are my most particular friends. A tay-ball indeed! why, Gunter . . ." Here I stopped: I felt I was committing myself.

"Gunter!" says the Mulligan, with another confounded slap on the shoulder. "Don't say another word: I'LL go widg you, my boy."

"YOU go, Mulligan?" says I: "why, really—I—it's not my party."

"Your hwhawt? hwhat's this letter? a'n't I an eligible young man?— Is the descendant of a thousand kings unfit company for a miserable tallow-chandthlering cockney? Are ye joking wid me? for, let me tell ye, I don't like them jokes. D'ye suppose I'm not as well bawrun and bred as yourself, or any Saxon friend ye ever had?"

"I never said you weren't, Mulligan," says I.

"Ye don't mean seriously that a Mulligan is not fit company for a Perkins?"

"My dear fellow, how could you think I could so far insult you?" says I. "Well, then," says he, "that's a matter settled, and we go."

What the deuce was I to do? I wrote to Mrs. Perkins; and that kind lady replied, that she would receive the Mulligan, or any other of my friends, with the greatest cordiality. "Fancy a party, all Mulligans!" thought I, with a secret terror.

MR. AND MRS. PERKINS, THEIR HOUSE, AND THEIR YOUNG PEOPLE.

Following Mrs. Perkins's orders, the present writer made his appearance very early at Pocklington Square: where the tastiness of all the decorations elicited my warmest admiration. Supper of course was in the dining-loom, superbly arranged by Messrs. Grigs and Spooner, the confectioners of the neighborhood. I assisted my respected friend Mr. Perkins and his butler in decanting the sherry, and saw, not without satisfaction, a large bath for wine under the sideboard, in which were already placed very many bottles of champagne.

The BACK DINING-ROOM, Mr. P.'s study (where the venerable man goes to sleep after dinner), was arranged on this occasion as a tea- room, Mrs. Flouncey (Miss Fanny's maid) officiating in a cap and pink ribbons, which became her exceedingly. Long, long before the arrival of the company, I remarked Master Thomas Perkins and Master Giles Bacon, his cousin (son of Sir Giles Bacon, Bart.), in this apartment, busy among the macaroons.

Mr. Gregory the butler, besides John the footman and Sir Giles's large man in the Bacon livery, and honest Grundsell, carpet-beater and green-grocer, of Little Pocklington Buildings, had at least half a dozen of aides-de-camp in black with white neck-cloths, like doctors of divinity.

The BACK DRAWING-ROOM door on the landing being taken off the hinges (and placed up stairs under Mr. Perkins's bed), the orifice was covered with muslin, and festooned with elegant wreaths of flowers. This was the Dancing Saloon. A linen was spread over the carpet; and a band—consisting of Mr. Clapperton, piano, Mr. Pinch, harp, and Herr Spoff, cornet-a-piston arrived at a pretty early hour, and were accommodated with some comfortable negus in the tea- room, previous to the commencement of their delightful labors. The boudoir to the left was fitted up as a card-room; the drawing-room was of course for the reception of the company,—the chandeliers and yellow damask being displayed this night in all their splendor; and the charming conservatory over the landing was ornamented by a few moon-like lamps, and the flowers arranged so that it had the appearance of a fairy bower. And Miss Perkins (as I took the liberty of stating to her mamma) looked like the fairy of that bower. It is this young creature's first year in PUBLIC LIFE: she has been educated, regardless of expense, at Hammersmith; and a simple white muslin dress and blue ceinture set off charms of which I beg to speak with respectful admiration.

My distinguished friend the Mulligan of Ballymulligan was good enough to come the very first of the party. By the way, how awkward it is to be the first of the party! and yet you know somebody must; but for my part, being timid, I always wait at the corner of the street in the cab, and watch until some other carriage comes up.

Well, as we were arranging the sherry in the decanters down the supper-tables, my friend arrived: "Hwhares me friend Mr. Titmarsh?" I heard him bawling out to Gregory in the passage, and presently he rushed into the supper-room, where Mr. and Mrs. Perkins and myself were, and as the waiter was announcing "Mr. Mulligan," "THE Mulligan of Ballymulligan, ye blackguard!" roared he, and stalked into the apartment, "apologoizing," as he said, for introducing himself.

Mr. and Mrs. Perkins did not perhaps wish to be seen in this room, which was for the present only lighted by a couple of candles; but HE was not at all abashed by the circumstance, and grasping them both warmly by the hands, he instantly made himself at home. "As friends of my dear and talented friend Mick," so he is pleased to call me, "I'm deloighted, madam, to be made known to ye. Don't consider me in the light of a mere acquaintance! As for you, my dear madam, you put me so much in moind of my own blessed mother, now resoiding at Ballymulligan Castle, that I begin to love ye at first soight." At which speech Mr. Perkins getting rather alarmed, asked the Mulligan whether he would take some wine, or go up stairs.

"Faix," says Mulligan "it's never too soon for good dhrink." And (although he smelt very much of whiskey already) he drank a tumbler of wine "to the improvement of an acqueentence which comminces in a manner so deloightful."

"Let's go up stairs, Mulligan," says I, and led the noble Irishman to the upper apartments, which were in a profound gloom, the candles not being yet illuminated, and where we surprised Miss Fanny, seated in the twilight at the piano, timidly trying the tunes of the polka which she danced so exquisitely that evening. She did not perceive the stranger at first; but how she started when the Mulligan loomed upon her.

"Heavenlee enchanthress!" says Mulligan, "don't floy at the approach of the humblest of your sleeves! Reshewm your pleece at that insthrument, which weeps harmonious, or smoils melojious, as you charrum it! Are you acqueented with the Oirish Melodies? Can ye play, 'Who fears to talk of Nointy-eight?' the 'Shan Van Voght?' or the 'Dirge of Ollam Fodhlah?'"

"Who's this mad chap that Titmarsh has brought?" I heard Master Bacon exclaim to Master Perkins. "Look! how frightened Fanny looks!"

"O poo! gals are ALWAYS frightened," Fanny's brother replied; but Giles Bacon, more violent, said, "I'll tell you what, Tom: if this goes on, we must pitch into him." And so I have no doubt they would, when another thundering knock coming, Gregory rushed into the room and began lighting all the candles, so as to produce an amazing brilliancy, Miss Fanny sprang up and ran to her mamma, and the young gentlemen slid down the banisters to receive the company in the hall.

EVERYBODY BEGINS TO COME, BUT ESPECIALLY MR. MINCHIN.

"It's only me and my sisters," Master Bacon said; though "only" meant eight in this instance. All the young ladies had fresh cheeks and purple elbows; all had white frocks, with hair more or less auburn: and so a party was already made of this blooming and numerous family, before the rest of the company began to arrive. The three Miss Meggots next came in their fly: Mr. Blades and his niece from 19 in the square: Captain and Mrs. Struther, and Miss Struther: Doctor Toddy's two daughters and their mamma: but where were the gentlemen? The Mulligan, great and active as he was, could not suffice among so many beauties. At last came a brisk neat little knock, and looking into the hall, I saw a gentleman taking off his clogs there, whilst Sir Giles Bacon's big footman was looking on with rather a contemptuous air.

"What name shall I enounce?" says he, with a wink at Gregory on the stair.

The gentleman in clogs said, with quiet dignity,—

    MR. FREDERICK MINCHIN.

"Pump Court, Temple," is printed on his cards in very small type: and he is a rising barrister of the Western Circuit. He is to be found at home of mornings: afterwards "at Westminster," as you read on his back door. "Binks and Minchin's Reports" are probably known to my legal friends: this is the Minchin in question.

He is decidedly genteel, and is rather in request at the balls of the Judges' and Serjeants' ladies: for he dances irreproachably, and goes out to dinner as much as ever he can.

He mostly dines at the Oxford and Cambridge Club, of which you can easily see by his appearance that he is a member; he takes the joint and his half-pint of wine, for Minchin does everything like a gentleman. He is rather of a literary turn; still makes Latin verses with some neatness; and before he was called, was remarkably fond of the flute.

When Mr. Minchin goes out in the evening, his clerk brings his bag to the Club, to dress; and if it is at all muddy, he turns up his trousers, so that he may come in without a speck. For such a party as this, he will have new gloves; otherwise Frederick, his clerk, is chiefly employed in cleaning them with India-rubber.

He has a number of pleasant stories about the Circuit and the University, which he tells with a simper to his neighbor at dinner; and has always the last joke of Mr. Baron Maule. He has a private fortune of five thousand pounds; he is a dutiful son; he has a sister married, in Harley Street; and Lady Jane Ranville has the best opinion of him, and says he is a most excellent and highly principled young man.

Her ladyship and daughter arrived just as Mr. Minchin had popped his clogs into the umbrella-stand; and the rank of that respected person, and the dignified manner in which he led her up stairs, caused all sneering on the part of the domestics to disappear.

THE BALL-ROOM DOOR.

A hundred of knocks follow Frederick Minchin's: in half an hour Messrs. Spoff, Pinch, and Clapperton have begun their music, and Mulligan, with one of the Miss Bacons, is dancing majestically in the first quadrille. My young friends Giles and Tom prefer the landing-place to the drawing-rooms, where they stop all night, robbing the refreshment-trays as they come up or down. Giles has eaten fourteen ices: he will have a dreadful stomach-ache to- morrow. Tom has eaten twelve, but he has had four more glasses of negus than Giles. Grundsell, the occasional waiter, from whom Master Tom buys quantities of ginger-beer, can of course deny him nothing. That is Grundsell, in the tights, with the tray. Meanwhile direct your attention to the three gentlemen at the door: they are conversing.

1st Gent.—Who's the man of the house—the bald man?

2nd Gent.—Of course. The man of the house is always bald. He's a stockbroker, I believe. Snooks brought me.

1st Gent.—Have you been to the tea-room? There's a pretty girl in the tea-room; blue eyes, pink ribbons, that kind of thing.

2nd Gent.—Who the deuce is that girl with those tremendous shoulders? Gad! I do wish somebody would smack 'em.

3rd Gent.—Sir—that young lady is my niece, sir,—my niece—my name is Blades, sir.

2nd Gent.—Well, Blades! smack your niece's shoulders: she deserves it, begad! she does. Come in, Jinks, present me to the Perkinses.— Hullo! here's an old country acquaintance—Lady Bacon, as I live! with all the piglings; she never goes out without the whole litter. (Exeunt 1st and 2nd Gents.)

LADY BACON, THE MISS BACONS, MR. FLAM.

Lady B.—Leonora! Maria! Amelia! here is the gentleman we met at Sir John Porkington's.

[The MISSES BACON, expecting to be asked to dance, smile simultaneously, and begin to smooth their tuckers.]

Mr. Flam.—Lady Bacon! I couldn't be mistaken in YOU! Won't you dance, Lady Bacon?

Lady B.—Go away, you droll creature!

Mr. Flam.—And these are your ladyship's seven lovely sisters, to judge from their likenesses to the charming Lady Bacon?

Lady B.—My sisters, he! he! my DAUGHTERS, Mr. Flam, and THEY dance, don't you, girls?

The Misses Bacon.—O yes!

Mr. Flam.—Gad! how I wish I was a dancing man!

[Exit FLAM.

MR. LARKINS.

I have not been able to do justice (only a Lawrence could do that) to my respected friend Mrs. Perkins, in this picture; but Larkins's portrait is considered very like. Adolphus Larkins has been long connected with Mr. Perkins's City establishment, and is asked to dine twice or thrice per annum. Evening-parties are the great enjoyment of this simple youth, who, after he has walked from Kentish Town to Thames Street, and passed twelve hours in severe labor there, and walked back again to Kentish Town, finds no greater pleasure than to attire his lean person in that elegant evening costume which you see, to walk into town again, and to dance at anybody's house who will invite him. Islington, Pentonville, Somers Town, are the scenes of many of his exploits; and I have seen this good-natured fellow performing figure-dances at Notting-hill, at a house where I am ashamed to say there was no supper, no negus even to speak of, nothing but the bare merits of the polka in which Adolphus revels. To describe this gentleman's infatuation for dancing, let me say, in a word, that he will even frequent boarding-house hops, rather than not go.

He has clogs, too, like Minchin: but nobody laughs at HIM. He gives himself no airs; but walks into a house with a knock and a demeanor so tremulous and humble, that the servants rather patronize him. He does not speak, or have any particular opinions, but when the time comes, begins to dance. He bleats out a word or two to his partner during this operation, seems very weak and sad during the whole performance, and, of course, is set to dance with the ugliest women everywhere.

The gentle, kind spirit! when I think of him night after night, hopping and jigging, and trudging off to Kentish Town, so gently, through the fogs, and mud, and darkness: I do not know whether I ought to admire him, because his enjoyments are so simple, and his dispositions so kindly; or laugh at him, because he draws his life so exquisitely mild. Well, well, we can't be all roaring lions in this world; there must be SOME lambs, and harmless, kindly, gregarious creatures for eating and shearing. See! even good- natured Mrs. Perkins is leading up the trembling Larkins to the tremendous Miss Bunion!

MISS BUNION.

The Poetess, author of "Heartstrings," "The Deadly Nightshade," "Passion Flowers," Though her poems breathe only of love, Miss B. has never been married. She is nearly six feet high; she loves waltzing beyond even poesy; and I think lobster-salad as much as either. She confesses to twenty-eight; in which case her first volume, "The Orphan of Gozo," (cut up by Mr. Rigby, in the Quarterly, with his usual kindness,) must have been published when she was three years old.

For a woman all soul, she certainly eats as much as any woman I ever saw. The sufferings she has had to endure, are, she says, beyond compare; the poems which she writes breathe a withering passion, a smouldering despair, an agony of spirit that would melt the soul of a drayman, were he to read them. Well, it is a comfort to see that she can dance of nights, and to know (for the habits of illustrious literary persons are always worth knowing) that she eats a hot mutton-chop for breakfast every morning of her blighted existence.

She lives in a boardinghouse at Brompton, and comes to the party in a fly.

MR. HICKS.

It is worth twopence to see Miss Bunion and Poseidon Hicks, the great poet, conversing with one another, and to talk of one to the other afterwards. How they hate each other! I (in my wicked way) have sent Hicks almost raving mad, by praising Bunion to him in confidence; and you can drive Bunion out of the room by a few judicious panegyrics of Hicks.

Hicks first burst upon the astonished world with poems, in the Byronic manner: "The Death-Shriek," "The Bastard of Lara," "The Atabal," "The Fire-Ship of Botzaris," and other works. His "Love Lays," in Mr. Moore's early style, were pronounced to be wonderfully precocious for a young gentleman then only thirteen, and in a commercial academy, at Tooting.

Subsequently, this great bard became less passionate and more thoughtful; and, at the age of twenty, wrote "Idiosyncracy" (in forty books, 4to.): "Ararat," "a stupendous epic," as the reviews said; and "The Megatheria," "a magnificent contribution to our pre- Adamite literature," according to the same authorities. Not having read these works, it would ill become me to judge them; but I know that poor Jingle, the publisher, always attributed his insolvency to the latter epic, which was magnificently printed in elephant folio.

Hicks has now taken a classical turn, and has brought out "Poseidon," "Iacchus," "Hephaestus," and I dare say is going through the mythology. But I should not like to try him at a passage of the Greek Delectus, any more than twenty thousand others of us who have had a "classical education."

Hicks was taken in an inspired attitude regarding the chandelier, and pretending he didn't know that Miss Pettifer was looking at him.

Her name is Anna Maria (daughter of Higgs and Pettifer, solicitors, Bedford Row); but Hicks calls her "Ianthe" in his album verses, and is himself an eminent drysalter in the city.

MISS MEGGOT.

Poor Miss Meggot is not so lucky as Miss Bunion. Nobody comes to dance with HER, though she has a new frock on, as she calls it, and rather a pretty foot, which she always manages to stick out.

She is forty-seven, the youngest of three sisters, who live a mouldy old house, near Middlesex Hospital, where they have lived for I don't know how many score of years; but this is certain: the eldest Miss Meggot saw the Gordon Riots out of that same parlor window, and tells the story how her father (physician to George III.) was robbed of his queue in the streets on that occasion. The two old ladies have taken the brevet rank, and are addressed as Mrs. Jane and Mrs. Betsy: one of them is at whist in the back drawing-room. But the youngest is still called Miss Nancy, and is considered quite a baby by her sisters.

She was going to be married once to a brave young officer, Ensign Angus Macquirk, of the Whistlebinkie Fencibles; but he fell at Quatre Bras, by the side of the gallant Snuffmull, his commander. Deeply, deeply did Miss Nancy deplore him.

But time has cicatrized the wounded heart. She is gay now, and would sing or dance, ay, or marry if anybody asked her.

Do go, my dear friend—I don't mean to ask her to marry, but to ask her to dance.—Never mind the looks of the thing. It will make her happy; and what does it cost you? Ah, my dear fellow! take this counsel: always dance with the old ladies—always dance with the governesses. It is a comfort to the poor things when they get up in their garret that somebody has had mercy on them. And such a handsome fellow as YOU too!

MISS RANVILLE, REV. MR. TOOP, MISS MULLINS, MR. WINTER.

Mr. W. Miss Mullins, look at Miss Ranville: what a picture of good humor.

Miss M.—Oh, you satirical creature!

Mr. W.—Do you know why she is so angry? she expected to dance with Captain Grig, and by some mistake, the Cambridge Professor got hold of her: isn't he a handsome man?

Miss M.—Oh, you droll wretch!

Mr. W.—Yes, he's a fellow of college—fellows mayn't marry, Miss Mullins—poor fellows, ay, Miss Mullins?

Miss M.—La!

Mr. W.—And Professor of Phlebotomy in the University. He flatters himself he is a man of the world, Miss Mullins, and always dances in the long vacation.

Miss M.—You malicious, wicked monster!

Mr. W.—Do you know Lady Jane Ranville? Miss Ranville's mamma. A ball once a year; footmen in canary-colored livery: Baker Street; six dinners in the season; starves all the year round; pride and poverty, you know; I've been to her ball ONCE. Ranville Ranville's her brother, and between you and me—but this, dear Miss Mullins, is a profound secret,—I think he's a greater fool than his sister.

Miss M.—Oh, you satirical, droll, malicious, wicked thing you!

Mr. W.—You do me injustice, Miss Mullins, indeed you do.

[Chaine Anglaise.]

MISS JOY, MR. AND MRS. JOY, MR. BOTTER.

Mr. B.—What spirits that girl has, Mrs. Joy!

Mr. J.—She's a sunshine in a house, Botter, a regular sunshine. When Mrs. J. here's in a bad humor, I . . .

Mrs. J.—Don't talk nonsense, Mr. Joy.

Mrs. B.—There's a hop, skip, and jump for you! Why, it beats Ellsler! Upon my conscience it does! It's her fourteenth quadrille too. There she goes! She's a jewel of a girl, though I say it that shouldn't.

Mrs. J. (laughing).—Why don't you marry her, Botter? Shall I speak to her? I dare say she'd have you. You're not so VERY old.

Mr. B.—Don't aggravate me, Mrs. J. You know when I lost my heart in the year 1817, at the opening of Waterloo Bridge, to a young lady who wouldn't have me, and left me to die in despair, and married Joy, of the Stock Exchange.

Mrs. J. Get away, you foolish old creature.

[MR. JOY looks on in ecstasies at Miss Joy's agility. LADY JANE RANVILLE, of Baker Street, pronounces her to be an exceedingly forward person. CAPTAIN DOBBS likes a girl who has plenty of go in her; and as for FRED SPARKS, he is over head and ears in love with her.]

MR. RANVILLE RANVILLE AND JACK HUBBARD.

This is Miss Ranville Ranville's brother, Mr. Ranville Ranville, of the Foreign Office, faithfully designed as he was playing at whist in the card-room. Talleyrand used to play at whist at the "Travellers'," that is why Ranville Ranville indulges in that diplomatic recreation. It is not his fault if he be not the greatest man in the room.

If you speak to him, he smiles sternly, and answers in monosyllables he would rather die than commit himself. He never has committed himself in his life. He was the first at school, and distinguished at Oxford. He is growing prematurely bald now, like Canning, and is quite proud of it. He rides in St. James's Park of a morning before breakfast. He dockets his tailor's bills, and nicks off his dinner-notes in diplomatic paragraphs, and keeps precis of them all. If he ever makes a joke, it is a quotation from Horace, like Sir Robert Peel. The only relaxation he permits himself, is to read Thucydides in the holidays.

Everybody asks him out to dinner, on account of his brass-buttons with the Queen's cipher, and to have the air of being well with the Foreign Office. "Where I dine," he says solemnly, "I think it is my duty to go to evening-parties." That is why he is here. He never dances, never sups, never drinks. He has gruel when he goes home to bed. I think it is in his brains.

He is such an ass and so respectable, that one wonders he has not succeeded in the world; and yet somehow they laugh at him; and you and I shall be Ministers as soon as he will.

Yonder, making believe to look over the print-books, is that merry rogue, Jack Hubbard.

See how jovial he looks! He is the life and soul of every party, and his impromptu singing after supper will make you die of laughing. He is meditating an impromptu now, and at the same time thinking about a bill that is coming due next Thursday. Happy dog!

MRS. TROTTER, MISS TROTTER, MISS TOADY, LORD METHUSELAH.

Dear Emma Trotter has been silent and rather ill-humored all the evening until now her pretty face lights up with smiles. Cannot you guess why? Pity the simple and affectionate creature! Lord Methuselah has not arrived until this moment: and see how the artless girl steps forward to greet him!

In the midst of all the selfishness and turmoil of the world, how charming it is to find virgin hearts quite unsullied, and to look on at little romantic pictures of mutual love! Lord Methuselah, though you know his age by the peerage—though he is old, wigged, gouty, rouged, wicked, has lighted up a pure flame in that gentle bosom. There was a talk about Tom Willoughby last year; and then, for a time, young Hawbuck (Sir John Hawbuck's youngest son) seemed the favored man; but Emma never knew her mind until she met the dear creature before you in a Rhine steamboat. "Why are you so late, Edward?" says she. Dear artless child!

Her mother looks on with tender satisfaction. One can appreciate the joys of such an admirable parent!

"Look at them!" says Miss Toady. "I vow and protest they're the handsomest couple in the room!"

Methuselah's grandchildren are rather jealous and angry, and Mademoiselle Ariane, of the French theatre, is furious. But there's no accounting for the mercenary envy of some people; and it is impossible to satisfy everybody.

MR. BEAUMORIS, MR. GRIG, MR. FLYNDERS.

Those three young men are described in a twinkling: Captain Grig of the Heavies; Mr. Beaumoris, the handsome young man; Tom Flinders (Flynders Flynders he now calls himself), the fat gentleman who dresses after Beaumoris.

Beaumoris is in the Treasury: he has a salary of eighty pounds a year, on which he maintains the best cab and horses of the season; and out of which he pays seventy guineas merely for his subscriptions to clubs. He hunts in Leicestershire, where great men mount him; he is a prodigious favorite behind the scenes at the theatres; you may get glimpses of him at Richmond, with all sorts of pink bonnets; and he is the sworn friend of half the most famous roues about town, such as Old Methuselah, Lord Billygoat, Lord Tarquin, and the rest: a respectable race. It is to oblige the former that the good-natured young fellow is here to-night; though it must not be imagined that he gives himself any airs of superiority. Dandy as he is, he is quite affable, and would borrow ten guineas from any man in the room, in the most jovial way possible.

It is neither Beau's birth, which is doubtful; nor his money, which is entirely negative; nor his honesty, which goes along with his money-qualification; nor his wit, for he can barely spell,—which recommend him to the fashionable world: but a sort of Grand Seigneur splendor and dandified je ne scais quoi, which make the man he is of him. The way in which his boots and gloves fit him is a wonder which no other man can achieve; and though he has not an atom of principle, it must be confessed that he invented the Taglioni shirt.

When I see these magnificent dandies yawning out of "White's," or caracoling in the Park on shining chargers, I like to think that Brummell was the greatest of them all, and that Brummell's father was a footman.

Flynders is Beaumoris's toady: lends him money: buys horses through his recommendation; dresses after him; clings to him in Pall Mall, and on the steps of the club; and talks about 'Bo' in all societies. It is his drag which carries down Bo's friends to the Derby, and his cheques pay for dinners to the pink bonnets. I don't believe the Perkinses know what a rogue it is, but fancy him a decent, reputable City man, like his father before him.

As for Captain Grig, what is there to tell about him? He performs the duties of his calling with perfect gravity. He is faultless on parade; excellent across country; amiable when drunk, rather slow when sober. He has not two ideas, and is a most good-natured, irreproachable, gallant, and stupid young officer.

CAVALIER SEUL.

This is my friend Bob Hely, performing the Cavalier seul in a quadrille. Remark the good-humored pleasure depicted in his countenance. Has he any secret grief? Has he a pain anywhere? No, dear Miss Jones, he is dancing like a true Briton, and with all the charming gayety and abandon of our race.

When Canaillard performs that Cavalier seul operation, does HE flinch? No: he puts on his most vainqueur look, he sticks his thumbs into the armholes of his waistcoat, and advances, retreats, pirouettes, and otherwise gambadoes, as though to say, "Regarde moi, O monde! Venez, O femmes, venez voir danser Canaillard!"

When De Bobwitz executes the same measure, he does it with smiling agility, and graceful ease.

But poor Hely, if he were advancing to a dentist, his face would not be more cheerful. All the eyes of the room are upon him, he thinks; and he thinks he looks like a fool.

Upon my word, if you press the point with me, dear Miss Jones, I think he is not very far from right. I think that while Frenchmen and Germans may dance, as it is their nature to do, there is a natural dignity about us Britons, which debars us from that enjoyment. I am rather of the Turkish opinion, that this should be done for us. I think . . .

"Good-by, you envious old fox-and-the-grapes," says Miss Jones, and the next moment I see her whirling by in a polka with Tom Tozer, at a pace which makes me shrink back with terror into the little boudoir.

M. CANAILLARD, CHEVALIER OF THE LEGION OF HONOR.

LIEUTENANT BARON DE BOBWITZ.

Canaillard. Oh, ces Anglais! quels hommes, mon Dieu! Comme ils sont habilles, comme ils dansent!

Bobwitz.—Ce sont de beaux hommes bourtant; point de tenue militaire, mais de grands gaillards; si je les avais dans ma compagnie de la Garde, j'en ferai de bons soldats.

Canaillard.—Est-il bete, cet Allemand! Les grands hommes ne font pas toujours de bons soldats, Monsieur. Il me semble que les soldats de France qui sont de ma taille, Monsieur, valent un peu mieux . . .

Bobwitz.—Vous croyez?

Canaillard.—Comment! je le crois, Monsieur? J'en suis sur! Il me semble, Monsieur, que nous l'avons prouve.

Bobwitz (impatiently).—Je m'en vais danser la Bolka. Serviteur, Monsieur.

Canaillard.—Butor! (He goes and looks at himself in the glass, when he is seized by Mrs. Perkins for the Polka.)

GRAND POLKA.

Though a quadrille seems to me as dreary as a funeral, yet to look at a polka, I own, is pleasant. See! Brown and Emily Bustleton are whirling round as light as two pigeons over a dovecot; Tozer, with that wicked whisking little Jones, spins along as merrily as a May-day sweep; Miss Joy is the partner of the happy Fred Sparks; and even Miss Ranville is pleased, for the faultless Captain Grig is toe and heel with her. Beaumoris, with rather a nonchalant air, takes a turn with Miss Trotter, at which Lord Methuseleh's wrinkled chops quiver uneasily. See! how the big Baron de Bobwitz spins lightly, and gravely, and gracefully round; and lo! the Frenchman staggering under the weight of Miss Bunion, who tramps and kicks like a young cart-horse.

But the most awful sight which met my view in this dance was the unfortunate Miss Little, to whom fate had assigned THE MULLIGAN as a partner. Like a pavid kid in the talons of an eagle, that young creature trembled in his huge Milesian grasp. Disdaining the recognized form of the dance, the Irish chieftain accommodated the music to the dance of his own green land, and performed a double shuffle jig, carrying Miss Little along with him. Miss Ranville and her Captain shrank back amazed; Miss Trotter skirried out of his way into the protection of the astonished Lord Methuselah; Fred Sparks could hardly move for laughing; while, on the contrary, Miss Joy was quite in pain for poor Sophy Little. As Canaillard and the Poetess came up, The Mulligan, in the height of his enthusiasm, lunged out a kick which sent Miss Bunion howling; and concluded with a tremendous Hurroo!—a war-cry which caused every Saxon heart to shudder and quail.

"Oh that the earth would open and kindly take me in!" I exclaimed mentally; and slunk off into the lower regions, where by this time half the company were at supper.

THE SUPPER.

The supper is going on behind the screen. There is no need to draw the supper. We all know that sort of transaction: the squabbling, and gobbling, and popping of champagne; the smell of musk and lobster-salad; the dowagers chumping away at plates of raised pie; the young lassies nibbling at little titbits, which the dexterous young gentlemen procure. Three large men, like doctors of divinity, wait behind the table, and furnish everything that appetite can ask for. I never, for my part, can eat any supper for wondering at those men. I believe if you were to ask them for mashed turnips, or a slice of crocodile, those astonishing people would serve you. What a contempt they must have for the guttling crowd to whom they minister—those solemn pastry-cook's men! How they must hate jellies, and game-pies, and champagne, in their hearts! How they must scorn my poor friend Grundsell behind the screen, who is sucking at a bottle!

This disguised green-grocer is a very well-known character in the neighborhood of Pocklington Square. He waits at the parties of the gentry in the neighborhood, and though, of course, despised in families where a footman is kept, is a person of much importance in female establishments.

Miss Jonas always employs him at her parties, and says to her page, "Vincent, send the butler, or send Desborough to me;" by which name she chooses to designate G. G.

When the Miss Frumps have post-horses to their carriage, and pay visits, Grundsell always goes behind. Those ladies have the greatest confidence in him, have been godmothers to fourteen of his children, and leave their house in his charge when they go to Bognor for the summer. He attended those ladies when they were presented at the last drawing-room of her Majesty Queen Charlotte.

GEORGE GRUNDSELL,
GREEN-GROCER AND SALESMAN,
9, LITTLE POCKLINGTON BUILDINGS,
LATE CONFIDENTIAL SERVANT IN THE FAMILY OF
THE LORD MAYOR OF LONDON.

        Carpets Beat.—Knives and Boots cleaned per contract.—
Errands
      faithfully performed—G. G. attends Ball and Dinner parties,
       and from his knowledge of the most distinguished Families
in
      London, confidently recommends his services to the
      distinguished neighbourhood of Pocklington Square.

Mr. Grundsell's state costume is a blue coat and copper buttons, a white waistcoat, and an immense frill and shirt-collar. He was for many years a private watchman, and once canvassed for the office of parish clerk of St. Peter's Pocklington. He can be intrusted with untold spoons; with anything, in fact, but liquor; and it was he who brought round the cards for MRS. PERKINS'S BALL.

AFTER SUPPER.

I do not intend to say any more about it. After the people had supped, they went back and danced. Some supped again. I gave Miss Bunion, with my own hands, four bumpers of champagne: and such a quantity of goose-liver and truffles, that I don't wonder she took a glass of cherry-brandy afterwards. The gray morning was in Pocklington Square as she drove away in her fly. So did the other people go away. How green and sallow some of the girls looked, and how awfully clear Mrs. Colonel Bludyer's rouge was! Lady Jane Ranville's great coach had roared away down the streets long before. Fred Minchin pattered off in his clogs: it was I who covered up Miss Meggot, and conducted her, with her two old sisters, to the carriage. Good old souls! They have shown their gratitude by asking me to tea next Tuesday. Methuselah is gone to finish the night at the club. "Mind to-morrow," Miss Trotter says, kissing her hand out of the carriage. Canaillard departs, asking the way to "Lesterre Squar." They all go away—life goes away.

Look at Miss Martin and young Ward! How tenderly the rogue is wrapping her up! how kindly she looks at him! The old folks are whispering behind as they wait for their carriage. What is their talk, think you? and when shall that pair make a match? When you see those pretty little creatures with their smiles and their blushes, and their pretty ways, would you like to be the Grand Bashaw?

"Mind and send me a large piece of cake," I go up and whisper archly to old Mr. Ward: and we look on rather sentimentally at the couple, almost the last in the rooms (there, I declare, go the musicians, and the clock is at five) —when Grundsell, with an air effare, rushes up to me and says, "For e'v'n sake, sir, go into the supper-room: there's that Hirish gent a-pitchin' into Mr. P."

THE MULLIGAN AND MR. PERKINS.

It was too true. I had taken him away after supper (he ran after Miss Little's carriage, who was dying in love with him as he fancied), but the brute had come back again. The doctors of divinity were putting up their condiments: everybody was gone; but the abominable Mulligan sat swinging his legs at the lonely supper- table!

Perkins was opposite, gasping at him.

The Mulligan.—I tell ye, ye are the butler, ye big fat man. Go get me some more champagne: it's good at this house.

Mr. Perkins (with dignity).—It IS good at this house; but—

The Mulligan.—Bht hwhat, ye goggling, bow-windowed jackass? Go get the wine, and we'll dthrink it together, my old buck.

Mr. Perkins.—My name, sir, is PERKINS.

The Mulligan.—Well, that rhymes with jerkins, my man of firkins; so don't let us have any more shirkings and lurkings, Mr. Perkins.

Mr. Perkins (with apoplectic energy).—Sir, I am the master of this house; and I order you to quit it. I'll not be insulted, sir. I'll send for a policeman, sir. What do you mean, Mr. Titmarsh, sir, by bringing this—this beast into my house, sir?

At this, with a scream like that of a Hyrcanian tiger, Mulligan of the hundred battles sprang forward at his prey; but we were beforehand with him. Mr. Gregory, Mr. Grundsell, Sir Giles Bacon's large man, the young gentlemen, and myself, rushed simultaneously upon the tipsy chieftain, and confined him. The doctors of divinity looked on with perfect indifference. That Mr. Perkins did not go off in a fit is a wonder. He was led away heaving and snorting frightfully.

Somebody smashed Mulligan's hat over his eyes, and I led him forth into the silent morning. The chirrup of the birds, the freshness of the rosy air, and a penn'orth of coffee that I got for him at a stall in the Regent Circus, revived him somewhat. When I quitted him, he was not angry but sad. He was desirous, it is true, of avenging the wrongs of Erin in battle line; he wished also to share the grave of Sarsfield and Hugh O'Neill; but he was sure that Miss Perkins, as well as Miss Little, was desperately in love with him; and I left him on a doorstep in tears.

"Is it best to be laughing-mad, or crying-mad, in the world?" says I moodily, coming into my street. Betsy the maid was already up and at work, on her knees, scouring the steps, and cheerfully beginning her honest daily labor.

OUR STREET

BY MR. M. A TITMARSH.

Our street, from the little nook which I occupy in it, and whence I and a fellow-lodger and friend of mine cynically observe it, presents a strange motley scene. We are in a state of transition. We are not as yet in the town, and we have left the country, where we were when I came to lodge with Mrs. Cammysole, my excellent landlady. I then took second-floor apartments at No. 17, Waddilove Street, and since, although I have never moved (having various little comforts about me), I find myself living at No. 46A, Pocklington Gardens.

Why is this? Why am I to pay eighteen shillings instead of fifteen? I was quite as happy in Waddilove Street; but the fact is, a great portion of that venerable old district has passed away, and we are being absorbed into the splendid new white-stuccoed Doric-porticoed genteel Pocklington quarter. Sir Thomas Gibbs Pocklington, M. P. for the borough of Lathanplaster, is the founder of the district and his own fortune. The Pocklington Estate Office is in the Square, on a line with Waddil—with Pocklington Gardens I mean. The old inn, the "Ram and Magpie," where the market- gardeners used to bait, came out this year with a new white face and title, the shield, of the "Pocklington Arms." Such a shield it is! Such quarterings! Howard, Cavendish, De Ros, De la Zouche, all mingled together.

Even our house, 46A, which Mrs. Cammysole has had painted white in compliment to the Gardens of which it now forms part, is a sort of impostor, and has no business to be called Gardens at all. Mr. Gibbs, Sir Thomas's agent and nephew, is furious at our daring to take the title which belongs to our betters. The very next door (No. 46, the Honorable Mrs. Mountnoddy,) is a house of five stories, shooting up proudly into the air, thirty feet above our old high-roofed low-roomed old tenement. Our house belongs to

Captain Bragg, not only the landlord but the son-in-law of Mrs. Cammysole, who lives a couple of hundred yards down the street, at "The Bungalow." He was the commander of the "Ram Chunder" East Indiaman, and has quarrelled with the Pocklingtons ever since he bought houses in the parish.

He it is who will not sell or alter his houses to suit the spirit of the times. He it is who, though he made the widow Cammysole change the name of her street, will not pull down the house next door, nor the baker's next, nor the iron-bedstead and feather warehouse ensuing, nor the little barber's with the pole, nor, I am ashamed to say, the tripe-shop, still standing. The barber powders the heads of the great footmen from Pocklington Gardens; they are so big that they can scarcely sit in his little premises. And the old tavern, the "East Indiaman," is kept by Bragg's ship-steward, and protests against the "Pocklington Arms."

Down the road is Pocklington Chapel, Rev. Oldham Slocum—in brick, with arched windows and a wooden belfry: sober, dingy, and hideous. In the centre of Pocklington Gardens rises St. Waltheof's, the Rev. Cyril Thuryfer and assistants—a splendid Anglo-Norman edifice, vast, rich, elaborate, bran new, and intensely old. Down Avemary Lane you may hear the clink of the little Romish chapel bell. And hard by is a large broad-shouldered Ebenezer (Rev. Jonas Gronow), out of the windows of which the hymns come booming all Sunday long.

Going westward along the line, we come presently to Comandine House (on a part of the gardens of which Comandine Gardens is about to be erected by his lordship); farther on, "The Pineries," Mr. and Lady Mary Mango: and so we get into the country, and out of Our Street altogether, as I may say. But in the half-mile, over which it may be said to extend, we find all sorts and conditions of people—from the Right Honorable Lord Comandine down to the present topographer; who being of no rank as it were, has the fortune to be treated on almost friendly footing by all, from his lordship down to the tradesman.

OUR HOUSE IN OUR STREET

We must begin our little descriptions where they say charity should begin—at home. Mrs. Cammysole, my landlady, will be rather surprised when she reads this, and finds that a good-natured tenant, who has never complained of her impositions for fifteen years, understands every one of her tricks, and treats them, not with anger, but with scorn—with silent scorn.

On the 18th of December, 1837, for instance, coming gently down stairs, and before my usual wont, I saw you seated in my arm-chair, peeping into a letter that came from my aunt in the country, just as if it had been addressed to you, and not to "M. A. Titmarsh, Esq." Did I make any disturbance? far from it; I slunk back to my bedroom (being enabled to walk silently in the beautiful pair of worsted slippers Miss Penelope J—s worked for me: they are worn out now, dear Penelope!) and then rattling open the door with a great noise, descending the stairs, singing "Son vergin vezzosa" at the top of my voice. You were not in my sitting-room, Mrs. Cammysole, when I entered that apartment.

You have been reading all my letters, papers, manuscripts, brouillons of verses, inchoate articles for the Morning Post and Morning Chronicle, invitations to dinner and tea—all my family letters, all Eliza Townley's letters, from the first, in which she declared that to be the bride of her beloved Michelagnolo was the fondest wish of her maiden heart, to the last, in which she announced that her Thomas was the best of husbands, and signed herself "Eliza Slogger;" all Mary Farmer's letters, all Emily Delamere's; all that poor foolish old Miss MacWhirter's, whom I would as soon marry as ——: in a word, I know that you, you hawk- beaked, keen-eyed, sleepless, indefatigable old Mrs. Cammysole, have read all my papers for these fifteen years.

I know that you cast your curious old eyes over all the manuscripts which you find in my coat-pockets and those of my pantaloons, as they hang in a drapery over the door-handle of my bedroom.

I know that you count the money in my green and gold purse, which Lucy Netterville gave me, and speculate on the manner in which I have laid out the difference between to-day and yesterday.

I know that you have an understanding with the laundress (to whom you say that you are all-powerful with me), threatening to take away my practice from her, unless she gets up gratis some of your fine linen.

I know that we both have a pennyworth of cream for breakfast, which is brought in in the same little can; and I know who has the most for her share.

I know how many lumps of sugar you take from each pound as it arrives. I have counted the lumps, you old thief, and for years have never said a word, except to Miss Clapperclaw, the first-floor lodger. Once I put a bottle of pale brandy into that cupboard, of which you and I only have keys, and the liquor wasted and wasted away until it was all gone. You drank the whole of it, you wicked old woman. You a lady, indeed!

I know your rage when they did me the honor to elect me a member of the "Poluphloisboiothalasses Club," and I ceased consequently to dine at home. When I DID dine at home,—on a beefsteak let us say,—I should like to know what you had for supper. You first amputated portions of the meat when raw; you abstracted more when cooked. Do you think I was taken in by your flimsy pretences? I wonder how you could dare to do such things before your maids (you a clergyman's daughter and widow, indeed), whom you yourself were always charging with roguery.

Yes, the insolence of the old woman is unbearable, and I must break out at last. If she goes off in a fit at reading this, I am sure I shan't mind. She has two unhappy wenches, against whom her old tongue is clacking from morning till night: she pounces on them at all hours. It was but this morning at eight, when poor Molly was brooming the steps, and the baker paying her by no means unmerited compliments, that my landlady came whirling out of the ground-floor front, and sent the poor girl whimpering into the kitchen.

Were it but for her conduct to her maids I was determined publicly to denounce her. These poor wretches she causes to lead the lives of demons; and not content with bullying them all day, she sleeps at night in the same room with them, so that she may have them up before daybreak, and scold them while they are dressing.

Certain it is, that between her and Miss Clapperclaw, on the first floor, the poor wenches lead a dismal life.

It is to you that I owe most of my knowledge of our neighbors; from you it is that most of the facts and observations contained in these brief pages are taken. Many a night, over our tea, have we talked amiably about our neighbors and their little failings; and as I know that you speak of mine pretty freely, why, let me say, my dear Bessy, that if we have not built up Our Street between us, at least we have pulled it to pieces.

THE BUNGALOW—CAPTAIN AND MRS. BRAGG.

Long, long ago, when Our Street was the country—a stagecoach between us and London passing four times a day—I do not care to own that it was a sight of Flora Cammysole's face, under the card of her mamma's "Lodgings to Let," which first caused me to become a tenant of Our Street. A fine good-humored lass she was then; and I gave her lessons (part out of the rent) in French and flower- painting. She has made a fine rich marriage since, although her eyes have often seemed to me to say, "Ah, Mr. T., why didn't you, when there was yet time, and we both of us were free, propose—you know what?" "Psha! Where was the money, my dear madam?"

Captain Bragg, then occupied in building Bungalow Lodge—Bragg, I say, living on the first floor, and entertaining sea-captains, merchants, and East Indian friends with his grand ship's plate, being disappointed in a project of marrying a director's daughter, who was also a second cousin once removed of a peer,—sent in a fury for Mrs. Cammysole, his landlady, and proposed to marry Flora off-hand, and settle four hundred a year upon her. Flora was ordered from the back-parlor (the ground-floor occupies the second- floor bedroom), and was on the spot made acquainted with the splendid offer which the first-floor had made her. She has been Mrs. Captain Bragg these twelve years.

Bragg to this day wears anchor-buttons, and has a dress-coat with a gold strap for epaulets, in case he should have a fancy to sport them. His house is covered with portraits, busts, and miniatures of himself. His wife is made to wear one of the latter. On his sideboard are pieces of plate, presented by the passengers of the "Ram Chunder" to Captain Bragg: "The 'Ram Chunder' East Indiaman, in a gale, off Table Bay;" "The Outward-bound Fleet, under convoy of her Majesty's frigate 'Loblollyboy,' Captain Gutch, beating off the French squadron, under Commodore Leloup (the 'Ram Chunder,' S.E. by E., is represented engaged with the 'Mirliton' corvette);" "The 'Ram Chunder' standing into the Hooghly, with Captain Bragg, his telescope and speaking-trumpet, on the poop;" "Captain Bragg presenting the Officers of the 'Ram Chunder' to General Bonaparte at St. Helena—TITMARSH" (this fine piece was painted by me when I was in favor with Bragg); in a word, Bragg and the "Ram Chunder" are all over the house.

Although I have eaten scores of dinners at Captain Bragg's charge, yet his hospitality is so insolent, that none of us who frequent his mahogany feel any obligation to our braggart entertainer.

After he has given one of his great heavy dinners he always takes an opportunity to tell you, in the most public way, how many bottles of wine were drunk. His pleasure is to make his guests tipsy, and to tell everybody how and when the period of inebriation arose. And Miss Clapperclaw tells me that he often comes over laughing and giggling to her, and pretending that he has brought ME into this condition—a calumny which I fling contemptuously in his face.

He scarcely gives any but men's parties, and invites the whole club home to dinner. What is the compliment of being asked, when the whole club is asked too, I should like to know? Men's parties are only good for boys. I hate a dinner where there are no women. Bragg sits at the head of his table, and bullies the solitary Mrs. Bragg.

He entertains us with stories of storms which he, Bragg, encountered— of dinners which he, Bragg, has received from the Governor-General of India—of jokes which he, Bragg, has heard; and however stale or odious they may be, poor Mrs. B. is always expected to laugh.

Woe be to her if she doesn't, or if she laughs at anybody else's jokes. I have seen Bragg go up to her and squeeze her arm with a savage grind of his teeth, and say, with an oath, "Hang it, madam, how dare you laugh when any man but your husband speaks to you? I forbid you to grin in that way. I forbid you to look sulky. I forbid you to look happy, or to look up, or to keep your eyes down to the ground. I desire you will not be trapesing through the rooms. I order you not to sit as still as a stone." He curses her if the wine is corked, or if the dinner is spoiled, or if she comes a minute too soon to the club for him, or arrives a minute too late. He forbids her to walk, except upon his arm. And the consequence of his ill treatment is, that Mrs. Cammysole and Mrs. Bragg respect him beyond measure, and think him the first of human beings.

"I never knew a woman who was constantly bullied by her husband who did not like him the better for it," Miss Clapperclaw says. And though this speech has some of Clapp's usual sardonic humor in it, I can't but think there is some truth in the remark.

LEVANT HOUSE CHAMBERS.

MR. RUMBOLD, A.R.A., AND MISS RUMBOLD.

When Lord Levant quitted the country and this neighborhood, in which the tradesmen still deplore him, No. 56, known as Levantine House, was let to the "Pococurante Club," which was speedily bankrupt (for we are too far from the centre of town to support a club of our own); it was subsequently hired by the West Diddlesex Railroad; and is now divided into sets of chambers, superintended by an acrimonious housekeeper, and by a porter in a sham livery: whom, if you don't find him at the door, you may as well seek at the "Grapes" public-house, in the little lane round the corner. He varnishes the japan-boots of the dandy lodgers; reads Mr. Pinkney's Morning Post before he lets him have it; and neglects the letters of the inmates of the chambers generally.

The great rooms, which were occupied as the salons of the noble Levant, the coffee-rooms of the "Pococurante" (a club where the play was furious, as I am told), and the board-room and manager's- room of the West Diddlesex, are tenanted now by a couple of artists: young Pinkney the miniaturist, and George Rumbold the historical painter. Miss Rumbold, his sister lives with him, by the way; but with that young lady of course we have nothing to do.

I knew both these gentlemen at Rome, where George wore a velvet doublet and a beard down to his chest, and used to talk about high art at the "Caffe Greco." How it smelled of smoke, that velveteen doublet of his, with which his stringy red beard was likewise perfumed! It was in his studio that I had the honor to be introduced to his sister, the fair Miss Clara: she had a large casque with a red horse-hair plume (I thought it had been a wisp of her brother's beard at first), and held a tin-headed spear in her hand, representing a Roman warrior in the great picture of "Caractacus" George was painting—a piece sixty-four feet by eighteen. The Roman warrior blushed to be discovered in that attitude: the tin-headed spear trembled in the whitest arm in the world. So she put it down, and taking off the helmet also, went and sat in a far corner of the studio, mending George's stockings; whilst we smoked a couple of pipes, and talked about Raphael being a good deal overrated.

I think he is; and have never disguised my opinion about the "Transfiguration.". And all the time we talked, there were Clara's eyes looking lucidly out from the dark corner in which she was sitting, working away at the stockings. The lucky fellow! They were in a dreadful state of bad repair when she came out to him at Rome, after the death of their father, the Reverend Miles Rumbold.

George, while at Rome, painted "Caractacus;" a picture of "Non Angli sed Angeli" of course; a picture of "Alfred in the Neatherd's Cottage," seventy-two feet by forty-eight—(an idea of the gigantic size and Michel-Angelesque proportions of this picture may be formed, when I state that the mere muffin, of which the outcast king is spoiling the baking, is two feet three in diameter) and the deaths of Socrates, of Remus, and of the Christians under Nero respectively. I shall never forget how lovely Clara looked in white muslin, with her hair down, in this latter picture, giving herself up to a ferocious Carnifex (for which Bob Gaunter the architect sat), and refusing to listen to the mild suggestions of an insinuating Flamen: which character was a gross caricature of myself.

None of George's pictures sold. He has enough to tapestry Trafalgar Square. He has painted, since he came back to England, "The Flaying of Marsyas," "The Smothering of the Little Boys in the Tower," "A Plague Scene during the Great Pestilence," "Ugolino on the Seventh Day after he was deprived of Victuals," For although these pictures have great merit, and the writhings of Marsyas, the convulsions of the little prince, the look of agony of St. Lawrence on the gridiron, are quite true to nature, yet the subjects somehow are not agreeable; and if he hadn't a small patrimony, my friend George would starve.

Fondness for art leads me a great deal to his studio. George is a gentleman, and has very good friends, and good pluck too. When we were at Rome, there was a great row between him and young Heeltap, Lord Boxmoor's son, who was uncivil to Miss Rumbold; (the young scoundrel—had I been a fighting man, I should like to have shot him myself!). Lady Betty Bulbul is very fond of Clara; and Tom Bulbul, who took George's message to Heeltap, is always hanging about the studio. At least I know that I find the young jackanapes there almost every day, bringing a new novel, or some poisonous French poetry, or a basket of flowers, or grapes, with Lady Betty's love to her dear Clara—a young rascal with white kids, and his hair curled every morning. What business has HE to be dangling about

George Rumbold's premises, and sticking up his ugly pug-face as a model for all George's pictures?

Miss Clapperclaw says Bulbul is evidently smitten, and Clara too. What! would she put up with such a little fribble as that, when there is a man of intellect and taste who—but I won't believe it. It is all the jealousy of women.

SOME OF THE SERVANTS IN OUR STREET.

These gentlemen have two clubs in our quarter—for the butlers at the "Indiaman," and for the gents in livery at the "Pocklington Arms"—of either of which societies I should like to be a member. I am sure they could not be so dull as our club at the "Poluphloisboio," where one meets the same neat, clean, respectable old fogies every day.

But with the best wishes, it is impossible for the present writer to join either the "Plate Club" or the " Uniform Club" (as these reunions are designated); for one could not shake hands with a friend who was standing behind your chair, or nod a How-d'ye-do? to the butler who was pouring you out a glass of wine;—so that what I know about the gents in our neighborhood is from mere casual observation. For instance, I have a slight acquaintance with (1) Thomas Spavin, who commonly wears an air of injured innocence, and is groom to Mr. Joseph Green, of Our Street. "I tell why the brougham 'oss is out of condition, and why Desperation broke out all in a lather! 'Osses will, this 'eavy weather; and Desperation was always the most mystest hoss I ever see.—I take him out with Mr. Anderson's 'ounds—I'm above it. I allis was too timid to ride to 'ounds by natur; and Colonel Sprigs' groom as says he saw me, is a liar,"

Such is the tenor of Mr. Spavin's remarks to his master. Whereas all the world in Our Street knows that Mr. Spavin spends at least a hundred a year in beer; that he keeps a betting-book; that he has lent Mr. Green's black brougham horse to the omnibus driver; and, at a time when Mr. G. supposed him at the veterinary surgeon's, has lent him to a livery stable, which has let him out to that gentleman himself, and actually driven him to dinner behind his own horse.

This conduct I can understand, but I cannot excuse—Mr. Spavin may; and I leave the matter to be settled betwixt himself and Mr. Green.

The second is Monsieur Sinbad, Mr. Clarence Bulbul's man, whom we all hate Clarence for keeping.

Mr. Sinbad is a foreigner, speaking no known language, but a mixture of every European dialect—so that he may be an Italian brigand, or a Tyrolese minstrel, or a Spanish smuggler, for what we know. I have heard say that he is neither of these, but an Irish Jew.

He wears studs, hair-oil, jewellery, and linen shirt-fronts, very finely embroidered, but not particular for whiteness. He generally appears in faded velvet waistcoats of a morning, and is always perfumed with stale tobacco. He wears large rings on his hands, which look as if he kept them up the chimney.

He does not appear to do anything earthly for Clarence Bulbul, except to smoke his cigars, and to practise on his guitar. He will not answer a bell, nor fetch a glass of water, nor go of an errand on which, au reste, Clarence dares not send him, being entirely afraid of his servant, and not daring to use him, or to abuse him, or to send him away.

3. Adams—Mr. Champignon's man—a good old man in an old livery coat with old worsted lace—so very old, deaf, surly, and faithful, that you wonder how he should have got into the family at all; who never kept a footman till last year, when they came into the street.

Miss Clapperclaw says she believes Adams to be Mrs. Champignon's father, and he certainly has a look of that lady; as Miss C. pointed out to me at dinner one night, whilst old Adams was blundering about amongst the hired men from Gunter's, and falling over the silver dishes.

4. Fipps, the buttoniest page in all the street: walks behind Mrs. Grimsby with her prayer-book, and protects her.

"If that woman wants a protector" (a female acquaintance remarks), "heaven be good to us! She is as big as an ogress, and has an upper lip which many a cornet of the Lifeguards might envy. Her poor dear husband was a big man, and she could beat him easily; and did too. Mrs. Grimsby indeed! Why, my dear Mr. Titmarsh, it is Glumdalca walking with Tom Thumb."

This observation of Miss C.'s is very true, and Mrs. Grimsby might carry her prayer-book to church herself. But Miss Clapperclaw, who is pretty well able to take care of herself too, was glad enough to have the protection of the page when she went out in the fly to pay visits, and before Mrs. Grimsby and she quarrelled at whist at Lady Pocklington's.

After this merely parenthetic observation, we come to 5, one of her ladyship's large men, Mr. Jeames—a gentleman of vast stature and proportions, who is almost nose to nose with us as we pass her ladyship's door on the outside of the omnibus. I think Jeames has a contempt for a man whom he witnesses in that position. I have fancied something like that feeling showed itself (as far as it may in a well-bred gentleman accustomed to society) in his behavior, while waiting behind my chair at dinner.

But I take Jeames to be, like most giants, good-natured, lazy, stupid, soft-hearted, and extremely fond of drink. One night, his lady being engaged to dinner at Nightingale House, I saw Mr. Jeames resting himself on a bench at the "Pocklington Arms:" where, as he had no liquor before him, he had probably exhausted his credit.

Little Spitfire, Mr. Clarence Bulbul's boy, the wickedest little varlet that ever hung on to a cab, was "chaffing" Mr. Jeames, holding up to his face a pot of porter almost as big as the young potifer himself.

"Vill you now, Big'un, or von't you?" Spitfire said. "If you're thirsty, vy don't you say so and squench it, old boy?"

"Don't ago on making fun of me—I can't abear chaffin'," was the reply of Mr. Jeames, and tears actually stood in his fine eyes as he looked at the porter and the screeching little imp before him.

Spitfire (real name unknown) gave him some of the drink: I am happy to say Jeames's face wore quite a different look when it rose gasping out of the porter; and I judge of his dispositions from the above trivial incident.

The last boy in the sketch, 6, need scarcely be particularized. Doctor's boy; was a charity-boy; stripes evidently added on to a pair of the doctor's clothes of last year—Miss Clapperclaw pointed this out to me with a giggle. Nothing escapes that old woman.

As we were walking in Kensington Gardens, she pointed me out Mrs. Bragg's nursery-maid, who sings so loud at church, engaged with a Lifeguardsman, whom she was trying to convert probably. My virtuous friend rose indignant at the sight.

"That's why these minxes like Kensington Gardens," she cried. "Look at the woman: she leaves the baby on the grass, for the giant to trample upon; and that little wretch of a Hastings Bragg is riding on the monster's cane."

Miss C. flew up and seized the infant, waking it out of its sleep, and causing all the gardens to echo with its squalling. "I'll teach you to be impudent to me," she said to the nursery-maid, with whom my vivacious old friend, I suppose, has had a difference; and she would not release the infant until she had rung the bell of Bungalow Lodge, where she gave it up to the footman.

The giant in scarlet had slunk down towards Knightsbridge meanwhile. The big rogues are always crossing the Park and the Gardens, and hankering about Our Street.

WHAT SOMETIMES HAPPENS IN OUR STREET.

It was before old Hunkington's house that the mutes were standing, as I passed and saw this group at the door. The charity-boy with the hoop is the son of the jolly-looking mute; he admires his father, who admires himself too, in those bran-new sables. The other infants are the spawn of the alleys about Our Street. Only the parson and the typhus fever visit those mysterious haunts, which lie crouched about our splendid houses like Lazarus at the threshold of Dives.

Those little ones come crawling abroad in the sunshine, to the annoyance of the beadles, and the horror of a number of good people in the street. They will bring up the rear of the procession anon, when the grand omnibus with the feathers, and the line coaches with the long-tailed black horses, and the gentleman's private carriages with the shutters up, pass along to Saint Waltheof's.

You can hear the slow bell tolling clear in the sunshine already, mingling with the crowing of "Punch," who is passing down the street with his show; and the two musics make a queer medley.

Not near so many people, I remark, engage "Punch" now as in the good old times. I suppose our quarter is growing too genteel for him.

Miss Bridget Jones, a poor curate's daughter in Wales, comes into all Hunkington's property, and will take his name, as I am told. Nobody ever heard of her before. I am sure Captain Hunkington, and his brother Barnwell Hunkington, must wish that the lucky young lady had never been heard of to the present day.

But they will have the consolation of thinking that they did their duty by their uncle, and consoled his declining years. It was but last month that Millwood Hunkington (the Captain) sent the old gentleman a service of plate; and Mrs. Barnwell got a reclining carriage at a great expense from Hobbs and Dobbs's, in which the old gentleman went out only once.

"It is a punishment on those Hunkingtons," Miss Clapperclaw remarks: "upon those people who have been always living beyond their little incomes, and always speculating upon what the old man would leave them, and always coaxing him with presents which they could not afford, and he did not want. It is a punishment upon those Hunkingtons to be so disappointed."

"Think of giving him plate," Miss C. justly says, "who had chests- full; and sending him a carriage, who could afford to buy all Long Acre. And everything goes to Miss Jones Hunkington. I wonder will she give the things back?" Miss Clapperclaw asks. "I wouldn't."

And indeed I don't think Miss Clapperclaw would.

SOMEBODY WHOM NOBODY KNOWS.

That pretty little house, the last in Pocklington Square, was lately occupied by a young widow lady who wore a pink bonnet, a short silk dress, sustained by a crinoline, and a light blue mantle, or over-jacket (Miss C. is not here to tell me the name of the garment); or else a black velvet pelisse, a yellow shawl, and a white bonnet; or else—but never mind the dress, which seemed to be of the handsomest sort money could buy—and who had very long glossy black ringlets, and a peculiarly brilliant complexion,—No. 96, Pocklington Square, I say, was lately occupied by a widow lady named Mrs. Stafford Molyneux.

The very first day on which an intimate and valued female friend of mine saw Mrs. Stafford Molyneux stepping into a brougham, with a splendid bay horse, and without a footman, (mark, if you please, that delicate sign of respectability,) and after a moment's examination of Mrs. S. M.'s toilette, her manners, little dog, carnation-colored parasol, Miss Elizabeth Clapperclaw clapped to the opera-glass with which she had been regarding the new inhabitant of Our Street, came away from the window in a great flurry, and began poking her fire in a fit of virtuous indignation.

"She's very pretty," said I, who had been looking over Miss C.'s shoulder at the widow with the flashing eyes and drooping ringlets.

"Hold your tongue, sir," said Miss Clapperclaw, tossing up her virgin head with an indignant blush on her nose. "It's a sin and a shame that such a creature should be riding in her carriage, forsooth, when honest people must go on foot."

Subsequent observations confirmed my revered fellow-lodger's anger and opinion. We have watched Hansom cabs standing before that lady's house for hours; we have seen broughams, with great flaring eyes, keeping watch there in the darkness; we have seen the vans from the comestible-shops drive up and discharge loads of wines, groceries, French plums, and other articles of luxurious horror. We have seen Count Wowski's drag, Lord Martingale's carriage, Mr. Deuceace's cab drive up there time after time; and (having remarked previously the pastry-cook's men arrive with the trays and entrees), we have known that this widow was giving dinners at the little house in Pocklington Square—dinners such as decent people could not hope to enjoy.

My excellent friend has been in a perfect fury when Mrs. Stafford Molyneux, in a black velvet riding-habit, with a hat and feather, has come out and mounted an odious gray horse, and has cantered down the street, followed by her groom upon a bay.

"It won't last long—it must end in shame and humiliation," my dear Miss C. has remarked, disappointed that the tiles and chimney-pots did not fall down upon Mrs. Stafford Molyneux's head, and crush that cantering, audacious woman.

But it was a consolation to see her when she walked out with a French maid, a couple of children, and a little dog hanging on to her by a blue ribbon. She always held down her head then—her head with the drooping black ringlets. The virtuous and well-disposed avoided her. I have seen the Square-keeper himself look puzzled as she passed; and Lady Kicklebury walking by with Miss K., her daughter, turn away from Mrs. Stafford Molyneux, and fling back at her a ruthless Parthian glance that ought to have killed any woman of decent sensibility.

That wretched woman, meanwhile, with her rouged cheeks (for rouge it IS, Miss Clapperclaw swears, and who is a better judge?) has walked on conscious, and yet somehow braving out the Street. You could read pride of her beauty, pride of her fine clothes, shame of her position, in her downcast black eyes.

As for Mademoiselle Trampoline, her French maid, she would stare the sun itself out of countenance. One day she tossed up her head as she passed under our windows with a look of scorn that drove Miss Clapperclaw back to the fireplace again.

It was Mrs. Stafford Molyneux's children, however, whom I pitied the most. Once her boy, in a flaring tartan, went up to speak to Master Roderick Lacy, whose maid was engaged ogling a policeman; and the children were going to make friends, being united with a hoop which Master Molyneux had, when Master Roderick's maid, rushing up, clutched her charge to her arms, and hurried away, leaving little Molyneux sad and wondering.

"Why won't he play with me, mamma?" Master Molyneux asked—and his mother's face blushed purple as she walked away.

"Ah—heaven help us and forgive us!" said I; but Miss C. can never forgive the mother or child; and she clapped her hands for joy one day when we saw the shutters up, bills in the windows, a carpet hanging out over the balcony, and a crowd of shabby Jews about the steps—giving token that the reign of Mrs. Stafford Molyneux was over. The pastry-cooks and their trays, the bay and the gray, the brougham and the groom, the noblemen and their cabs, were all gone; and the tradesmen in the neighborhood were crying out that they were done.

"Serve the odious minx right!" says Miss C.; and she played at piquet that night with more vigor than I have known her manifest for these last ten years.

What is it that makes certain old ladies so savage upon certain subjects? Miss C. is a good woman; pays her rent and her tradesmen; gives plenty to the poor; is brisk with her tongue— kind-hearted in the main; but if Mrs. Stafford Molyneux and her children were plunged into a caldron of boiling vinegar, I think my revered friend would not take them out.

THE MAN IN POSSESSION.

For another misfortune which occurred in Our Street we were much more compassionate. We liked Danby Dixon, and his wife Fanny Dixon still more. Miss C. had a paper of biscuits and a box of preserved apricots always in the cupboard, ready for Dixon's children— provisions by the way which she locked up under Mrs. Cammysole's nose, so that our landlady could by no possibility lay a hand on them.

Dixon and his wife had the neatest little house possible, (No. 16, opposite 96,) and were liked and respected by the whole street. He was called Dandy Dixon when he was in the dragoons, and was a light weight, and rather famous as a gentleman rider. On his marriage, he sold out and got fat: and was indeed a florid, contented, and jovial gentleman.

His little wife was charming—to see her in pink with some miniature Dixons, in pink too, round about her, or in that beautiful gray dress, with the deep black lace flounces, which she wore at my Lord Comandine's on the night of the private theatricals, would have done any man good. To hear her sing any of my little ballads, "Knowest Thou the Willow-tree?" for instance, or "The Rose upon my Balcony," or "The Humming of the Honey-bee," (far superior in MY judgment, and in that of SOME GOOD JUDGES likewise, to that humbug Clarence Bulbul's ballads,)—to hear her, I say, sing these, was to be in a sort of small Elysium. Dear, dear little Fanny Dixon! she was like a little chirping bird of Paradise. It was a shame that storms should ever ruffle such a tender plumage.

Well, never mind about sentiment. Danby Dixon, the owner of this little treasure, an ex-captain of Dragoons, and having nothing to do, and a small income, wisely thought he would employ his spare time, and increase his revenue. He became a director of the Cornaro Life Insurance Company, of the Tregulpho tin-mines, and of four or five railroad companies. It was amusing to see him swaggering about the City in his clinking boots, and with his high and mighty dragoon manners. For a time his talk about shares after dinner was perfectly intolerable; and I for one was always glad to leave him in the company of sundry very dubious capitalists who frequented his house, and walk up to hear Mrs. Fanny warbling at the piano with her little children about her knees.

It was only last season that they set up a carriage—the modestest little vehicle conceivable—driven by Kirby, who had been in Dixon's troop in the regiment, and had followed him into private life as coachman, footman, and page.

One day lately I went into Dixon's house, hearing that some calamities had befallen him, the particulars of which Miss Clapperclaw was desirous to know. The creditors of the Tregulpho Mines had got a verdict against him as one of the directors of that company; the engineer of the Little Diddlesex Junction had sued him for two thousand three hundred pounds—the charges of that scientific man for six weeks' labor in surveying the line. His brother directors were to be discovered nowhere: Windham, Dodgin, Mizzlington, and the rest, were all gone long ago.

When I entered, the door was open: there was a smell of smoke in the dining-room, where a gentleman at noonday was seated with a pipe and a pot of beer: a man in possession indeed, in that comfortable pretty parlor, by that snug round table where I have so often seen Fanny Dixon's smiling face.

Kirby, the ex-dragoon, was scowling at the fellow, who lay upon a little settee reading the newspaper, with an evident desire to kill him. Mrs. Kirby, his wife, held little Danby, poor Dixon's son and heir. Dixon's portrait smiled over the sideboard still, and his wife was up stairs in an agony of fear, with the poor little daughters of this bankrupt, broken family.

This poor soul had actually come down and paid a visit to the man in possession. She had sent wine and dinner to "the gentleman down stairs," as she called him in her terror. She had tried to move his heart, by representing to him how innocent Captain Dixon was, and how he had always paid, and always remained at home when everybody else had fled. As if her tears and simple tales and entreaties could move that man in possession out of the house, or induce him to pay the costs of the action which her husband had lost.

Danby meanwhile was at Boulogne, sickening after his wife and children. They sold everything in his house—all his smart furniture and neat little stock of plate; his wardrobe and his linen, "the property of a gentleman gone abroad;" his carriage by the best maker; and his wine selected without regard to expense. His house was shut up as completely as his opposite neighbor's; and a new tenant is just having it fresh painted inside and out, as if poor Dixon had left an infection behind.

Kirby and his wife went across the water with the children and Mrs. Fanny—she has a small settlement; and I am bound to say that our mutual friend Miss Elizabeth C. went down with Mrs. Dixon in the fly to the Tower Stairs, and stopped in Lombard Street by the way.

So it is that the world wags: that honest men and knaves alike are always having ups and downs of fortune, and that we are perpetually changing tenants in Our Street.

THE LION OF THE STREET.

What people can find in Clarence Bulbul, who has lately taken upon himself the rank and dignity of Lion of Our Street, I have always been at a loss to conjecture.

"He has written an Eastern book of considerable merit," Miss Clapperclaw says; but hang it, has not everybody written an Eastern book? I should like to meet anybody in society now who has not been up to the second cataract. An Eastern book forsooth! My Lord Castleroyal has done one—an honest one; my Lord Youngent another— an amusing one; my Lord Woolsey another—a pious one; there is "The Cutlet and the Cabob"— a sentimental one; "Timbuctoothen"—a humorous one, all ludicrously overrated, in my opinion: not including my own little book, of which a copy or two is still to be had, by the way.

Well, then, Clarence Bulbul, because he has made part of the little tour that all of us know, comes back and gives himself airs, forsooth, and howls as if he were just out of the great Libyan desert.

When we go and see him, that Irish Jew courier, whom I have before had the honor to describe, looks up from the novel which he is reading in the ante-room, and says, "Mon maitre est au divan," or, "Monsieur trouvera Monsieur dans son serail," and relapses into the Comte de Montecristo again.

Yes, the impudent wretch has actually a room in his apartments on the ground-floor of his mother's house, which he calls his harem. When Lady Betty Bulbul (they are of the Nightingale family) or Miss Blanche comes down to visit him, their slippers are placed at the door, and he receives them on an ottoman, and these infatuated women will actually light his pipe for him.

Little Spitfire, the groom, hangs about the drawing-room, outside the harem forsooth! so that he may be ready when Clarence Bulbul claps hands for him to bring the pipes and coffee.

He has coffee and pipes for everybody. I should like you to have seen the face of old Bowly, his college-tutor, called upon to sit cross-legged on a divan, a little cup of bitter black Mocha put into his hand, and a large amber-muzzled pipe stuck into his mouth by Spitfire, before he could so much as say it was a fine day. Bowly almost thought he had compromised his principles by consenting so far to this Turkish manner.

Bulbul's dinners are, I own, very good; his pilaffs and curries excellent. He tried to make us eat rice with our fingers, it is true; but he scalded his own hands in the business, and invariably bedizened his shirt; so he has left off the Turkish practice, for dinner at least, and uses a fork like a Christian.

But it is in society that he is most remarkable; and here he would, I own, be odious, but he becomes delightful, because all the men hate him so. A perfect chorus of abuse is raised round about him. "Confounded impostor," says one; "Impudent jackass," says another; "Miserable puppy," cries a third; "I'd like to wring his neck," says Bruff, scowling over his shoulder at him. Clarence meanwhile nods, winks, smiles, and patronizes them all with the easiest good- humor. He is a fellow who would poke an archbishop in the apron, or clap a duke on the shoulder, as coolly as he would address you and me.

I saw him the other night at Mrs. Bumpsher's grand let-off. He flung himself down cross-legged on a pink satin sofa, so that you could see Mrs. Bumpsher quiver with rage in the distance, Bruff growl with fury from the further room, and Miss Pim, on whose frock Bulbul's feet rested, look up like a timid fawn.

"Fan me, Miss Pim," said he of the cushion. "You look like a perfect Peri to-night. You remind me of a girl I once knew in Circassia—Ameena, the sister of Schamyl Bey. Do you know, Miss Pim, that you would fetch twenty thousand piastres in the market at Constantinople?"

"Law, Mr. Bulbul!" is all Miss Pim can ejaculate; and having talked over Miss Pim, Clarence goes off to another houri, whom he fascinates in a similar manner. He charmed Mrs. Waddy by telling her that she was the exact figure of the Pasha of Egypt's second wife. He gave Miss Tokely a piece of the sack in which Zuleika was drowned; and he actually persuaded that poor little silly Miss Vain to turn Mahometan, and sent her up to the Turkish ambassador's to look out for a mufti.

THE DOVE OF OUR STREET.

If Bulbul is our Lion, Young Oriel may be described as The Dove of our colony. He is almost as great a pasha among the ladies as Bulbul. They crowd in flocks to see him at Saint Waltheof's, where the immense height of his forehead, the rigid asceticism of his surplice, the twang with which he intones the service, and the namby-pamby mysticism of his sermons, have turned all the dear girls' heads for some time past. While we were having a rubber at Mrs. Chauntry's, whose daughters are following the new mode, I heard the following talk (which made me revoke by the way) going on, in what was formerly called the young ladies' room, but is now styled the Oratory:—

THE ORATORY.

MISS CHAUNTRY.   MISS ISABEL CHAUNTRY.
MISS DE L'AISLE.   MISS PYX.
REV. L. ORIEL.   REV. O. SLOCUM—[In the further room.]

Miss Chauntry (sighing).—Is it wrong to be in the Guards, dear Mr. Oriel?

Miss Pyx.—She will make Frank de Boots sell out when he marries.

Mr. Oriel.—To be in the Guards, dear sister? The church has always encouraged the army. Saint Martin of Tours was in the army; Saint Louis was in the army; Saint Waltheof, our patron, Saint Witikind of Aldermanbury, Saint Wamba, and Saint Walloff were in the army. Saint Wapshot was captain of the guard of Queen Boadicea; and Saint Werewolf was a major in the Danish cavalry. The holy Saint Ignatius of Loyola carried a pike, as we know; and—

Miss De l'Aisle.—Will you take some tea, dear Mr. Oriel?

Oriel.—This is not one of MY feast days, Sister Emma. It is the feast of Saint Wagstatf of Walthamstow.

The Young Ladies.—And we must not even take tea?

Oriel.—Dear sisters, I said not so. YOU may do as you list; but I am strong (with a heart-broken sigh); don't ply me (he reels). I took a little water and a parched pea after matins. To-morrow is a flesh day, and—and I shall be better then.

Rev. O. Slocum (from within).—Madam, I take your heart with my small trump.

Oriel.—Yes, better! dear sister; it is only a passing—a— weakness.

Miss I. Chauntry.—He's dying of fever.

Miss Chauntry.—I'm so glad De Boots need not leave the Blues.

Miss Pyx.—He wears sackcloth and cinders inside his waistcoat.

Miss De l'Aisle.—He's told me to-night he's going to—to— Ro-o-ome. [Miss De l'Aisle bursts into tears.]

Rev. O. Slocum.—My lord, I have the highest club, which gives the trick and two by honors.

Thus, you see, we have a variety of clergymen in Our Street. Mr. Oriel is of the pointed Gothic school, while old Slocum is of the good old tawny port-wine school: and it must be confessed that Mr. Gronow, at Ebenezer, has a hearty abhorrence for both.

As for Gronow, I pity him, if his future lot should fall where Mr. Oriel supposes that it will.

And as for Oriel, he has not even the benefit of purgatory, which he would accord to his neighbor Ebenezer; while old Slocum pronounces both to be a couple of humbugs; and Mr. Mole, the demure little beetle-browed chaplain of the little church of Avemary Lane, keeps his sly eyes down to the ground when he passes any one of his black-coated brethren.

There is only one point on which, my friends, they seem agreed. Slocum likes port, but who ever heard that he neglected his poor? Gronow, if he comminates his neighbor's congregation, is the affectionate father of his own. Oriel, if he loves pointed Gothic and parched peas for breakfast, has a prodigious soup-kitchen for his poor; and as for little Father Mole, who never lifts his eyes from the ground, ask our doctor at what bedsides he finds him, and how he soothes poverty, and braves misery and infection.

THE BUMPSHERS.

No. 6, Pocklington Gardens, (the house with the quantity of flowers in the windows, and the awning over the entrance,) George Bumpsher, Esquire, M.P. for Humborough (and the Beanstalks, Kent).

For some time after this gorgeous family came into our quarter, I mistook a bald-headed, stout person, whom I used to see looking through the flowers on the upper windows, for Bumpsher himself, or for the butler of the family; whereas it was no other than Mrs. Bumpsher, without her chestnut wig, and who is at least three times the size of her husband.

The Bumpshers and the house of Mango at the Pineries vie together in their desire to dominate over the neighborhood; and each votes the other a vulgar and purse-proud family. The fact is, both are City people. Bumpsher, in his mercantile capacity, is a wholesale stationer in Thames Street; and his wife was the daughter of an eminent bill-broking firm, not a thousand miles from Lombard Street.

He does not sport a coronet and supporters upon his London plate and carriages; but his country-house is emblazoned all over with those heraldic decorations. He puts on an order when he goes abroad, and is Count Bumpsher of the Roman States—which title he purchased from the late Pope (through Prince Polonia the banker) for a couple of thousand scudi.

It is as good as a coronation to see him and Mrs. Bumpsher go to Court. I wonder the carriage can hold them both. On those days Mrs. Bumpsher holds her own drawing-room before her Majesty's; and we are invited to come and see her sitting in state, upon the largest sofa in her rooms. She has need of a stout one, I promise you. Her very feathers must weigh something considerable. The diamonds on her stomacher would embroider a full-sized carpet-bag. She has rubies, ribbons, cameos, emeralds, gold serpents, opals, and Valenciennes lace, as if she were an immense sample out of Howell and James's shop.

She took up with little Pinkney at Rome, where he made a charming picture of her, representing her as about eighteen, with a cherub in her lap, who has some liking to Bryanstone Bumpsher, her enormous, vulgar son; now a cornet in the Blues, and anything but a cherub, as those would say who saw him in his uniform jacket.

I remember Pinkney when he was painting the picture, Bryanstone being then a youth in what they call a skeleton suit (as if such a pig of a child could ever have been dressed in anything resembling a skeleton)—I remember, I say, Mrs. B. sitting to Pinkney in a sort of Egerian costume, her boy by her side, whose head the artist turned round and directed it towards a piece of gingerbread, which he was to have at the end of the sitting.

Pinkney, indeed, a painter!—a contemptible little humbug, a parasite of the great! He has painted Mrs. Bumpsher younger every year for these last ten years—and you see in the advertisements of all her parties his odious little name stuck in at the end of the list. I'm sure, for my part, I'd scorn to enter her doors, or be the toady of any woman.

JOLLY NEWBOY, ESQ., M.P.

How different it is with the Newboys, now, where I have an entree (having indeed had the honor in former days to give lessons to both the ladies)—and where such a quack as Pinkney would never be allowed to enter! A merrier house the whole quarter cannot furnish. It is there you meet people of all ranks and degrees, not only from our quarter, but from the rest of the town. It is there that our great man, the Right Honorable Lord Comandine, came up and spoke to me in so encouraging a manner that I hope to be invited to one of his lordship's excellent dinners (of which I shall not fail to give a very flattering description) before the season is over. It is there you find yourself talking to statesmen, poets, and artists—not sham poets like Bulbul, or quack artists like that Pinkney—but to the best members of all society. It is there I made this sketch, while Miss Chesterforth was singing a deep-toned tragic ballad, and her mother scowling behind her. What a buzz and clack and chatter there was in the room to be sure! When Miss Chesterforth sings, everybody begins to talk. Hicks and old Fogy were on Ireland: Bass was roaring into old Pump's ears (or into his horn rather) about the Navigation Laws; I was engaged talking to the charming Mrs. Short; while Charley Bonham (a mere prig, in whom I am surprised that the women can see anything,) was pouring out his fulsome rhapsodies in the ears of Diana White. Lovely, lovely Diana White! were it not for three or four other engagements, I know a heart that would suit you to a T.

Newboy's I pronounce to be the jolliest house in the street. He has only of late had a rush of prosperity, and turned Parliament man; for his distant cousin, of the ancient house of Newboy of ——shire, dying, Fred—then making believe to practise at the bar, and living with the utmost modesty in Gray's Inn Road—found himself master of a fortune, and a great house in the country; of which getting tired, as in the course of nature he should, he came up to London, and took that fine mansion in our Gardens. He represents Mumborough in Parliament, a seat which has been time out of mind occupied by a Newboy.

Though he does not speak, being a great deal too rich, sensible, and lazy, he somehow occupies himself with reading blue-books, and indeed talks a great deal too much good sense of late over his dinner-table, where there is always a cover for the present writer.

He falls asleep pretty assiduously too after that meal—a practice which I can well pardon in him—for, between ourselves, his wife, Maria Newboy, and his sister, Clarissa, are the loveliest and kindest of their sex, and I would rather hear their innocent prattle, and lively talk about their neighbors, than the best wisdom from the wisest man that ever wore a beard.

Like a wise and good man, he leaves the question of his household entirely to the women. They like going to the play. They like going to Greenwich. They like coming to a party at Bachelor's hall. They are up to all sorts of fun, in a word; in which taste the good-natured Newboy acquiesces, provided he is left to follow his own.

It was only on the 17th of the month, that, having had the honor to dine at the house, when, after dinner, which took place at eight, we left Newboy to his blue-books, and went up stairs and sang a little to the guitar afterwards—it was only on the 17th December, the night of Lady Sowerby's party, that the following dialogue took place in the boudoir, whither Newboy, blue-books in hand, had ascended.

He was curled up with his House of Commons boots on his wife's arm-chair, reading his eternal blue-books, when Mrs. N. entered from her apartment, dressed for the evening.

Mrs. N.—Frederick, won't you come?

Mr. N.—Where?

Mrs. N.—To Lady Sowerby's.

Mr. N.—I'd rather go to the Black Hole in Calcutta. Besides, this Sanitary Report is really the most interesting—[he begins to read.]

Mrs. N.—(piqued)—Well, Mr. Titmarsh will go with us.

Mr. N.—Will he? I wish him joy.

At this juncture Miss Clarissa Newboy enters in a pink paletot, trimmed with swansdown—looking like an angel—and we exchange glances of—what shall I say?—of sympathy on both parts, and consummate rapture on mine. But this is by-play.

Mrs. N.—Good night, Frederick. I think we shall be late.

Mr. N.—You won't wake me, I dare say; and you don't expect a public man to sit up.

Mrs. N.—It's not you, it's the servants. Cocker sleeps very heavily. The maids are best in bed, and are all ill with the influenza. I say, Frederick dear, don't you think you had better give me YOUR CHUBB KEY?

This astonishing proposal, which violates every recognized law of society—this demand which alters all the existing state of things— this fact of a woman asking for a door-key, struck me with a terror which I cannot describe, and impressed me with the fact of the vast progress of Our Street. The door-key! What would our grandmothers, who dwelt in this place when it was a rustic suburb, think of its condition now, when husbands stay at home, and wives go abroad with the latchkey?

The evening at Lady Sowerby's was the most delicious we have spent for long, long days.

Thus it will be seen that everybody of any consideration in Our Street takes a line. Mrs. Minimy (34) takes the homoeopathic line, and has soirees of doctors of that faith. Lady Pocklington takes the capitalist line; and those stupid and splendid dinners of hers are devoured by loan-contractors and railroad princes. Mrs. Trimmer (38) comes out in the scientific line, and indulges us in rational evenings, where history is the lightest subject admitted, and geology and the sanitary condition of the metropolis form the general themes of conversation. Mrs. Brumby plays finely on the bassoon, and has evenings dedicated to Sebastian Bach, and enlivened with Handel. At Mrs. Maskleyn's they are mad for charades and theatricals.

They performed last Christmas in a French piece, by Alexandre Dumas, I believe—"La Duchesse de Montefiasco," of which I forget the plot, but everybody was in love with everybody else's wife, except the hero, Don Alonzo, who was ardently attached to the Duchess, who turned out to be his grandmother. The piece was translated by Lord Fiddle-faddle, Tom Bulbul being the Don Alonzo; and Mrs. Roland Calidore (who never misses an opportunity of acting in a piece in which she can let down her hair) was the Duchess.

ALONZO.

```
You know how well he loves you, and you wonder
To see Alonzo suffer, Cunegunda?—
Ask if the chamois suffer when they feel
Plunged in their panting sides the hunter's steel?
Or when the soaring heron or eagle proud,
Pierced by my shaft, comes tumbling from the cloud,
Ask if the royal birds no anguish know,
```

The victims of Alonzo's twanging bow?
Then ask him if he suffers—him who dies,
Pierced by the poisoned glance that glitters from your eyes!
                              [He staggers from the effect of the
poison

THE DUCHESS.

Alonzo loves—Alonzo loves! and whom?
His grandmother! Oh, hide me, gracious tomb!
                              [Her Grace faints away.

Such acting as Tom Bulbul's I never saw. Tom lisps atrociously, and uttered the passage, "You athk me if I thuffer," in the most absurd way. Miss Clapperclaw says he acted pretty well, and that I only joke about him because I am envious, and wanted to act a part myself.—I envious indeed!

But of all the assemblies, feastings, junketings, dejeunes, soirees, conversaziones, dinner-parties, in Our Street, I know of none pleasanter than the banquets at Tom Fairfax's; one of which this enormous provision-consumer gives seven times a week. He lives in one of the little houses of the old Waddilove Street quarter, built long before Pocklington Square and Pocklington Gardens and the Pocklington family itself had made their appearance in this world.

Tom, though he has a small income, and lives in a small house, yet sits down one of a party of twelve to dinner every day of his life; these twelve consisting of Mrs. Fairfax, the nine Misses Fairfax, and Master Thomas Fairfax—the son and heir to twopence halfpenny a year.

It is awkward just now to go and beg pot-luck from such a family as this; because, though a guest is always welcome, we are thirteen at table—an unlucky number, it is said. This evil is only temporary, and will be remedied presently, when the family will be thirteen WITHOUT the occasional guest, to judge from all appearances.

Early in the morning Mrs. Fairfax rises, and cuts bread and butter from six o'clock till eight; during which time the nursery operations upon the nine little graces are going on. If his wife has to rise early to cut the bread and butter, I warrant Fairfax must be up betimes to earn it. He is a clerk in a Government office; to which duty he trudges daily, refusing even twopenny omnibuses. Every time he goes to the shoemaker's he has to order eleven pairs of shoes, and so can't afford to spare his own. He teaches the children

Latin every morning, and is already thinking when Tom shall be inducted into that language. He works in his garden for an hour before breakfast. His work over by three o'clock, he tramps home at four, and exchanges his dapper coat for his dressing-gown—a ragged but honorable garment.

Which is the best, his old coat or Sir John's bran-new one? Which is the most comfortable and becoming, Mrs. Fairfax's black velvet gown (which she has worn at the Pocklington Square parties these twelve years, and in which I protest she looks like a queen), or that new robe which the milliner has just brought home to Mrs. Bumpsher's, and into which she will squeeze herself on Christmas- day?

Miss Clapperclaw says that we are all so charmingly contented with ourselves that not one of us would change with his neighbor; and so, rich and poor, high and low, one person is about as happy as another in Our Street.

DOCTOR BIRCH AND HIS YOUNG FRIENDS

by MR. M. A. TITMARSH

THE DOCTOR AND HIS STAFF.

There is no need to say why I became assistant-master and professor of the English and French languages, flower-painting, and the German flute, in Doctor Birch's Academy, at Rodwell Regis. Good folks may depend on this, that it was not for CHOICE that I left lodgings near London, and a genteel society, for an under-master's desk in that old school. I promise you the fare at the usher's table, the getting up at five o'clock in the morning, the walking out with little boys in the fields, (who used to play me tricks, and never could be got to respect my awful and responsible character as teacher in the school,) Miss Birch's vulgar insolence, Jack Birch's glum condescension, and the poor old Doctor's patronage, were not matters in themselves pleasurable: and that that patronage and those dinners were sometimes cruel hard to swallow. Never mind—my connection with the place is over now, and I hope they have got a more efficient under-master.

Jack Birch (Rev. J. Birch, of St. Neot's Hall, Oxford,) is partner with his father the Doctor, and takes some of the classes. About his Greek I can't say much; but I will construe him in Latin any day. A more supercilious little prig, (giving himself airs, too, about his cousin, Miss Raby, who lives with the Doctor,) a more empty, pompous little coxcomb I never saw. His white neck-cloth looked as if it choked him. He used to try and look over that starch upon me and Prince the assistant, as if he were a couple of footmen. He didn't do much business in the school; but occupied his time in writing sanctified letters to the boys' parents, and in composing dreary sermons to preach to them.

The real master of the school is Prince; an Oxford man too: shy, haughty, and learned; crammed with Greek and a quantity of useless learning; uncommonly kind to the small boys; pitiless with the fools and the braggarts; respected of all for his honesty, his learning, his bravery, (for he hit out once in a boat-row in a way which astonished the boys and the bargemen,) and for a latent power about him, which all saw and confessed somehow. Jack Birch could never look him in the face. Old Miss Z. dared not put off any of HER airs upon him. Miss Rosa made him the lowest of curtsies. Miss Raby said she was afraid of him. Good old Prince! we have sat many a night smoking in the Doctor's harness-room, whither we retired when our boys were gone to bed, and our cares and canes put by.

After Jack Birch had taken his degree at Oxford—a process which he effected with great difficulty—this place, which used to be called "Birch's," "Dr. Birch's Academy," and what not, became suddenly "Archbishop Wigsby's College of Rodwell Regis." They took down the old blue board with the gold letters, which has been used to mend the pigsty since. Birch had a large school-room run up in the Gothic taste, with statuettes, and a little belfry, and a bust of Archbishop Wigsby in the middle of the school. He put the six senior boys into caps and gowns, which had rather a good effect as the lads sauntered down the street of the town, but which certainly provoked the contempt and hostility of the bargemen; and so great was his rage for academic costumes and ordinances, that he would have put me myself into a lay gown, with red knots and fringes, but that I flatly resisted, and said that a writing-master had no business with such paraphernalia.

By the way, I have forgotten to mention the Doctor himself. And what shall I say of him? Well, he has a very crisp gown and bands, a solemn aspect, a tremendous loud voice, and a grand air with the boys' parents; whom he receives in a study covered round with the best-bound books, which imposes upon many—upon the women especially—and makes them fancy that this is a Doctor indeed. But law bless you! He never reads the books, or opens one of them; except that in which he keeps his bands—a Dugdale's "Monasticon," which looks like a book, but is in reality a cupboard, where he has his port, almond-cakes, and decanter of wine. He gets up his classics with translations, or what the boys call cribs; they pass wicked tricks upon him when he hears the forms. The elder wags go to his study and ask him to help them in hard bits of Herodotus or Thucydides: he says he will look over the passage, and flies for refuge to Mr. Prince, or to the crib.

He keeps the flogging department in his own hands; finding that his son was too savage. He has awful brows and a big voice. But his roar frightens nobody. It is only a lion's skin; or, so to say, a muff.

Little Mordant made a picture of him with large ears, like a well- known domestic animal, and had his own justly boxed for the caricature. The Doctor discovered him in the fact, and was in a flaming rage, and threatened whipping at first; but in the course of the day an opportune basket of game arriving from Mordant's father, the Doctor became mollified, and has burnt the picture with the ears. However, I have one wafered up in my desk by the hand of the same little rascal.

THE COCK OF THE SCHOOL.

I am growing an old fellow, and have seen many great folks in the course of my travels and time: Louis Philippe coming out of the Tuileries; his Majesty the King of Prussia and the Reichsverweser accolading each other at Cologne at my elbow; Admiral Sir Charles Napier (in an omnibus once), the Duke of Wellington, the immortal Goethe at Weimar, the late benevolent Pope Gregory XVI., and a score more of the famous in this world—the whom whenever one looks at, one has a mild shock of awe and tremor. I like this feeling and decent fear and trembling with which a modest spirit salutes a GREAT MAN.

Well, I have seen generals capering on horseback at the head of their crimson battalions; bishops sailing down cathedral aisles, with downcast eyes, pressing their trencher caps to their hearts with their fat white hands; college heads when her Majesty is on a visit; the doctor in all his glory at the head of his school on speech-day: a great sight and all great men these. I have never met the late Mr. Thomas Cribb, but I have no doubt should have regarded him with the same feeling of awe with which I look every day at George Champion, the Cock of Dr. Birch's school.

When, I say, I reflect as I go up and set him a sum, that he could whop me in two minutes, double up Prince and the other assistant, and pitch the Doctor out of window, I can't but think how great, how generous, how magnanimous a creature this is, that sits quite quiet and good-natured, and works his equation, and ponders through his Greek play. He might take the school-room pillars and pull the house down if he liked. He might close the door, and demolish every one of us, like Antar the lover or Ibla; but he lets us live. He never thrashes anybody without a cause; when woe betide the tyrant or the sneak!

I think that to be strong, and able to whop everybody—(not to do it, mind you, but to feel that you were able to do it,)—would be the greatest of all gifts. There is a serene good humor which plays about George Champion's broad face, which shows the consciousness of this power, and lights up his honest blue eyes with a magnanimous calm.

He is invictus. Even when a cub there was no beating this lion. Six years ago the undaunted little warrior actually stood up to Frank Davison,—

(the Indian officer now—poor little Charley's brother, whom Miss Raby nursed so affectionately,)—then seventeen years old, and the Cock of Birch's. They were obliged to drag off the boy, and Frank, with admiration and regard for him, prophesied the great things he would do. Legends of combats are preserved fondly in schools; they have stories of such at Rodwell Regis, performed in the old Doctor's time, forty years ago.

Champion's affair with the Young Tutbury Pet, who was down here in training,—with Black the bargeman,—with the three head boys of Doctor Wapshot's academy, whom he caught maltreating an outlying day-boy of ours, known to all the Rodwell Regis men. He was always victorious. He is modest and kind, like all great men. He has a good, brave, honest understanding. He cannot make verses like young Pinder, or read Greek like Wells the Prefect, who is a perfect young abyss of learning, and knows enough, Prince says, to furnish any six first-class men; but he does his work in a sound downright way, and he is made to be the bravest of soldiers, the best of country parsons, an honest English gentleman wherever he may go.

Old Champion's chief friend and attendant is Young Jack Hall, whom he saved, when drowning, out of the Miller's Pool. The attachment of the two is curious to witness. The smaller lad gambolling, playing tricks round the bigger one, and perpetually making fun of his protector. They are never far apart, and of holidays you may meet them miles away from the school,— George sauntering heavily down the lanes with his big stick, and little Jack larking with the pretty girls in the cottage-windows.

George has a boat on the river, in which, however, he commonly lies smoking, whilst Jack sculls him. He does not play at cricket, except when the school plays the county, or at Lord's in the holidays. The boys can't stand his bowling, and when he hits, it is like trying to catch a cannon-ball. I have seen him at tennis. It is a splendid sight to behold the young fellow bounding over the court with streaming yellow hair, like young Apollo in a flannel jacket.

The other head boys are Lawrence the captain, Bunce, famous chiefly for his magnificent appetite, and Pitman, surnamed Roscius, for his love of the drama. Add to these Swanky, called Macassar, from his partiality to that condiment, and who has varnished boots, wears white gloves on Sundays, and looks out for Miss Pinkerton's school (transferred from Chiswick to Rodwell Regis, and conducted by the nieces of the late Miss Barbara Pinkerton, the friend of our great lexicographer, upon the principles approved by him, and practised by that admirable woman,) as it passes into church.

Representations have been made concerning Mr. Horace Swanky's behavior; rumors have been uttered about notes in verse, conveyed in three-cornered puffs, by Mrs. Ruggles, who serves Miss Pinkerton's young ladies on Fridays,—and how Miss Didow, to whom the tart and enclosure were addressed, tried to make away with herself by swallowing a ball of cotton. But I pass over these absurd reports, as likely to affect the reputation of an admirable seminary conducted by irreproachable females. As they go into church Miss P. driving in her flock of lambkins with the crook of her parasol, how can it be helped if her forces and ours sometimes collide, as the boys are on their way up to the organ-loft? And I don't believe a word about the three-cornered puff, but rather that it was the invention of that jealous Miss Birch, who is jealous of Miss Raby, jealous of everybody who is good and handsome, and who has HER OWN ENDS in view, or I am very much in error.

THE DEAR BROTHERS.


```
THE DOCTOR.
MR. TIPPER, Uncle to the Masters Boxall.
BOXALL MAJOR, BOXALL MINOR, BROWN, JONES, SMITH, ROBINSON,
   TIFFIN MINIMUS.
```

```
B. Go it, old Boxall!
J. Give it him, young Boxall!
R. Pitch into him, old Boxall!
S. Two to one on young Boxall!
```

[Enter TIFFIN MINIMUS, running.

Tiffin Minimus.—Boxalls! you're wanted. (The Doctor to Mr. Tipper.) —Every boy in the school loves them, my dear sir; your nephews are a credit to my establishment. They are orderly, well-conducted, gentlemanlike boys. Let us enter and find them at their studies.

[Enter The DOCTOR and Mr. TIPPER.

GRAND TABLEAU.

THE LITTLE SCHOOL-ROOM.

What they call the little school-room is a small room at the other end of the great school; through which you go to the Doctor's private house, and where Miss Raby sits with her pupils. She has a half-dozen very small ones over whom she presides and teaches them in her simple way, until they are big or learned enough to face the great school-room. Many of them are in a hurry for promotion, the graceless little simpletons, and know no more than their elders when they are well off.

She keeps the accounts, writes out the bills, superintends the linen, and sews on the general shirt-buttons. Think of having such a woman at home to sew on one's shirt-buttons! But peace, peace, thou foolish heart!

Miss Raby is the Doctor's niece. Her mother was a beauty (quite unlike old Zoe therefore); and she married a pupil in the old Doctor's time who was killed afterwards, a captain in the East India service, at the siege of Bhurtpore. Hence a number of Indian children come to the Doctor's; for Raby was very much liked, and the uncle's kind reception of the orphan has been a good speculation for the school-keeper.

It is wonderful how brightly and gayly that little quick creature does her duty. She is the first to rise, and the last to sleep, if any business is to be done. She sees the other two women go off to parties in the town without even so much as wishing to join them. It is Cinderella, only contented to stay at home—content to bear Zoe's scorn and to admit Rosa's superior charms,—and to do her utmost to repay her uncle for his great kindness in housing her.

So you see she works as much as three maid-servants for the wages of one. She is as thankful when the Doctor gives her a new gown, as if he had presented her with a fortune; laughs at his stories most good-humoredly, listens to Zoe's scolding most meekly, admires Rosa with all her heart, and only goes out of the way when Jack Birch shows his sallow face: for she can't bear him, and always finds work when he comes near.

How different she is when some folks approach her! I won't be presumptuous; but I think, I think, I have made a not unfavorable impression in some quarters. However, let us be mum on this subject. I like to see her, because she always looks good-humored; because she is always kind, because she is always modest, because she is fond of those poor little brats,—orphans some of them— because she is rather pretty, I dare say, or because I think so, which comes to the same thing.

Though she is kind to all, it must be owned she shows the most gross favoritism towards the amiable children. She brings them cakes from dessert, and regales them with Zoe's preserves; spends many of her little shillings in presents for her favorites, and will tell them stories by the hour. She has one very sad story about a little boy, who died long ago: the younger children are never weary of hearing about him; and Miss Raby has shown to one of them a lock of the little chap's hair, which she keeps in her work- box to this day.

A HOPELESS CASE.

Let us, people who are so uncommonly clever and learned, have a great tenderness and pity for the poor folks who are not endowed with the prodigious talents which we have. I have always had a regard for dunces;—those of my own school-days were amongst the pleasantest of the fellows, and have turned out by no means the dullest in life; whereas many a youth who could turn off Latin hexameters by the yard, and construe Greek quite glibly, is no better than a feeble prig now, with not a pennyworth more brains than were in his head before his beard grew.

Those poor dunces! Talk of being the last man, ah! what a pang it must be to be the last boy—huge, misshapen, fourteen years of age, and "taken up" by a chap who is but six years old, and can't speak quite plain yet!

Master Hulker is in that condition at Birch's. He is the most honest, kind, active, plucky, generous creature. He can do many things better than most boys. He can go up a tree, pump, play at cricket, dive and swim perfectly—he can eat twice as much as almost any lady (as Miss Birch well knows), he has a pretty talent at carving figures with his hack-knife, he makes and paints little coaches, he can take a watch to pieces and put it together again. He can do everything but learn his lesson; and then he sticks at the bottom of the school hopeless. As the little boys are drafted in from Miss Raby's class, (it is true she is one of the best instructresses in the world,) they enter and hop over poor Hulker. He would be handed over to the governess, only he is too big. Sometimes, I used to think that this desperate stupidity was a stratagem of the poor rascal's, and that he shammed dulness, so that he might be degraded into Miss Raby's class—if she would teach ME, I know, before George, I would put on a pinafore and a little jacket—but no, it is a natural incapacity for the Latin Grammar.

If you could see his grammar, it is a perfect curiosity of dog's ears. The leaves and cover are all curled and ragged. Many of the pages are worn away with the rubbing of his elbows as he sits poring over the hopeless volume, with the blows of his fists as he thumps it madly, or with the poor fellow's tears. You see him wiping them away with the back of his hand, as he tries and tries, and can't do it.

When I think of that Latin Grammar, and that infernal As in praesenti, and of other things which I was made to learn in my youth; upon my conscience, I am surprised that we ever survived it. When one thinks of the boys who have been caned because they could not master that intolerable jargon! Good Lord, what a pitiful chorus these poor little creatures send up! Be gentle with them, ye schoolmasters, and only whop those who WON'T learn.

The Doctor has operated upon Hulker (between ourselves), but the boy was so little affected you would have thought he had taken chloroform. Birch is weary of whipping now, and leaves the boy to go his own gait. Prince, when he hears the lesson, and who cannot help making fun of a fool, adopts the sarcastic manner with Master Hulker, and says, "Mr. Hulker, may I take the liberty to inquire if your brilliant intellect has enabled you to perceive the difference between those words which grammarians have defined as substantive and adjective nouns?—if not, perhaps Mr. Ferdinand Timmins will instruct you." And Timmins hops over Hulker's head.

I wish Prince would leave off girding at the poor lad. He is a boy, and his mother is a widow woman, who loves him with all her might. There is a famous sneer about the suckling of fools and the chronicling of small beer; but remember it was a rascal who uttered it.

A WORD ABOUT MISS BIRCH.

"The gentlemen, and especially the younger and more tender of these pupils, will have the advantage of the constant superintendence and affectionate care of Miss Zoe Birch, sister of the principal: whose clearest aim will be to supply (as far as may be) the absent maternal friend."—Prospectus of Rodwell Regis School.

This is all very well in the Doctor's prospectus, and Miss Zoe Birch—(a pretty blossom it is, fifty-five years old, during two score of which she has dosed herself with pills; with a nose as red and a face as sour as a crab-apple)—this is all mighty well in a prospectus. But I should like to know who would take Miss Zoe for a mother, or would have her for one?

The only persons in the house who are not afraid of her are Miss Rosa and I—no, I am afraid of her, though I DO know the story about the French usher in 1830—but all the rest tremble before the woman, from the Doctor down to poor Francis the knife-boy, whom she bullies into his miserable blacking-hole.

The Doctor is a pompous and outwardly severe man—but inwardly weak and easy; loving a joke and a glass of port-wine. I get on with him, therefore, much better than Mr. Prince, who scorns him for an ass, and under whose keen eyes the worthy Doctor writhes like a convicted impostor; and many a sunshiny afternoon would he have said, "Mr. T., sir, shall we try another glass of that yellow sealed wine which you seem to like?" (and which he likes even better than I do,) had not the old harridan of a Zoe been down upon us, and insisted on turning me out with her abominable weak coffee. She a mother indeed! A sour-milk generation she would have nursed. She is always croaking, scolding, bullying—yowling at the housemaids, snarling at Miss Raby, bowwowing after the little boys, barking after the big ones. She knows how much every boy eats to an ounce; and her delight is to ply with fat the little ones who can't bear it, and with raw meat those who hate underdone. It was she who caused the Doctor to be eaten out three times; and nearly created a rebellion in the school because she insisted on his flogging Goliath Longman.

The only time that woman is happy is when she comes in of a morning to the little boys' dormitories with a cup of hot Epsom salts, and a sippet of bread. Boo!—the very notion makes me quiver. She stands over them. I saw her do it to young Byles only a few days since; and her presence makes the abomination doubly abominable.

As for attending them in real illness, do you suppose that she would watch a single night for any one of them? Not she. When poor little Charley Davison (that child a lock of whose soft hair I have said how Miss Raby still keeps) lay ill of scarlet fever in the holidays—for the Colonel, the father of these boys, was in India—it was Anne Raby who tended the child, who watched him all through the fever, who never left him while it lasted, or until she had closed the little eyes that were never to brighten or moisten more. Anny watched and deplored him; but it was Miss Birch who wrote the letter announcing his demise, and got the gold chain and locket which the Colonel ordered as a memento of his gratitude. It was through a row with Miss Birch that Frank Davison ran away. I promise you that after he joined his regiment in India, the Ahmednuggur Irregulars, which his gallant father commands, there came over no more annual shawls and presents to Dr. and Miss Birch; and that if she fancied the Colonel was coming home to marry her (on account of her tenderness to his motherless children, which he was always writing about), THAT notion was very soon given up. But these affairs are of early date, seven years back, and I only heard of them in a very confused manner from Miss Raby, who was a girl, and had just come to Rodwell Regis. She is always very much moved when she speaks about those boys; which is but seldom. I take it the death of the little one still grieves her tender heart.

Yes, it is Miss Birch, who has turned away seventeen ushers and second-masters in eleven years, and half as many French masters, I suppose, since the departure of her FAVORITE, M. Grinche, with her gold watch, but this is only surmise—that is, from hearsay, and from Miss Rosa taunting her aunt, as she does sometimes, in her graceful way: but besides this, I have another way of keeping her in order.

Whenever she is particularly odious or insolent to Miss Raby, I have but to introduce raspberry jam into the conversation, and the woman holds her tongue. She will understand me. I need not say more.

NOTE, 12th December. I MAY speak now. I have left the place and don't mind. I say then at once, and without caring twopence for the consequences, that I saw this woman, this MOTHER of the boys, EATING JAM WITH A SPOON OUT OF MASTER WIGGINS'S TRUNK IN THE

BOX- ROOM: and of this I am ready to take an affidavit any day.

BRIGGS IN LUCK.

If this story does not carry its own moral, what fable does, I wonder? Before the arrival of that hamper, Master Briggs was in no better repute than any other young gentleman of the lower school; and in fact I had occasion myself, only lately, to correct Master Brown for kicking his friend's shins during the writing-lesson. But how this basket, directed by his mother's housekeeper and marked "Glass with care," (whence I conclude that it contains some jam and some bottles of wine, probably, as well as the usual cake and game-pie, and half a sovereign for the elder Master B., and five new shillings for Master Decimus Briggs)—how, I say, the arrival of this basket alters all Master Briggs's circumstances in life, and the estimation in which many persons regard him!

If he is a good-hearted boy, as I have reason to think, the very first thing he will do, before inspecting the contents of the hamper, or cutting into them with the knife which Master Brown has so considerately lent him, will be to read over the letter from home which lies on the top of the parcel. He does so, as I remark to Miss Raby (for whom I happened to be mending pens when the little circumstance arose), with a flushed face and winking eyes. Look how the other boys are peering into the basket as he reads.—I say to her, "Isn't it a pretty picture?" Part of the letter is in a very large hand. This is from his little sister. And I would wager that she netted the little purse which he has just taken out of it, and which Master Lynx is eying.

"You are a droll man, and remark all sorts of queer things," Miss Raby says, smiling, and plying her swift needle and fingers as quick as possible.

"I am glad we are both on the spot, and that the little fellow lies under our guns as it were, and so is protected from some such brutal school-pirate as young Duval for instance, who would rob him, probably, of some of those good things; good in themselves, and better because fresh from home. See, there is a pie as I said, and which I dare say is better than those which are served at our table (but you never take any notice of such kind of things, Miss Raby), a cake of course, a bottle of currant-wine, jam-pots, and no end of pears in the straw. With their money little Briggs will be able to pay the tick which that imprudent child has run up with Mrs. Ruggles; and I shall let Briggs Major pay for the pencil-case which Bullock sold to him.—It will be a lesson to the young prodigal for the future. But, I say, what a change there will be in his life for some time to come, and at least until his present wealth is spent! The boys who bully him will mollify towards him, and accept his pie and sweetmeats. They will have feasts in the bedroom; and that wine will taste more delicious to them than the best out of the Doctor's cellar. The cronies will be invited. Young Master Wagg will tell his most dreadful story and sing his best song for a slice of that pie. What a jolly night they will have! When we go the rounds at night, Mr. Prince and I will take care to make a noise before we come to Briggs's room, so that the boys may have time to put the light out, to push the things away, and to scud into bed. Doctor Spry may be put in requisition the next morning."

"Nonsense! you absurd creature," cries out Miss Raby, laughing; and I lay down the twelfth pen very nicely mended.

"Yes; after luxury comes the doctor, I say; after extravagance a hole in the breeches pocket. To judge from his disposition, Briggs Major will not be much better off a couple of days hence than he is now; and, if I am not mistaken, will end life a poor man. Brown will be kicking his shins before a week is over, depend upon it. There are boys and men of all sorts, Miss R. —There are selfish sneaks who hoard until the store they daren't use grows mouldy— there are spendthrifts who fling away, parasites who flatter and lick its shoes, and snarling curs who hate and envy, good fortune."

I put down the last of the pens, brushing away with it the quill- chips from her desk first, and she looked at me with a kind, wondering face. I brushed them away, clicked the penknife into my pocket, made her a bow, and walked off—for the bell was ringing for school.

A YOUNG FELLOW WHO IS PRETTY SURE TO SUCCEED.

If Master Briggs is destined in all probability to be a poor man, the chances are that Mr. Bullock will have a very different lot, he is a son of a partner of the eminent banking firm of Bullock and Hulker, Lombard street, and very high in the upper school—quite out of my jurisdiction, consequently.

He writes the most beautiful current-hand ever seen; and the way in which he mastered arithmetic (going away into recondite and wonderful rules in the Tutor's Assistant, which some masters even dare not approach,) is described by the Doctor in terms of admiration. He is Mr. Prince's best algebra pupil; and a very fair classic, too; doing everything well for which he has a mind.

He does not busy himself with the sports of his comrades, and holds a cricket-bat no better than Miss Raby would. He employs the play- hours in improving his mind, and reading the newspaper; he is a profound politician, and, it must be owned, on the liberal side. The elder boys despise him rather; and when champion Major passes, he turns his head, and looks down. I don't like the expression of Bullock's narrow green eyes, as they follow the elder Champion, who does not seem to know or care how much the other hates him.

No. Mr. Bullock, though perhaps the cleverest and most accomplished boy in the school, associates with the quite little boys when he is minded for society. To these he is quite affable, courteous, and winning. He never fagged or thrashed one of them. He has done the verses and corrected the exercises of many, and many is the little lad to whom he has lent a little money.

It is true he charges at the rate of a penny a week for every sixpence lent out; but many a fellow to whom tarts are a present necessity is happy to pay this interest for the loan. These transactions are kept secret. Mr. Bullock, in rather a whining tone, when he takes Master Green aside and does the requisite business for him, says, "You know you'll go and talk about it everywhere. I don't want to lend you the money, I want to buy something with it. It's only to oblige you; and yet I am sure you will go and make fun of me." Whereon, of course, Green, eager for the money, vows solemnly that the transaction shall be confidential, and only speaks when the payment of the interest becomes oppressive.

Thus it is that Mr. Bullock's practices are at all known. At a very early period, indeed, his commercial genius manifested itself: and by happy speculations in toffey; by composing a sweet drink made of stick-liquorice and brown sugar, and selling it at a profit to the younger children; by purchasing a series of novels, which he let out at an adequate remuneration; by doing boys' exercises for a penny, and other processes, he showed the bent of his mind. At the end of the half-year he always went home richer than when he arrived at school, with his purse full of money.

Nobody knows how much he brought: but the accounts are fabulous. Twenty, thirty, fifty—it is impossible to say how many sovereigns. When joked about his money, he turns pale and swears he has not a shilling: whereas he has had a banker's account ever since he was thirteen.

At the present moment he is employed in negotiating the sale of a knife with Master Green, and is pointing out to the latter the beauty of the six blades, and that he need not pay until after the holidays.

Champion Major has sworn that he will break every bone in his skin the next time that he cheats a little boy, and is bearing down upon him. Let us come away. It is frightful to see that big peaceful clever coward moaning under well-deserved blows and whining for mercy.

DUVAL THE PIRATE.

JONES MINIMUS passes, laden with tarts.

```
Duval.—Hullo! you small boy with the tarts!  Come here, sir.
Jones Minimus.—Please, Duval, they ain't mine.
Duval.—Oh, you abominable young story-teller.
                              [He confiscates the goods.
```

I think I like young Duval's mode of levying contributions better than Bullock's. The former's, at least, has the merit of more candor. Duval is the pirate of Birch's, and lies in wait for small boys laden with money or provender. He scents plunder from afar off: and pounces out on it. Woe betide the little fellow when Duval boards him!

There was a youth here whose money I used to keep, as he was of an extravagant and weak taste; and I doled it out to him in weekly shillings, sufficient for the purchase of the necessary tarts. This boy came to me one day for half a sovereign, for a very particular purpose, he said. I afterwards found he wanted to lend the money to Duval.

The young ogre burst out laughing, when in a great wrath and fury I ordered him to refund to the little boy: and proposed a bill of exchange at three months. It is true Duval's father does not pay the Doctor, and the lad never has a shilling, save that which he levies; and though he is always bragging about the splendor of Freenystown, Co. Cork, and the fox-hounds his father keeps, and the claret they drink there—there comes no remittance from Castle Freeny in these bad times to the honest Doctor; who is a kindly man enough, and never yet turned an insolvent boy out of doors.

THE DORMITORIES.

MASTER HEWLETT AND MASTER NIGHTINGALE
(Rather a cold winter night.)

Hewlett (flinging a shoe at Master Nightingale's bed, with which he hits that young gentleman).—Hullo, you! Get up and bring me that shoe!

Nightingale.—Yes, Hewlett. (He gets up.)

Hewlett.—Don't drop it, and be very careful of it, sir.

Nightingale.—Yes, Hewlett.

Hewlett.—Silence in the dormitory! Any boy who opens his mouth, I'll murder him. Now, sir, are not you the boy what can sing?

Nightingale.—Yes, Hewlett.

Hewlett.—Chant, then, till I go to sleep, and if I wake when you stop, you'll have this at your head.

[Master HEWLETT lays his Bluchers on the bed, ready to shy at Master Nightingale's head in the case contemplated.]

Nightingale (timidly).—Please, Hewlett?

Hewlett.—Well, sir?

Nightingale.—May I put on my trousers, please?

Hewlett.—No, sir. Go on, or I'll—

Nightingale.—

"Through pleasures and palaces Though we may roam, Be it ever so humble There's no place like home."

A CAPTURE AND A RESCUE.

My young friend, Patrick Champion, George's younger brother, is a late arrival among us; has much of the family quality and good nature; is not in the least a tyrant to the small boys, but is as eager as Amadis to fight. He is boxing his way up the school, emulating his great brother. He fixes his eye on a boy above him in strength or size, and you hear somehow that a difference has arisen between them at football, and they have their coats off presently. He has thrashed himself over the heads of many youths in this manner: for instance, if Champion can lick Dobson, who can thrash Hobson, how much more, then, can he thrash Hobson? Thus he works up and establishes his position in the school. Nor does Mr. Prince think it advisable that we ushers should walk much in the way when these little differences are being settled, unless there is some gross disparity, or danger is apprehended.

For instance, I own to having seen this row as I was shaving at my bedroom window. I did not hasten down to prevent its consequences. Fogle had confiscated a top, the property of Snivins; the which, as the little wretch was always pegging it at my toes, I did not regret. Snivins whimpered; and young Champion came up, lusting for battle. Directly he made out Fogle, he steered for him, pulling up his coat-sleeves, and clearing for action.

"Who spoke to YOU, young Champion?" Fogle said, and he flung down the top to Master Snivins. I knew there would be no fight; and perhaps Champion, too, was disappointed,

THE GARDEN, WHERE THE PARLOR-BOARDERS GO.

Noblemen have been rather scarce at Birch's—but the heir of a great Prince has been living with the Doctor for some years.—He is Lord George Gaunt's eldest son, the noble Plantagenet Gaunt Gaunt, and nephew of the Most Honorable the Marquis of Steyne.

They are very proud of him at the Doctor's—and the two Misses and Papa, whenever a stranger comes down whom they want to dazzle, are pretty sure to bring Lord Steyne into the conversation, mention the last party at Gaunt House, and cursorily to remark that they have with them a young friend who will be, in all human probability, Marquis of Steyne and Earl of Gaunt,

Plantagenet does not care much about these future honors: provided he can get some brown sugar on his bread-and-butter, or sit with three chairs and play at coach-and-horses quite quietly by himself, he is tolerably happy. He saunters in and out of school when he likes, and looks at the masters and other boys with a listless grin. He used to be taken to church, but he laughed and talked in odd places, so they are forced to leave him at home now. He will sit with a bit of string and play cat's-cradle for many hours. He likes to go and join the very small children at their games. Some are frightened at him; but they soon cease to fear, and order him about. I have seen him go and fetch tarts from Mrs. Ruggles for a boy of eight years old; and cry bitterly if he did not get a piece. He cannot speak quite plain, but very nearly; and is not more, I suppose, than three-and-twenty.

Of course at home they know his age, though they never come and see him. But they forget that Miss Rosa Birch is no longer a young chit as she was ten years ago, when Gaunt was brought to the school. On the contrary, she has had no small experience in the tender passion, and is at this moment smitten with a disinterested affection for Plantagenet Gaunt.

Next to a little doll with a burnt nose, which he hides away in cunning places, Mr. Gaunt is very fond of Miss Rosa too. What a pretty match it would make! and how pleased they would be at Gaunt House, if the grandson and heir of the great Marquis of Steyne, the descendant of a hundred Gaunts and Tudors, should marry Miss Birch, thc schoolmaster's daughter! It is true she has the sense on her side, and poor Plantagenet is only an idiot: but there he is, a zany, with such expectations and such a pedigree!

If Miss Rosa would run away with Mr. Gaunt, she would leave off bullying her cousin, Miss Anny Raby. Shall I put her up to the notion, and offer to lend her the money to run away? Mr. Gaunt is not allowed money. He had some once, but Bullock took him into a corner, and got it from him. He has a moderate tick opened at a tart-woman's. He stops at Rodwell Regis through the year: school- time and holiday-time, it is all the same to him. Nobody asks about him, or thinks about him, save twice a year, when the Doctor goes to Gaunt House, and gets the amount of his bills, and a glass of wine in the steward's room.

And yet you see somehow that he is a gentleman. His manner is different to that of the owners of that coarse table and parlor at which he is a boarder (I do not speak of Miss R. of course, for HER manners are as good as those of a duchess). When he caught Miss Rosa boxing little Fiddes's ears, his face grew red, and he broke into a fierce inarticulate rage. After that, and for some days, he used to shrink from her; but they are reconciled now. I saw them this afternoon in the garden where only the parlor-boarders walk. He was playful, and touched her with his stick. She raised her handsome eyes in surprise, and smiled on him very kindly.

The thing was so clear, that I thought it my duty to speak to old Zoe about it. The wicked old catamaran told me she wished that some people would mind their own business, and hold their tongues— that some persons were paid to teach writing, and not to tell tales and make mischief: and I have since been thinking whether I ought to communicate with the Doctor.

THE OLD PUPIL.

As I came into the playgrounds this morning, I saw a dashing young fellow, with a tanned face and a blond moustache, who was walking up and down the green arm-in-arm with Champion Major, and followed by a little crowd of boys.

They were talking of old times evidently. "What had become of Irvine and Smith?"—"Where was Bill Harris and Jones: not Squinny Jones, but Cocky Jones?"—and so forth. The gentleman was no stranger; he was an old pupil evidently, come to see if any of his old comrades remained, and revisit the cari luoghi of his youth.

Champion was evidently proud of his arm-fellow, he espied his brother, young Champion, and introduced him. "Come here, sir," he called. "The young 'un wasn't here in your time, Davison." "Pat, sir," said he, "this is Captain Davison, one of Birch's boys. Ask him who was among the first in the lines at Sobraon?"

Pat's face kindled up as he looked Davison full in the face, and held out his hand. Old Champion and Davison both blushed. The infantry set up a "Hurray, hurray, hurray," Champion leading, and waving his wide-awake. I protest that the scene did one good to witness. Here was the hero and cock of the school come back to see his old haunts and cronies. He had always remembered them. Since he had seen them last, he had faced death and achieved honor. But for my dignity I would have shied up my hat too.

With a resolute step, and his arm still linked in Champion's, Captain Davison now advanced, followed by a wake of little boys, to that corner of the green where Mrs. Ruggles has her tart stand.

"Hullo, Mother Ruggles! don't you remember me?" he said, and shook her by the hand.

"Lor, if it ain't Davison Major!" she said. "Well, Davison Major, you owe me fourpence for two sausage-rolls from when you went away."

Davison laughed, and all the little crew of boys set up a similar chorus.

"I buy the whole shop," he said. "Now, young 'uns—eat away!"

Then there was such a "Hurray! hurray!" as surpassed the former cheer in loudness. Everybody engaged in it except Piggy Duff, who made an instant dash at the three-cornered puffs, but was stopped by Champion, who said there should be a fair distribution. And so there was, and no one lacked, neither of raspberry, open tarts, nor of mellifluous bulls'-eyes, nor of polonies, beautiful to the sight and taste.

The hurraying brought out the old Doctor himself, who put his hand up to his spectacles and started when he saw the old pupil. Each blushed when he recognized the other; for seven years ago they had parted not good friends.

"What—Davison?" the Doctor said, with a tremulous voice. "God bless you, my dear fellow!"—and they shook hands. "A half holiday, of course, boys," he added, and there was another hurray: there was to be no end to the cheering that day.

"How's—how's the family, sir?" Captain Davison asked.

"Come in and see. Rosa's grown quite a lady. Dine with us, of course. Champion Major, come to dinner at five. Mr. Titmarsh, the pleasure of your company?" The Doctor swung open the garden gate: the old master and pupil entered the house reconciled.

I thought I would first peep into Miss Raby's room, and tell her of this event. She was working away at her linen there, as usual quiet and cheerful.

"You should put up," I said with a smile; "the Doctor has given us a half-holiday."

"I never have holidays," Miss Raby replied.

Then I told her of the scene I had just witnessed, of the arrival of the old pupil, the purchase of the tarts, the proclamation of the holiday, and the shouts of the boys of "Hurray, Davison!"

"WHO is it?" cried out Miss Raby, starting and turning as white as a sheet.

I told her it was Captain Davison from India; and described the appearance and behavior of the Captain. When I had finished speaking, she asked me to go and get her a glass of water; she felt unwell. But she was gone when I came back with the water.

I know all now. After sitting for a quarter of an hour with the Doctor, who attributed his guest's uneasiness no doubt to his desire to see Miss Rosa Birch, Davison started up and said he wanted to see Miss Raby. "You remember, sir, how kind she was to my little brother, sir?" he said. Whereupon the Doctor, with a look of surprise, that anybody should want to see Miss Raby, said she was in the little school-room; whither the Captain went, knowing the way from old times.

A few minutes afterwards, Miss B. and Miss Z. returned from a drive with Plantagenet Gaunt in their one-horse fly, and being informed of Davison's arrival, and that he was closeted with Miss Raby in the little school-room, of course made for that apartment at once. I was coming into it from the other door. I wanted to know whether she had drunk the water.

This is what both parties saw. The two were in this very attitude. "Well, upon my word!" cries out Miss Zoe; but Davison did not let go his hold; and Miss Raby's head only sank down on his hand.

"You must get another governess, sir, for the little boys," Frank Davison said to the Doctor. "Anny Raby has promised to come with me."

You may suppose I shut to the door on my side. And when I returned to the little school-room, it was black and empty. Everybody was gone. I could hear the boys shouting at play in the green outside. The glass of water was on the table where I had placed it. I took it and drank it myself, to the health of Anny Raby and her husband. It was rather a choker.

But of course I wasn't going to stop on at Birch's. When his young friends reassemble on the 1st of February next, they will have two new masters. Prince resigned too, and is at present living with me at my old lodgings at Mrs. Cammysole's. If any nobleman or gentleman wants a private tutor for his son, a note to the Rev. F. Prince will find him there.

Miss Clapperclaw says we are both a couple of old fools; and that she knew when I set off last year to Rodwell Regis, after meeting the two young ladies at a party at General Champion's house in our street, that I was going on a goose's errand. I shall dine there on Christmas-day; and so I wish a merry Christmas to all young and old boys.

EPILOGUE.

The play is done; the curtain drops,
Slow falling, to the prompter's bell:
A moment yet the actor stops,
And looks around, to say farewell.
It is an irksome word and task;
And when he's laughed and said his say,
He shows, as he removes the mask,
A face that's anything but gay.

One word, ere yet the evening ends,
Let's close it with a parting rhyme,
And pledge a hand to all young friends,
As fits the merry Christmas time.
On life's wide scene you, too, have parts,
That Fate ere long shall bid you play;
Good night! with honest gentle hearts
A kindly greeting go alway!

Good night! I'd say the griefs, the joys,
Just hinted in this mimic page,
The triumphs and defeats of boys,
Are but repeated in our age.
I'd say, your woes were not less keen,
Your hopes more vain, than those of men,
Your pangs or pleasures of fifteen,
At forty-five played o'er again.

I'd say, we suffer and we strive
Not less nor more as men than boys;
With grizzled beards at forty-five,
As erst at twelve, in corduroys.
And if, in time of sacred youth,
We learned at home to love and pray,
Pray heaven, that early love and truth
May never wholly pass away.

And in the world, as in the school,
I'd say, how fate may change and shift;
The prize be sometimes with the fool,

The race not always to the swift.
The strong may yield, the good may fall,
The great man be a vulgar clown,
The knave be lifted over all,
The kind cast pitilessly down.

Who knows the inscrutable design?
Blessed be He who took and gave:
Why should your mother, Charles, not mine,
Be weeping at her darling's grave?*
We bow to heaven that will'd it so,
That darkly rules the fate of all,
That sends the respite or the blow,
That's free to give or to recall.

This crowns his feast with wine and wit:
Who brought him to that mirth and state?
His betters, see, below him sit,
Or hunger hopeless at the gate.
Who bade the mud from Dives' Wheel
To spurn the rags of Lazarus?
Come, brother, in that dust we'll kneel,
Confessing heaven that ruled it thus.

So each shall mourn in life's advance,
Dear hopes, dear friends, untimely killed;
Shall grieve for many a forfeit chance,
A longing passion unfulfilled.
Amen: whatever Fate be sent,—
Pray God the heart may kindly glow,
Although the head with cares be bent,
And whitened with the winter snow.

Come wealth or want, come good or ill,
Let young and old accept their part,
And bow before the Awful Will,
And bear it with an honest heart.
Who misses, or who wins the prize?
Go, lose or conquer as you can.
But if you fail, or if you rise,
Be each, pray God, a gentleman,

A gentleman, or old or young:
(Bear kindly with my humble lays,)
The sacred chorus first was sung
Upon the first of Christmas days.
The shepherds heard it overhead—
The joyful angels raised it then:

Glory to heaven on high, it said,
And peace on earth to gentle men.

My song, save this, is little worth;
I lay the weary pen aside,
And wish you health, and love, and mirth,
As fits the solemn Christmas tide.
As fits the holy Christmas birth,
Be this, good friends, our carol still—
Be peace on earth, be peace on earth,
To men of gentle will.

* C. B., ob. Dec. 1843, aet. 42.

PREFACE TO THE SECOND EDITION: BEING AN ESSAY ON THUNDER AND SMALL BEER.

Any reader who may have a fancy to purchase a copy of this present edition of the "History of the Kickleburys Abroad," had best be warned in time, that the Times newspaper does not approve of the work, and has but a bad opinion both of the author and his readers. Nothing can be fairer than this statement: if you happen to take up the poor little volume at a railroad station, and read this sentence, lay the book down, and buy something else. You are warned. What more can the author say? If after this you WILL buy, —amen! pay your money, take your book, and fall to. Between ourselves, honest reader, it is no very strong potation which the present purveyor offers to you. It will not trouble your head much in the drinking. It was intended for that sort of negus which is offered at Christmas parties and of which ladies and children may partake with refreshment and cheerfulness. Last year I tried a brew which was old, bitter, and strong; and scarce any one would drink it. This year we send round a milder tap, and it is liked by customers: though the critics (who like strong ale, the rogues!) turn up their noses. In heaven's name, Mr. Smith, serve round the liquor to the gentle-folks. Pray, dear madam, another glass; it is Christmas time, it will do you no harm. It is not intended to keep long, this sort of drink. (Come, froth up, Mr. Publisher, and pass quickly round!) And as for the professional gentlemen, we must get a stronger sort for THEM some day.

The Times' gentleman (a very difficult gent to please) is the loudest and noisiest of all, and has made more hideous faces over the refreshment offered to him than any other critic. There is no use shirking this statement! when a man has been abused in the Times, he can't hide it, any more than he could hide the knowledge of his having been committed to prison by Mr. Henry, or publicly caned in Pall Mall. You see it in your friends' eyes when they meet you. They know it. They have chuckled over it to a man. They whisper about it at the club, and look over the paper at you. My next-door neighbor came to see me this morning, and I saw by his face that he had the whole story pat. "Hem!" says he, "well, I HAVE heard of it; and the fact is, they were talking about you at dinner last night, and mentioning that the Times had—ahem!— 'walked into you.'"

"My good M——" I say—and M—— will corroborate, if need be, the statement I make here—"here is the Times' article, dated January 4th, which states so and so, and here is a letter from the publisher, likewise dated January 4th, and which says:—

"MY DEAR Sir,—Having this day sold the last copy of the first edition (of x thousand) of the 'Kickleburys Abroad,' and having orders for more, had we not better proceed to a second edition? and will you permit me to enclose an order on,"

Singular coincidence! And if every author who was so abused by a critic had a similar note from a publisher, good Lord! how easily would we take the critic's censure!

"Yes, yes," you say; "it is all very well for a writer to affect to be indifferent to a critique from the Times. You bear it as a boy bears a flogging at school, without crying out; but don't swagger and brag as if you liked it."

Let us have truth before all. I would rather have a good word than a bad one from any person: but if a critic abuses me from a high place, and it is worth my while, I will appeal. If I can show that the judge who is delivering sentence against me, and laying down the law and making a pretence of learning, has no learning and no law, and is neither more nor less than a pompous noodle, who ought not to be heard in any respectable court, I will do so; and then, dear friends, perhaps you will have something to laugh at in this book.—

"THE KICKLEBURYS ABROAD.

"It has been customary, of late years, for the purveyors of amusing literature—the popular authors of the day—to put forth certain opuscules, denominated 'Christmas Books,' with the ostensible intention of swelling the tide of exhilaration, or other expansive emotions, incident upon the exodus of the old and the inauguration of the new year. We have said that their ostensible intention was such, because there is another motive for these productions, locked up (as the popular author deems) in his own breast, but which betrays itself, in the quality of the work, as his principal incentive. Oh! that any muse should be set upon a high stool to cast up accounts and balance a ledger! Yet so it is; and the popular author finds it convenient to fill up the declared deficit, and place himself in a position the more effectually to encounter those liabilities which sternly assert themselves contemporaneously and in contrast with the careless and free-handed tendencies of the season by the emission of Christmas books—a kind of literary assignats, representing to the emitter expunged debts, to the receiver an investment of enigmatical value. For the most part bearing the stamp of their origin in the vacuity of the writer's exchequer rather than in the fulness of his genius, they suggest by their feeble flavor the rinsings of a void brain after the more important concoctions of the expired year. Indeed, we should as little think of taking these compositions as examples of the merits of their authors as we should think of measuring the valuable services of Mr. Walker, the postman, or Mr. Bell, the dust- collector, by the copy of verses they leave at our doors as a provocative of the expected annual gratuity—effusions with which they may fairly be classed for their intrinsic worth no less than their ultimate purport.

"In the Christmas book presently under notice, the author appears (under the thin disguise of Mr. Michael Angelo Titmarsh) in 'propria persona' as the popular author, the contributor to Punch, the remorseless pursuer of unconscious vulgarity and feeble- mindedness, launched upon a tour of relaxation to the Rhine. But though exercising, as is the wont of popular authors in their moments of leisure, a plentiful reserve of those higher qualities to which they are indebted for their fame, his professional instincts are not altogether in abeyance. From the moment his eye lights upon a luckless family group embarked on the same steamer with himself, the sight of his accustomed quarry—vulgarity, imbecility, and affectation—reanimates his relaxed sinews, and, playfully fastening his satiric fangs upon the familiar prey, he dallies with it in mimic ferocity like a satiated mouser.

"Though faintly and carelessly indicated, the characters are those with which the author loves to surround himself. A tuft-hunting county baronet's widow, an inane captain of dragoons, a graceless young baronet, a lady with groundless pretensions to feeble health and poesy, an obsequious nonentity her husband, and a flimsy and artificial young lady, are the personages in whom we are expected to find amusement. Two individuals alone form an exception to the above category, and are offered to the respectful admiration of the reader,—the one, a shadowy serjeant-at-law, Mr. Titmarsh's travelling companion, who escapes with a few side puffs of flattery, which the author struggles not to render ironical, and a mysterious countess, spoken of in a tone of religious reverence, and apparently introduced that we may learn by what delicate discriminations our adoration of rank should be regulated.

"To those who love to hug themselves in a sense of superiority by admeasurement with the most worthless of their species, in their most worthless aspects, the Kickleburys on the Rhine will afford an agreeable treat, especially as the purveyor of the feast offers his own moments of human weakness as a modest entree in this banquet of erring mortality. To our own, perhaps unphilosophical, taste the aspirations towards sentimental perfection of another popular author are infinitely preferable to these sardonic divings after the pearl of truth, whose lustre is eclipsed in the display of the diseased oyster. Much, in the present instance, perhaps all, the disagreeable effect of his subject is no doubt attributable to the absence of Mr. Thackeray's usual brilliancy of style. A few flashes, however, occur, such as the description of M. Lenoir's gaming establishment, with the momentous crisis to which it was subjected, and the quaint and imaginative sallies evoked by the whole town of Rougetnoirbourg and its lawful prince. These, with the illustrations, which are spirited enough, redeem the book from an absolute ban. Mr. Thackeray's pencil is more congenial than his pen. He cannot draw his men and women with their skins off, and, therefore, the effigies of his characters are pleasanter to contemplate than the flayed anatomies of the letter-press."

There is the whole article. And the reader will see (in the paragraph preceding that memorable one which winds up with the diseased oyster) that he must be a worthless creature for daring to like the book, as he could only do so from a desire to hug himself in a sense of superiority by admeasurement with the most worthless of his fellow-creatures!

The reader is worthless for liking a book of which all the characters are worthless, except two, which are offered to his respectful admiration; and of these two the author does not respect one, but struggles not to laugh in his face; whilst he apparently speaks of another in a tone of religious reverence, because the lady is a countess, and because he (the author) is a sneak. So reader, author, characters, are rogues all. Be there any honest men left, Hal? About Printing-house Square, mayhap you may light on an honest man, a squeamish man, a proper moral man, a man that shall talk you Latin by the half-column if you will but hear him.

And what a style it is, that great man's! What hoighth of foine language entoirely! How he can discoorse you in English for all the world as if it was Latin! For instance, suppose you and I had to announce the important news that some writers published what are called Christmas books; that Christmas books are so called because they are published at Christmas: and that the purpose of the authors is to try and amuse people. Suppose, I say, we had, by the sheer force of intellect, or by other means of observation or information, discovered these great truths, we should have announced them in so many words. And there it is that the difference lies between a great writer and a poor one; and we may see how an inferior man may fling a chance away. How does my friend of the Times put these propositions? "It has been customary," says he, "of late years for the purveyors of amusing literature to put forth certain opuscules, denominated Christmas books, with the ostensible intention of swelling the tide of exhilaration, or other expansive emotions, incident upon the exodus of the old or the inauguration of the new year." That is something like a sentence; not a word scarcely but's in Latin, and the longest and handsomest out of the whole dictionary. That is proper economy—as you see a buck from Holywell Street put every pinchbeck pin, ring, and chain which he possesses about his shirt, hands, and waistcoat, and then go and cut a dash in the Park, or swagger with his order to the theatre. It costs him no more to wear all his ornaments about his distinguished person than to leave them at home. If you can be a swell at a cheap rate, why not? And I protest, for my part, I had no idea what I was really about in writing and submitting my little book for sale, until my friend the critic, looking at the article, and examining it with the eyes of a connoisseur, pronounced that what I had fancied simply to be a book was in fact "an opuscule denominated so-and-so, and ostensibly intended to swell the tide of expansive emotion incident upon the inauguration of the new year." I can hardly believe as much even now—so little do we know what we really are after, until men of genius come and interpret.

And besides the ostensible intention, the reader will perceive that my judge has discovered another latent motive, which I had "locked up in my own breast." The sly rogue! (if we may so speak of the court.) There is no keeping anything from him; and this truth, like the rest, has come out, and is all over England by this time. Oh, that all England, which has bought the judge's charge, would purchase the prisoner's plea in mitigation! "Oh, that any muse should be set on a high stool," says the bench, "to cast up accounts and balance a ledger! Yet so it is; and the popular author finds it convenient to fill up the declared deficit by the emission of Christmas books—a kind of assignats that bear the stamp of their origin in the vacuity of the writer's exchequer." There is a trope for you! You rascal, you wrote because you wanted money! His lordship has found out what you were at, and that there is a deficit in your till. But he goes on to say that we poor devils are to be pitied in our necessity; and that these compositions are no more to be taken as examples of our merits than the verses which the dustman leaves at his lordship's door, "as a provocative of the expected annual gratuity," are to be considered as measuring his, the scavenger's, valuable services—nevertheless the author's and the scavenger's "effusions may fairly be classed, for their intrinsic worth, no less than their ultimate purport."

Heaven bless his lordship on the bench—What a gentle manlike badinage he has, and what a charming and playful wit always at hand! What a sense he has for a simile, or what Mrs. Malaprop calls an odorous comparison, and how gracefully he conducts it to "its ultimate purport." A gentleman writing a poor little book is a scavenger asking for a Christmas-box!

As I try this small beer which has called down such a deal of thunder, I can't help thinking that it is not Jove who has interfered (the case was scarce worthy of his divine vindictiveness); but the Thunderer's man, Jupiter Jeames, taking his master's place, adopting his manner, and trying to dazzle and roar like his awful employer. That figure of the dustman has hardly been flung from heaven: that "ultimate purport" is a subject which the Immortal would hardly handle. Well, well; let us allow that the book is not worthy of such a polite critic—that the beer is not strong enough for a gentleman who has taste and experience in beer.

That opinion no man can ask his honor to alter; but (the beer being the question), why make unpleasant allusions to the Gazette, and hint at the probable bankruptcy of the brewer? Why twit me with my poverty; and what can the Times' critic know about the vacuity of my exchequer? Did he ever lend me any money? Does he not himself write for money? (and who would grudge it to such a polite and generous and learned author?) If he finds no disgrace in being paid, why should I? If he has ever been poor, why should he joke at my empty exchequer? Of course such a genius is paid for his work: with such neat logic, such a pure style, such a charming poetical turn of phrase, of course a critic gets money. Why, a man who can say of a Christmas book that "it is an opuscule denominated so-and-so, and ostensibly intended to swell the tide of expansive emotion incident upon the exodus of the old year," must evidently have had immense sums and care expended on his early education, and deserves a splendid return. You can't go into the market, and get scholarship like THAT, without paying for it: even the flogging that such a writer must have had in early youth (if he was at a public school where the rods were paid for), must have cost his parents a good sum. Where would you find any but an accomplished classical scholar to compare the books of the present (or indeed any other) writer to "sardonic divings after the pearl of truth, whose lustre is eclipsed in the display of the diseased oyster;" mere Billingsgate doesn't turn out oysters like these; they are of the Lucrine lake:—this satirist has pickled his rods in Latin brine. Fancy, not merely a diver, but a sardonic diver: and the expression of his confounded countenance on discovering not only a pearl, but an eclipsed pearl, which was in a diseased oyster! I say it is only by an uncommon and happy combination of taste, genius, and industry, that a man can arrive at uttering such sentiments in such fine language,—that such a man ought to be well paid, as I have no doubt he is, and that he is worthily employed to write literary articles, in large type, in the leading journal of Europe. Don't we want men of eminence and polite learning to sit on the literary bench, and to direct the public opinion?

But when this profound scholar compares me to a scavenger who leaves a copy of verses at his door and begs for a Christmas-box, I must again cry out and say, "My dear sir, it is true your simile is offensive, but can you make it out? Are you not hasty in your figures and illusions?" If I might give a hint to so consummate a rhetorician, you should be more careful in making your figures figures, and your similes like: for instance, when you talk of a book "swelling the tide of exhilaration incident to the inauguration of the new year," or of a book "bearing the stamp of its origin in vacuity," of a man diving sardonically; or of a pearl eclipsed in the display of a diseased oyster—there are some people who will not apprehend your meaning: some will doubt whether you had a meaning: some even will question your great powers, and say, "Is this man to be a critic in a newspaper, which knows what English, and Latin too, and what sense and scholarship, are?" I don't quarrel with you—I take for granted your wit and learning, your modesty and benevolence—but why scavenger—Jupiter Jeames—why scavenger? A gentleman, whose biography the Examiner was fond of quoting before it took its present serious and orthodox turn, was pursued by an outraged wife to the very last stage of his existence with an appeal almost as pathetic—Ah, sir, why scavenger?

How can I be like a dustman that rings for a Christmas-box at your hall-door? I never was there in my life. I never left at your door a copy of verses provocative of an annual gratuity, as your noble honor styles it. Who are you? If you are the man I take you to be, it must have been you who asked the publisher for my book, and not I who sent it in, and begged a gratuity of your worship. You abused me out of the Times' window; but if ever your noble honor sent me a gratuity out of your own door, may I never drive another dust-cart. "Provocative of a gratuity!" O splendid swell! How much was it your worship sent out to me by the footman? Every farthing you have paid I will restore to your lordship, and I swear I shall not be a halfpenny the poorer.

As before, and on similar seasons and occasions, I have compared myself to a person following a not dissimilar calling: let me suppose now, for a minute, that I am a writer of a Christmas farce, who sits in the pit, and sees the performance of his own piece. There comes applause, hissing, yawning, laughter, as may be: but the loudest critic of all is our friend the cheap buck, who sits yonder and makes his remarks, so that all the audience may hear. "THIS a farce!" says Beau Tibbs: "demmy! it's the work of a poor devil who writes for money,—confound his vulgarity! This a farce! Why isn't it a tragedy, or a comedy, or an epic poem, stap my vitals? This a farce indeed! It's a feller as sends round his 'at, and appeals to charity. Let's 'ave our money back again, I say." And he swaggers off;—and you find the fellow came with an author's order.

But if, in spite of Tibbs, our "kyind friends," the little farce, which was meant to amuse Christmas (or what my classical friend calls Exodus), is asked for, even up to Twelfth Night,—shall the publisher stop because Tibbs is dissatisfied? Whenever that capitalist calls to get his money back, he may see the letter from the respected publisher, informing the author that all the copies are sold, and that there are demands for a new edition. Up with the curtain, then! Vivat Regina! and no money returned, except the Times "gratuity!"

M. A. TITMARSH.

January 5, 1851.

THE KICKLEBURYS ON THE RHINE.

The cabman, when he brought us to the wharf, and made his usual charge of six times his legal fare, before the settlement of which he pretended to refuse the privilege of an exeat regno to our luggage, glared like a disappointed fiend when Lankin, calling up the faithful Hutchison, his clerk, who was in attendance, said to him, "Hutchison, you will pay this man. My name is Serjeant Lankin, my chambers are in Pump Court. My clerk will settle with you, sir." The cabman trembled; we stepped on board; our lightsome luggage was speedily whisked away by the crew; our berths had been secured by the previous agency of Hutchison; and a couple of tickets, on which were written, "Mr. Serjeant Lankin," "Mr. Titmarsh," (Lankin's, by the way, incomparably the best and comfortablest sleeping place,) were pinned on to two of the curtains of the beds in a side cabin when we descended.

Who was on board? There were Jews, with Sunday papers and fruit; there were couriers and servants straggling about; there were those bearded foreign visitors of England, who always seem to decline to shave or wash themselves on the day of a voyage, and, on the eve of quitting our country, appear inclined to carry away as much as possible of its soil on their hands and linen: there were parties already cozily established on deck under the awning; and steady- going travellers for'ard, smoking already the pleasant morning cigar, and watching the phenomena of departure.

The bell rings: they leave off bawling, "Anybody else for the shore?" The last grape and Bell's Life merchant has scuffled over the plank: the Johns of the departing nobility and gentry line the brink of the quay, and touch their hats: Hutchison touches his hat to me—to ME, heaven bless him! I turn round inexpressibly affected and delighted, and whom do I see but Captain Hicks!

"Hallo! YOU here?" says Hicks, in a tone which seems to mean, "Confound you, you are everywhere."

Hicks is one of those young men who seem to be everywhere a great deal too often.

How are they always getting leave from their regiments? If they are not wanted in this country, (as wanted they cannot be, for you see them sprawling over the railing in Rotten Row all day, and shaking their heels at every ball in town,)—if they are not wanted in this country, I say, why the deuce are they not sent off to India, or to Demerara, or to Sierra Leone, by Jove?—the farther the better; and I should wish a good unwholesome climate to try 'em, and make 'em hardy. Here is this Hicks, then—Captain Launcelot Hicks, if you please—whose life is nothing but breakfast, smoking, riding-school, billiards, mess, polking, billiards, and smoking again, and da capo—pulling down his moustaches, and going to take a tour after the immense labors of the season.

"How do you do, Captain Hicks?" I say. "Where are you going?"

"Oh, I am going to the Whine," says Hicks; "evewybody goes to the Whine." The WHINE indeed! I dare say he can no more spell properly than he can speak.

"Who is on board—anybody?" I ask, with the air of a man of fashion. "To whom does that immense pile of luggage belong—under charge of the lady's-maid, the courier, and the British footman? A large white K is painted on all the boxes."

"How the deuce should I know?" says Hicks, looking, as I fancy, both red and angry, and strutting off with his great cavalry lurch and swagger: whilst my friend the Serjeant looks at him lost in admiration, and surveys his shining little boots, his chains and breloques, his whiskers and ambrosial moustaches, his gloves and other dandifications, with a pleased wonder; as the ladies of the Sultan's harem surveyed the great Lady from Park Lane who paid them a visit; or the simple subjects of Montezuma looked at one of Cortes's heavy dragoons.

"That must be a marquis at least," whispers Lankin, who consults me on points of society, and is pleased to have a great opinion of my experience.

I burst out in a scornful laugh. "THAT!" I say; "he is a captain of dragoons, and his father an attorney in Bedford Row. The whiskers of a roturier, my good Lankin, grow as long as the beard of a Plantagenet. It don't require much noble blood to learn the polka. If you were younger, Lankin, we might go for a shilling a night, and dance every evening at M. Laurent's Casino, and skip about in a little time as well as that fellow. Only we despise the kind of thing you know,—only we're too grave, and too steady."

"And too fat," whispers Lankin, with a laugh.

"Speak for yourself, you maypole," says I. "If you can't dance yourself, people can dance round you—put a wreath of flowers upon your old poll, stick you up in a village green, and so make use of you."

"I should gladly be turned into anything so pleasant," Lankin answers; "and so, at least, get a chance of seeing a pretty girl now and then. They don't show in Pump Court, or at the University Club, where I dine. You are a lucky fellow, Titmarsh, and go about in the world. As for me, I never—"

"And the judges' wives, you rogue?" I say. "Well, no man is satisfied; and the only reason I have to be angry with the captain yonder is, that, the other night, at Mrs. Perkins's, being in conversation with a charming young creature—who knows all my favorite passages in Tennyson, and takes a most delightful little line of opposition in the Church controversy—just as we were in the very closest, dearest, pleasantest part of the talk, comes up young Hotspur yonder, and whisks her away in a polka. What have you and I to do with polkas, Lankin? He took her down to supper— what have you and I to do with suppers?"

"Our duty is to leave them alone," said the philosophical Serjeant. "And now about breakfast—shall we have some?" And as he spoke, a savory little procession of stewards and stewards' boys, with drab tin dish-covers, passed from the caboose, and descended the stairs to the cabin. The vessel had passed Greenwich by this time, and had worked its way out of the mast-forest which guards the approaches of our city.

The owners of those innumerable boxes, bags, oil-skins, guitar- cases, whereon the letter K was engraven, appeared to be three ladies, with a slim gentleman of two or three and thirty, who was probably the husband of one of them. He had numberless shawls under his arm and guardianship. He had a strap full of Murray's Handbooks and Continental Guides in his keeping; and a little collection of parasols and umbrellas, bound together, and to be carried in state before the chief of the party, like the lictor's fasces before the consul.

The chief of the party was evidently the stout lady. One parasol being left free, she waved it about, and commanded the luggage and the menials to and fro. "Horace, we will sit there," she exclaimed, pointing to a comfortable place on the deck. Horace went and placed the shawls and the Guidebooks. "Hirsch, avy vou conty les bagages? tront sett morso ong too?" The German courier said, "Oui, miladi," and bowed a rather sulky assent. "Bowman, you will see that Finch is comfortable, and send her to me." The gigantic Bowman, a gentleman in an undress uniform, with very large and splendid armorial buttons, and with traces of the powder of the season still lingering in his hair, bows, and speeds upon my lady's errand.

I recognize Hirsch, a well-known face upon the European high-road, where he has travelled with many acquaintances. With whom is he making the tour now?—Mr. Hirsch is acting as courier to Mr. and Mrs. Horace Milliken. They have not been married many months, and they are travelling, Hirsch says, with a contraction of his bushy eyebrows, with miladi, Mrs. Milliken's mamma. "And who is her ladyship?" Hirsch's brow contracts into deeper furrows. "It is Miladi Gigglebury," he says, "Mr. Didmarsh. Berhabs you know her." He scowls round at her, as she calls out loudly, "Hirsch, Hirsch!" and obeys that summons.

It is the great Lady Kicklebury of Pocklington Square, about whom I remember Mrs. Perkins made so much ado at her last ball; and whom old Perkins conducted to supper. When Sir Thomas Kicklebury died (he was one of the first tenants of the Square), who does not remember the scutcheon with the coronet with two balls, that flamed over No. 36? Her son was at Eton then, and has subsequently taken an honorary degree at Oxford, and been an ornament of Platt's and the "Oswestry Club." He fled into St. James's from the great house in Pocklington Square, and from St. James's to Italy and the Mediterranean, where he has been for some time in a wholesome exile. Her eldest daughter's marriage with Lord Roughhead was talked about last year; but Lord Roughhead, it is known, married Miss Brent; and Horace Milliken, very much to his surprise, found himself the affianced husband of Miss Lavinia Kicklebury, after an agitating evening at Lady Polkimore's, when Miss Lavinia, feeling herself faint, went out on to the leads (the terrace, Lady Polkimore WILL call it), on the arm of Mr. Milliken. They were married in January: it's not a bad match for Miss K. Lady Kicklebury goes and stops for six months of the year at Pigeoncot with her daughter and son-in-law; and now that they are come abroad, she comes too. She must be with Lavinia, under the present circumstances.

When I am arm-in-arm, I tell this story glibly off to Lankin, who is astonished at my knowledge of the world, and says, "Why, Titmarsh, you know everything."

"I DO know a few things, Lankin my boy," is my answer. "A man don't live in society, and PRETTY GOOD society, let me tell you, for nothing."

The fact is, that all the above details are known to almost any man in our neighborhood. Lady Kicklebury does not meet with US much, and has greater folks than we can pretend to be at her parties. But we know about THEM. She'll condescend to come to Perkins's, WITH WHOSE FIRM SHE BANKS; and she MAY overdraw HER ACCOUNT: but of that, of course, I know nothing.

When Lankin and I go down stairs to breakfast, we find, if not the best, at least the most conspicuous places in occupation of Lady Kicklebury's party, and the hulking London footman making a darkness in the cabin, as he stoops through it bearing cups and plates to his employers.

[Why do they always put mud into coffee on board steamers? Why does the tea generally taste of boiled boots? Why is the milk scarce and thin? And why do they have those bleeding legs of boiled mutton for dinner? I ask why? In the steamers of other nations you are well fed. Is it impossible that Britannia, who confessedly rules the waves, should attend to the victuals a little, and that meat should be well cooked under a Union Jack? I just put in this question, this most interesting question, in a momentous parenthesis, and resume the tale.]

When Lankin and I descend to the cabin, then, the tables are full of gobbling people; and, though there DO seem to be a couple of places near Lady Kicklebury, immediately she sees our eyes directed to the inviting gap, she slides out, and with her ample robe covers even more than that large space to which by art and nature she is entitled, and calling out, "Horace, Horace!" and nodding, and winking, and pointing, she causes her son-in-law to extend the wing on his side. We are cut of THAT chance of a breakfast. We shall have the tea at its third water, and those two damp black mutton- chops, which nobody else will take, will fall to our cold share.

At this minute a voice, clear and sweet, from a tall lady in a black veil, says, "Mr. Titmarsh," and I start and murmur an ejaculation of respectful surprise, as I recognize no less a person than the Right Honorable the Countess of Knightsbridge, taking her tea, breaking up little bits of toast with her slim fingers, and sitting between a Belgian horse-dealer and a German violoncello- player who has a conge after the opera—like any other mortal.

I whisper her ladyship's name to Lankin. The Serjeant looks towards her with curiosity and awe. Even he, in his Pump Court solitudes, has heard of that star of fashion—that admired amongst men, and even women—that Diana severe yet simple, the accomplished Aurelia of Knightsbridge. Her husband has but a small share of HER qualities. How should he? The turf

and the fox-chase are his delights—the smoking-room at the "Travellers'"—
nay, shall we say it?—the illuminated arcades of "Vauxhall," and the
gambols of the dishevelled Terpsichore. Knightsbridge has his faults—ah!
even the peerage of England is not exempt from them. With Diana for his
wife, he flies the halls where she sits severe and serene, and is to be found
(shrouded in smoke, 'tis true,) in those caves where the contrite chimney-
sweep sings his terrible death chant, or the Bacchanalian judge administers
a satiric law. Lord Knightsbridge has his faults, then; but he has the gout at
Rougetnoirbourg, near the Rhine, and thither his wife is hastening to
minister to him.

"I have done," says Lady Knightsbridge, with a gentle bow, as she rises;
"you may have this place, Mr. Titmarsh; and I am sorry my breakfast is
over: I should have prolonged it had I thought that YOU were coming to sit
by me. Thank you—my glove." (Such an absurd little glove, by the way).
"We shall meet on the deck when you have done."

And she moves away with an august curtsy. I can't tell how it is, or what
it is, in that lady; but she says, "How do you do?" as nobody else knows
how to say it. In all her actions, motions, thoughts, I would wager there is
the same calm grace and harmony. She is not very handsome, being very
thin, and rather sad-looking. She is not very witty, being only up to the
conversation, whatever it may be; and yet, if she were in black serge, I think
one could not help seeing that she was a Princess, and Serene Highness; and
if she were a hundred years old, she could not be but beautiful. I saw her
performing her devotions in Antwerp Cathedral, and forgot to look at
anything else there;—so calm and pure, such a sainted figure hers seemed.

When this great lady did the present writer the honor to shake his hand
(I had the honor to teach writing and the rudiments of Latin to the young
and intelligent Lord Viscount Pimlico), there seemed to be a commotion in
the Kicklebury party—heads were nodded together, and turned towards
Lady Knightsbridge: in whose honor, when Lady Kicklebury had
sufficiently reconnoitred her with her eye-glass, the baronet's lady rose and
swept a reverential curtsy, backing until she fell up against the cushions at
the stern of the boat. Lady Knightsbridge did not see this salute, for she did
not acknowledge it, but walked away slimly (she seems to glide in and out
of the room), and disappeared up the stair to the deck.

Lankin and I took our places, the horse-dealer making room for us; and
I could not help looking, with a little air of triumph, over to the Kicklebury

faction, as much as to say, "You fine folks, with your large footman and supercilious airs, see what WE can do."

As I looked—smiling, and nodding, and laughing at me, in a knowing, pretty way, and then leaning to mamma as if in explanation, what face should I see but that of the young lady at Mrs. Perkins's, with whom I had had that pleasant conversation which had been interrupted by the demand of Captain Hicks for a dance? So, then, that was Miss Kicklebury, about whom Miss Perkins, my young friend, has so often spoken to me: the young ladies were in conversation when I had the happiness of joining them; and Miss P. went away presently, to look to her guests)—that is Miss Fanny Kicklebury.

A sudden pang shot athwart my bosom—Lankin might have perceived it, but the honest Serjeant was so awe-stricken by his late interview with the Countess of Knightsbridge, that his mind was unfit to grapple with other subjects—a pang of feeling (which I concealed under the grin and graceful bow wherewith Miss Fanny's salutations were acknowledged) tore my heart-strings—as I thought of—I need not say—of HICKS.

He had danced with her, he had supped with her—he was here, on board the boat. Where was that dragoon? I looked round for him. In quite a far corner,—but so that he could command the Kicklebury party, I thought,— he was eating his breakfast, the great healthy oaf, and consuming one broiled egg after another.

In the course of the afternoon, all parties, as it may be supposed, emerged upon deck again, and Miss Fanny and her mamma began walking the quarter-deck with a quick pace, like a couple of post-captains. When Miss Fanny saw me, she stopped and smiled, and recognized the gentleman who had amused her so at Mrs. Perkins's. What a dear sweet creature Eliza Perkins was! They had been at school together. She was going to write to Eliza everything that happened on the voyage.

"EVERYTHING?" I said, in my particularly sarcastic manner.

"Well, everything that was worth telling. There was a great number of things that were very stupid, and of people that were very stupid. Everything that YOU say, Mr. Titmarsh, I am sure I may put down. You have seen Mr. Titmarsh's funny books, mamma?"

Mamma said she had heard—she had no doubt they were very amusing. "Was not that—ahem—Lady Knightsbridge, to whom I saw you speaking, sir?"

"Yes; she is going to nurse Lord Knightsbridge, who has the gout at

Rougetnoirbourg."

"Indeed! how very fortunate! what an extraordinary coincidence! We are going too," said Lady Kicklebury.

I remarked "that everybody was going to Rougetnoirbourg this year; and I heard of two gentlemen—Count Carambole and Colonel Cannon—who had been obliged to sleep there on a billiard-table for want of a bed."

"My son Kicklebury—are you acquainted with Sir Thomas Kicklebury?" her ladyship said, with great stateliness—"is at Noirbourg, and will take lodgings for us. The springs are particularly recommended for my daughter, Mrs. Milliken and, at great personal sacrifice, I am going thither myself:, but what will not a mother do, Mr. Titmarsh? Did I understand you to say that you have the— the entree at Knightsbridge House? The parties are not what they used to be, I am told. Not that I have any knowledge. I am but a poor country baronet's widow, Mr. Titmarsh; though the Kickleburys date from Henry III., and MY family is not of the most modern in the country. You have heard of General Guff, my father, perhaps? aide-de-camp to the Duke of York, and wounded by his Royal Highness's side at the bombardment of Valenciennes. WE move IN OUR OWN SPHERE."

"Mrs. Perkins is a very kind creature," I said, "and it was a very pleasant ball. Did you not think so, Miss Kicklebury?"

"I thought it odious," said Miss Fanny. "I mean, it WAS pleasant until that—that stupid man—what was his name?—came and took me away to dance with him."

"What! don't you care for a red coat and moustaches?" I asked.

"I adore genius, Mr. Titmarsh," said the young lady, with a most killing look of her beautiful blue eyes, "and I have every one of your works by heart—all, except the last, which I can't endure. I think it's wicked, positively wicked—My darling Scott—how can you? And are you going to make a Christmas-book this year?"

"Shall I tell you about it?"

"Oh, do tell us about it," said the lively, charming creature, clapping her hands: and we began to talk, being near Lavinia (Mrs. Milliken) and her husband, who was ceaselessly occupied in fetching and carrying books, biscuits, pillows and cloaks, scent-bottles, the Italian greyhound, and the thousand and one necessities of the pale and interesting bride. Oh, how she did fidget! how she did grumble! how she altered and twisted her position!

and how she did make poor Milliken trot!

After Miss Fanny and I had talked, and I had told her my plan, which she pronounced to be delightful, she continued:—"I never was so provoked in my life, Mr. Titmarsh, as when that odious man came and interrupted that dear delightful conversation."

"On your word? The odious man is on board the boat: I see him smoking just by the funnel yonder, look! and looking at us."

"He is very stupid," said Fanny; "and all that I adore is intellect, dear Mr. Titmarsh."

"But why is he on board?" said I, with a fin sourire.

"Why is he on board? Why is everybody on board? How do we meet? (and oh, how glad I am to meet you again!) You don't suppose that I know how the horrid man came here?"

"Eh! he may be fascinated by a pair of blue eyes, Miss Fanny! Others have been so," I said.

"Don't be cruel to a poor girl, you wicked, satirical creature," she said. "I think Captain Hicks odious—there! and I was quite angry when I saw him on the boat. Mamma does not know him, and she was so angry with me for dancing with him that night: though there was nobody of any particular mark at poor dear Mrs. Perkins's—that is, except YOU, Mr. Titmarsh."

"And I am not a dancing man," I said, with a sigh.

"I hate dancing men; they can do nothing but dance."

"O yes, they can. Some of them can smoke, and some can ride, and some of them can even spell very well."

"You wicked, satirical person. I'm quite afraid of you!"

"And some of them call the Rhine the 'Whine,'" I said, giving an admirable imitation of poor Hicks's drawling manner.

Fanny looked hard at me, with a peculiar expression on her face. At last she laughed. "Oh, you wicked, wicked man," she said, "what a capital mimic you are, and so full of cleverness! Do bring up Captain Hicks—isn't that his name?—and trot him out for us. Bring him up, and introduce him to mamma: do now, go!"

Mamma, in the meanwhile, had waited her time, and was just going to step down the cabin stairs as Lady Knightsbridge ascended from them. To draw back, to make a most profound curtsy, to exclaim, "Lady Knightsbridge! I have had the honor of seeing your ladyship at—hum—hum—hum" (this word I could not catch)—"House,"—all these feats were performed by Lady Kicklebury in one instant, and acknowledged with the usual calmness by the younger lady.

"And may I hope," continues Lady Kicklebury, "that that most beautiful of all children—a mother may say so—that Lord Pimlico has recovered his hooping-cough? We were so anxious about him. Our medical attendant is Mr. Topham, and he used to come from Knightsbridge House to Pocklington Square, often and often. I am interested about the hooping-cough. My own dear boy had it most severely; that dear girl, my eldest daughter, whom you see stretched on the bench—she is in a very delicate state, and only lately married—not such a match as I could have wished: but Mr. Milliken is of a good family, distantly related to your ladyship's. A Milliken, in George the Third's reign, married a Boltimore, and the Boltimores, I think, are your first-cousins. They married this year, and Lavinia is so fond of me, that she can't part with me, and I have come abroad just to please her. We are going to Noirbourg. I think I heard from my son that Lord Knightsbridge was at Noirbourg."

"I believe I have had the pleasure of seeing Sir Thomas Kicklebury at Knightsbridge House," Lady Knightsbridge said, with something of sadness.

"Indeed!" and Kicklebury had never told her! He laughed at her when she talked about great people: he told her all sorts of ridiculous stories when upon this theme. But, at any rate, the acquaintance was made: Lady Kicklebury would not leave Lady Knightsbridge; and, even in the throes of sea-sickness, and the secret recesses of the cabin, WOULD talk to her about the world, Lord Pimlico, and her father, General Guff, late aide-de-camp to the Duke of York.

That those throes of sickness ensued, I need not say. A short time after passing Ramsgate, Serjeant Lankin, who had been exceedingly gay and satirical—(in his calm way; he quotes Horace, my favorite bits as an author, to myself, and has a quiet snigger, and, so to speak, amontillado flavor, exceedingly pleasant)—Lankin, with a rueful and livid countenance, descended into his berth, in the which that six foot of serjeant packed himself I don't know how.

When Lady Knightsbridge went down, down went Kicklebury. Milliken and his wife stayed, and were ill together on deck. A palm of glory ought to be awarded to that man for his angelic patience, energy, and suffering. It was he who went for Mrs. Milliken's maid, who wouldn't come to her mistress; it was he, the shyest of men, who stormed the ladies' cabin—that maritime harem—in order to get her mother's bottle of salts; it was he who went for the brandy-and-water, and begged, and prayed, and besought his adored Lavinia to taste a leetle drop. Lavinia's reply was, "Don't—go away —don't tease, Horace," and so forth. And, when not wanted, the gentle creature subsided on the bench, by his wife's feet, and was sick in silence.

[Mem—In married life, it seems to me, that it is almost always Milliken and wife, or just the contrary. The angels minister to the tyrants; or the gentle, hen-pecked husband cowers before the superior partlet. if ever I marry, I know the sort of woman I will choose; and I won't try her temper by over-indulgence, and destroy her fine qualities by a ruinous subserviency to her wishes.]

Little Miss Fanny stayed on deck, as well as her sister, and looked at the stars of heaven, as they began to shine there, and at the Foreland lights as we passed them. I would have talked with her; I would have suggested images of poesy, and thoughts of beauty; I would have whispered the word of sentiment—the delicate allusion— the breathing of the soul that longs to find a congenial heart—the sorrows and aspirations of the wounded spirit, stricken and sad, yet not QUITE despairing; still knowing that the hope-plant lurked in its crushed ruins—still able to gaze on the stars and the ocean, and love their blazing sheen, their boundless azure. I would, I say, have taken the opportunity of that stilly night to lay bare to her the treasures of a heart that, I am happy to say, is young still; but circumstances forbade the frank outpouring of my poet soul: in a word, I was obliged to go and lie down on the flat of my back, and endeavor to control OTHER emotions which struggled in my breast.

Once, in the night-watches, I arose, and came on deck; the vessel was not, methought, pitching much; and yet—and yet Neptune was inexorable. The placid stars looked down, but they gave me no peace. Lavinia Milliken seemed asleep, and her Horace, in a death- like torpor, was huddled at her feet. Miss Fanny had quitted the larboard side of the ship, and had gone to starboard; and I thought that there was a gentleman beside her; but I could not see very clearly, and returned to the horrid crib, where Lankin was asleep, and the German fiddler underneath him was snoring like his own violoncello.

In the morning we were all as brisk as bees. We were in the smooth waters of the lazy Scheldt. The stewards began preparing breakfast with that matutinal eagerness which they always show. The sleepers in the cabin were roused from their horse-hair couches by the stewards' boys nudging, and pushing, and flapping table-cloths over them. I shaved and made a neat toilette, and came upon deck just as we lay off that little Dutch fort, which is, I dare say, described in "Murray's Guide-book," and about which I had some rare banter with poor Hicks and Lady Kicklebury, whose sense of humor is certainly not very keen. He had, somehow, joined her ladyship's party, and they were looking at the fort, and its tri-colored flag— that floats familiar in Vandevelde's pictures—and at the lazy shipping, and the tall roofs, and dumpy church towers, and flat pastures, lying before us in a Cuyplike haze.

I am sorry to say, I told them the most awful fibs about that fort. How it had been defended by the Dutch patriot, Van Swammerdam, against the united forces of the Duke of Alva and Marshal Turenne, whose leg was shot off as he was leading the last unsuccessful assault, and who turned round to his aide-de-camp and said, "Allez dire an Premier Consul, que je meurs avec regret de ne pas avoir assez fait pour la France!" which gave Lady Kicklebury an opportunity to placer her story of the Duke of York, and the bombardment of Valenciennes; and caused young Hicks to look at me in a puzzled and appealing manner and hint that I was "chaffing."

"Chaffing indeed!" says I, with a particularly arch eye-twinkle at Miss Fanny. "I wouldn't make fun of you, Captain Hicks! If you doubt my historical accuracy, look at the 'Biographie Universelle.' I say—look at the 'Biographie Universelle.'"

He said, "O—ah—the 'Biogwaphie Universelle' may be all vewy well, and that; but I never can make out whether you are joking or not, somehow; and I always fancy you are going to CAWICKACHAW me. Ha, ha!" And he laughed, the good-natured dragoon laughed, and fancied he had made a joke.

I entreated him not to be so severe upon me; and again he said, "Haw haw!" and told me, "I mustn't expect to have it all MY OWN WAY, and if I gave a hit, I must expect a Punch in return. Haw haw!" Oh, you honest young Hicks!

Everybody, indeed, was in high spirits. The fog cleared off, the sun shone, the ladies chatted and laughed, even Mrs. Milliken was in good humor ("My wife is all intellect," Milliken says, looking at her with admiration), and talked with us freely and gayly. She was kind enough to say that it was a great pleasure to meet with a literary and well-informed person—that one often lived with people that did not comprehend one. She asked if my companion, that tall gentleman—Mr. Serjeant Lankin, was he? —was literary. And when I said that Lankin knew more Greek, and more Latin, and more law, and more history, and more everything, than all the passengers put together, she vouchsafed to look at him with interest, and enter into a conversation with my modest friend the Serjeant. Then it was that her adoring husband said "his Lavinia was all intellect;"— Lady Kicklebury saying that SHE was not a literary woman: that in HER day few acquirements were requisite for the British female; but that she knew THE SPIRIT OF THE AGE, and her DUTY AS A MOTHER, and that "Lavinia and Fanny had had the best masters and the best education which money and constant maternal solicitude could impart." If our matrons are virtuous, as they are, and it is Britain's boast, permit me to say that they certainly know it.

The conversation growing powerfully intellectual under Mrs. Milliken, poor Hicks naturally became uneasy, and put an end to literature by admiring the ladies' head-dresses. "Cab-heads, hoods, what do you call 'em?" he asked of Miss Kicklebury. Indeed, she and her sister wore a couple of those blue silk over-bonnets, which have lately become the fashion, and which I never should have mentioned but for the young lady's reply.

"Those hoods!" she said—"WE CALL THOSE HOODS UGLIES! Captain Hicks."

Oh, how pretty she looked as she said it! The blue eyes looked up under the blue hood, so archly and gayly; ever so many dimples began playing about her face; her little voice rang so fresh and sweet, that a heart which has never loved a tree or flower but the vegetable in question was sure to perish—a heart worn down and sickened by repeated disappointment, mockery, faithlessness—a heart whereof despair is an accustomed tenant, and in whose desolate and lonely depths dwells an abiding gloom, began to throb once more—began to beckon Hope from the window—began to admit sunshine—began to—O Folly, Folly! O Fanny! O Miss K., how lovely you looked as you said, "We call those hoods Uglies!" Ugly indeed!

This is a chronicle of feelings and characters, not of events and places, so much. All this time our vessel was making rapid way up the river, and we saw before us the slim towers of the noble cathedral of Antwerp soaring in the rosy sunshine. Lankin and I had agreed to go to the "Grand

Laboureur," or the Place de Meir. They give you a particular kind of jam-tarts there—called Nun's tarts, I think—that I remember, these twenty years, as the very best tarts—as good as the tarts which we ate when we were boys. The "Laboureur" is a dear old quiet comfortable hotel; and there is no man in England who likes a good dinner better than Lankin.

"What hotel do you go to?" I asked of Lady Kicklebury.

"We go to the 'Saint Antoine' of course. Everybody goes to the 'Saint Antoine,'" her ladyship said. "We propose to rest here; to do the Rubens's; and to proceed to Cologne to-morrow. Horace, call Finch and Bowman; and your courier, if he will have the condescension to wait upon ME, will perhaps look to the baggage."

"I think, Lankin," said I, "as everybody seems going to the 'Saint Antoine,' we may as well go, and not spoil the party."

"I think I'll go too," says Hicks; as if HE belonged to the party.

And oh, it was a great sight when we landed, and at every place at which we paused afterwards, to see Hirsch over the Kicklebury baggage, and hear his polyglot maledictions at the porters! If a man sometimes feels sad and lonely at his bachelor condition, if SOME feelings of envy pervade his heart, at seeing beauty on another's arm, and kind eyes directed towards a happier mug than his own—at least there are some consolations in travelling, when a fellow has but one little portmanteau or bag which he can easily shoulder, and thinks of the innumerable bags and trunks which the married man and the father drags after him. The married Briton on a tour is but a luggage overseer: his luggage is his morning thought, and his nightly terror. When he floats along the Rhine he has one eye on a ruin, and the other on his luggage. When he is in the railroad he is always thinking, or ordered by his wife to think, "is the luggage safe?" It clings round him. It never leaves him (except when it DOES leave him, as a trunk or two will, and make him doubly miserable). His carpet-bags lie on his chest at night, and his wife's forgotten bandbox haunts his turbid dreams.

I think it was after she found that Lady Kicklebury proposed to go to the "Grand Saint Antoine" that Lady Knightsbridge put herself with her maid into a carriage and went to the other inn. We saw her at the cathedral, where she kept aloof from our party. Milliken went up the tower, and so did Miss Fanny. I am too old a traveller to mount up those immeasurable stairs, for the purpose of making myself dizzy by gazing upon a vast map of low countries stretched beneath me, and waited with Mrs. Milliken and her mother below.

When the tower-climbers descended, we asked Miss Fanny and her brother what they had seen.

"We saw Captain Hicks up there," remarked Milliken. "And I am very glad you didn't come, Lavinia my love. The excitement would have been too much for you, quite too much."

All this while Lady Kicklebury was looking at Fanny, and Fanny was holding her eyes down; and I knew that between her and this poor Hicks there could be nothing serious, for she had laughed at him and mimicked him to me half a dozen times in the course of the day.

We "do the Rubens's," as Lady Kicklebury says; we trudge from cathedral to picture-gallery, from church to church. We see the calm old city, with its towers and gables, the bourse, and the vast town-hall; and I have the honor to give Lady Kicklebury my arm during these peregrinations, and to hear a hundred particulars regarding her ladyship's life and family. How Milliken has been recently building at Pigeoncot; how he will have two thousand a year more when his uncle dies; how she had peremptorily to put a stop to the assiduities of that unprincipled young man, Lord Roughhead, whom Lavinia always detested, and who married Miss Brent out of sheer pique. It was a great escape for her darling Lavinia. Roughhead is a most wild and dissipated young man, one of Kicklebury's Christchurch friends, of whom her son has too many, alas! and she enters into many particulars respecting the conduct of Kicklebury—the unhappy boy's smoking, his love of billiards, his fondness for the turf: she fears he has already injured his income, she fears he is even now playing at Noirbourg; she is going thither to wean him, if possible, from his companions and his gayeties—what may not a mother effect? She only wrote to him the day before they left London to announce that she was marching on him with her family. He is in many respects like his poor father— the same openness and frankness, the same easy disposition: alas! the same love of pleasure. But she had reformed the father, and will do her utmost to call back her dear misguided boy. She had an advantageous match for him in view—a lady not beautiful in person, it is true, but possessed of every good principle, and a very, very handsome fortune. It was under pretence of flying from this lady that Kicklebury left town. But she knew better.

I say young men will be young men, and sow their wild oats; and think to myself that the invasion of his mamma will be perhaps more surprising than pleasant to young Sir Thomas Kicklebury, and that she possibly talks about herself and her family, and her virtues and her daughters, a little too much: but she WILL make a confidant of me, and all the time we are doing the Rubens's she is talking of the pictures at Kicklebury, of her portrait by Lawrence, pronounced to be his finest work, of Lavinia's talent for drawing, and the expense of Fanny's music-masters; of her house in town (where she hopes to see me); of her parties which were stopped by the illness of her butler. She talks Kicklebury until I am sick. And oh, Miss Fanny, all of this I endure, like an old fool, for an occasional sight of your bright eyes and rosy face!

[Another parenthesis.—"We hope to see you in town, Mr. Titmarsh." Foolish mockery! If all the people whom one has met abroad, and who have said, "We hope to meet you often in town," had but made any the slightest efforts to realize their hopes by sending a simple line of invitation through the penny post, what an enormous dinner acquaintance one would have had! But I mistrust people who say, "We hope to see you in town."]

Lankin comes in at the end of the day, just before dinnertime. He has paced the whole town by himself—church, tower, and fortifications, and Rubens, and all. He is full of Egmont and Alva. He is up to all the history of the siege, when Chassee defended, and the French attacked the place. After dinner we stroll along the quays; and over the quiet cigar in the hotel court, Monsieur Lankin discourses about the Rubens pictures, in a way which shows that the learned Serjeant has an eye for pictorial beauty as well as other beauties in this world, and can rightly admire the vast energy, the prodigal genius, the royal splendor of the King of Antwerp. In the most modest way in the world he has remarked a student making clever sketches at the Museum, and has ordered a couple of copies from him of the famous Vandyke and the wondrous adoration of the Magi, "a greater picture," says he, "than even the cathedral picture; in which opinion those may agree who like." He says he thinks Miss Kicklebury is a pretty little thing; that all my swans are geese; and that as for that old woman, with her airs and graces, she is the most intolerable old nuisance in the world. There is much good judgment, but there is too much sardonic humor about Lankin. He cannot appreciate women properly. He is spoiled by being an old bachelor, and living in that dingy old Pump Court; where, by the way, he has a cellar fit for a Pontiff. We go to rest; they have given us humble lodgings high up in the building, which we accept like philosophers who travel with but a portmanteau apiece. The Kickleburys have the grand suite, as becomes their dignity. Which, which of those twinkling lights illumines the chamber of Miss Fanny?

Hicks is sitting in the court too, smoking his cigar. He and Lankin met in the fortifications. Lankin says he is a sensible fellow, and seems to know his profession. "Every man can talk well about something," the Serjeant says. "And one man can about everything," says I; at which Lankin blushes; and we take our flaring tallow candles and go to bed. He has us up an hour before the starting time, and we have that period to admire Herr Oberkellner, who swaggers as becomes the Oberkellner of a house frequented by ambassadors; who contradicts us to our faces, and whose own countenance is ornamented with yesterday's beard, of which, or of any part of his clothing, the graceful youth does not appear to have divested himself since last we left him. We recognize, somewhat dingy and faded, the elaborate shirt-front which appeared at yesterday's banquet. Farewell, Herr Oberkellner! May we never see your handsome countenance, washed or unwashed, shaven or unshorn, again!

"Here come the ladies: "Good morning, Miss Fanny." I hope you slept well, Lady Kicklebury?" "A tremendous bill?" "No wonder; how can you expect otherwise, when you have such a bad dinner?" Hearken to Hirsch's comminations over the luggage! Look at the honest Belgian soldiers, and that fat Freyschutz on guard, his rifle in one hand, and the other hand in his pocket. Captain Hicks bursts into a laugh at the sight of the fat Freyschutz, and says, "By Jove, Titmarsh, you must cawickachaw him." And we take our seats at length and at leisure, and the railway trumpets blow, and (save for a brief halt) we never stop till night, trumpeting by green flats and pastures, by broad canals and old towns, through Liege and Verviers, through Aix and Cologne, till we are landed at Bonn at nightfall.

We all have supper, or tea—we have become pretty intimate—we look at the strangers' book, as a matter of course, in the great room of the "Star Hotel." Why, everybody is on the Rhine! Here are the names of half one's acquaintance.

"I see Lord and Lady Exborough are gone on," says Lady Kicklebury, whose eye fastens naturally on her kindred aristocracy. "Lord and Lady Wyebridge and suite, Lady Zedland and her family."

"Hallo! here's Cutler of the Onety-oneth, and MacMull of the Greens, en route to Noirbourg," says Hicks, confidentially. "Know MacMull? Devilish good fellow—such a fellow to smoke."

Lankin, too, reads and grins. "Why, are they going the Rhenish circuit?" he says, and reads:

Sir Thomas Minos, Lady Minos, nebst Begleitung, aus England.

Sir John AEacus, mit Familie und Dienerschaft, aus England.

Sir Roger Raadamanthus.

Thomas Smith, Serjeant.

Serjeant Brown and Mrs. Brown, aus England.

Serjeant Tomkins, Anglais. Madame Tomkins, Mesdemoiselles Tomkins.

Monsieur Kewsy, Conseiller de S. M. la Reine d'Angleterre. Mrs. Kewsy, three Miss Kewsys.

And to this list Lankin, laughing, had put down his own name, and that of the reader's obedient servant, under the august autograph of Lady Kicklebury, who signed for herself, her son-in-law, and her suite.

Yes, we all flock the one after the other, we faithful English folks. We can buy Harvey Sauce, and Cayenne Pepper, and Morison's Pills, in every city in the world. We carry our nation everywhere with us; and are in our island, wherever we go. Toto divisos orbe— always separated from the people in the midst of whom we are.

When we came to the steamer next morning, "the castled crag of Drachenfels" rose up in the sunrise before, and looked as pink as the cheeks of Master Jacky, when they have been just washed in the morning. How that rosy light, too, did become Miss Fanny's pretty dimples, to be sure! How good a cigar is at the early dawn! I maintain that it has a flavor which it does not possess at later hours, and that it partakes of the freshness of all Nature. And wine, too: wine is never so good as at breakfast; only one can't drink it, for tipsiness's sake.

See! there is a young fellow drinking soda-water and brandy already. He puts down his glass with a gasp of satisfaction. It is evident that he had need of that fortifier and refresher. He puts down the beaker and says, "How are you, Titmarsh? I was SO cut last night. My eyes, wasn't I! Not in the least: that's all."

It is the youthful descendant and heir of an ancient line: the noble Earl of Grimsby's son, Viscount Talboys. He is travelling with the Rev. Baring Leader, his tutor; who, having a great natural turn and liking towards the aristocracy, and having inspected Lady Kicklebury's cards on her trunks, has introduced himself to her ladyship already, and has inquired after Sir Thomas Kicklebury, whom he remembers perfectly, and whom he had often the happiness of meeting when Sir Thomas was an undergraduate at Oxford. There are few characters more amiable, and delightful to watch and contemplate, than some of those middle-aged Oxford bucks who hang about the university and live with the young tufts. Leader can talk racing and boating with the fastest young Christchurch gentleman. Leader occasionally rides to cover with Lord Talboys; is a good shot, and seldom walks out without a setter or a spaniel at his heels. Leader knows the "Peerage" and the "Racing Calendar" as well as the Oxford cram-books. Leader comes up to town and dines with Lord Grimsby. Leader goes to Court every two years. He is the greatest swell in his common-room. He drinks claret, and can't stand port-wine any longer; and the old fellows of his college admire him, and pet him, and get all their knowledge of the world and the aristocracy from him. I admire those kind old dons when they appear affable and jaunty, men of the world, members of the "Camford and Oxbridge Club," upon the London pavement. I like to see them over the Morning Post in the common-room; with a "Ha, I see Lady Rackstraw has another daughter." "Poppleton there has been at another party at X——— House, and YOU weren't asked, my boy."—"Lord Coverdale has got a large party staying at Coverdale. Did you know him at Christchurch? He was a very handsome man before he broke his nose fighting the bargeman at Iffly: a light weight, but a beautiful sparrer," Let me add that Leader, although he does love a tuft, has a kind heart: as his mother and sisters in Yorkshire know; as all the village knows too—which is proud of his position in the great world, and welcomes him very kindly when he comes down and takes the duty at Christmas, and preaches to them one or two of "the very sermons which Lord Grimsby was good enough to like, when I delivered them at Talboys."

"You are not acquainted with Lord Talboys?" Leader asks, with a degage air. "I shall have much pleasure in introducing you to him. Talboys, let me introduce you to Lady Kicklebury. Sir Thomas Kicklebury was not at Christchurch in your time; but you have heard of him, I dare say. Your son has left a reputation at Oxford."

"I should think I have, too. He walked a hundred miles in a hundred hours. They said he bet that he'd drink a hundred pints of beer in a hundred hours: but I don't think he could do it—not strong beer; don't think any man could. The beer here isn't worth a—"

"My dear Talboys," says Leader, with a winning smile, "I suppose Lady Kicklebury is not a judge of beer—and what an unromantic subject of conversation here, under the castled crag immortalized by Byron."

"What the deuce does it mean about peasant-girls with dark blue eyes, and hands that offer corn and wine?" asks Talboys. "I'VE never seen any peasant-girls, except the—ugliest set of women I ever looked at."

"The poet's license. I see, Miliken, you are making a charming sketch. You used to draw when you were at Brasenose, Milliken; and play—yes, you played the violoncello."

Mr. Milliken still possessed these accomplishments. He was taken up that very evening by a soldier at Coblentz, for making a sketch of Ehrenbreitstein. Mrs. Milliken sketches immensely too, and writes poetry: such dreary pictures, such dreary poems! but professional people are proverbially jealous; and I doubt whether our fellow-passenger, the German, would even allow that Milliken could play the violoncello.

Lady Kicklebury gives Miss Fanny a nudge when Lord Talboys appears, and orders her to exert all her fascinations. How the old lady coaxes, and she wheedles! She pours out the Talboys' pedigree upon him; and asks after his aunt, and his mother's family. Is he going to Noirbourg? How delightful! There is nothing like British spirits; and to see an English matron well set upon a young man of large fortune and high rank, is a great and curious sight.

And yet, somehow, the British doggedness does not always answer. "Do you know that old woman in the drab jacket, Titmarsh?" my hereditary legislator asks of me. "What the devil is she bothering ME for, about my aunts, and setting her daughter at me? I ain't such a fool as that. I ain't clever, Titmarsh; I never said I was. I never pretend to be clever, and that— but why does that old fool bother ME, hay? Heigho! I'm devilish thirsty. I was devilish cut last night. I think I must have another go-off. Hallo you! Kellner! Garsong! Ody soda, Oter petty vare do dyvee de Conac. That's your sort; isn't it, Leader?"

"You will speak French well enough, if you practise," says Leader with a tender voice; "practice is everything. Shall we dine at the table-d'hote? Waiter! put down the name of Viscount Talboys and Mr. Leader, if you please."

The boat is full of all sorts and conditions of men. For'ard, there are peasants and soldiers: stumpy, placid-looking little warriors for the most part, smoking feeble cigars and looking quite harmless under their enormous helmets. A poor stunted dull-looking boy of sixteen, staggering before a black-striped sentry-box, with an enormous musket on his shoulder, does not seem to me a martial or awe-inspiring object. Has it not been said that we carry our prejudices everywhere, and only admire what we are accustomed to admire in our own country?

Yonder walks a handsome young soldier who has just been marrying a wife. How happy they seem! and how pleased that everybody should remark their happiness. It is a fact that in the full sunshine, and before a couple of hundred people on board the Joseph Miller steamer, the soldier absolutely kissed Mrs. Soldier; at which the sweet Fanny Kicklebury was made to blush.

We were standing together looking at the various groups: the pretty peasant-woman (really pretty for once,) with the red head-dress and fluttering ribbons, and the child in her arms; the jolly fat old gentleman, who was drinking Rhine-wine before noon, and turning his back upon all the castles, towers, and ruins, which reflected their crumbling peaks in the water; upon the handsome young students who came with us from Bonn, with their national colors in their caps, with their picturesque looks, their yellow ringlets, their budding moustaches, and with cuts upon almost every one of their noses, obtained in duels at the university: most picturesque are these young fellows, indeed—but ah, why need they have such black hands?

Near us is a type, too: a man who adorns his own tale, and points his own moral. "Yonder, in his carriage, sits the Count de Reineck, who won't travel without that dismal old chariot, though it is shabby, costly, and clumsy, and though the wicked red republicans come and smoke under his very nose. Yes, Miss Fanny, it is the lusty young Germany, pulling the nose of the worn-out old world."

"Law, what DO you mean, Mr. Titmarsh?" cries the dear Fanny.

"And here comes Mademoiselle de Reineck, with her companion. You see she is wearing out one of the faded silk gowns which she has spoiled at the Residenz during the season: for the Reinecks are economical, though they are proud; and forced, like many other insolvent grandees, to do and to wear shabby things.

"It is very kind of the young countess to call her companion 'Louise,' and to let Louise call her 'Laure;' but if faces may be trusted,—and we can read in one countenance conceit and tyranny; deceit and slyness in another,—dear Louise has to suffer some hard raps from dear Laure: and, to judge from her dress, I don't think poor Louise has her salary paid very regularly.

"What a comfort it is to live in a country where there is neither insolence nor bankruptcy among the great folks, nor cringing, nor flattery among the small. Isn't it, Miss Fanny?"

Miss Fanny says, that she can't understand whether I am joking or serious; and her mamma calls her away to look at the ruins of Wigginstein. Everybody looks at Wigginstein. You are told in Murray to look at Wigginstein.

Lankin, who has been standing by, with a grin every now and then upon his sardonic countenance, comes up and says, "Titmarsh, how can you be so impertinent?"

"Impertinent! as how?"

"The girl must understand what you mean; and you shouldn't laugh at her own mother to her. Did you ever see anything like the way in which that horrible woman is following the young lord about?"

"See! You see it every day, my dear fellow; only the trick is better done, and Lady Kicklebury is rather a clumsy practitioner. See! why nobody is better aware of the springes which are set to catch him than that young fellow himself, who is as knowing as any veteran in May Fair. And you don't suppose that Lady Kicklebury fancies that she is doing anything mean, or anything wrong? Heaven bless you! she never did anything wrong in her life. She has no idea but that everything she says, and thinks, and does is right. And no doubt she never did rob a church: and was a faithful wife to Sir Thomas, and pays her tradesmen. Confound her virtue! It is that which makes her so wonderful—that brass armor in which she walks impenetrable —not knowing what pity is, or charity; crying sometimes when she is vexed, or thwarted, but laughing never; cringing, and domineering by the same natural instinct—never doubting about herself above all. Let us rise, and revolt against those people, Lankin. Let us war with them, and smite them utterly. It is to use against these, especially, that Scorn and Satire were invented."

"And the animal you attack," says Lankin, "is provided with a hide to defend him—it is a common ordinance of nature."

And so we pass by tower and town, and float up the Rhine. We don't describe the river. Who does not know it? How you see people asleep in the cabins at the most picturesque parts, and angry to be awakened when they fire off those stupid guns for the echoes! It is as familiar to numbers of people as Greenwich; and we know the merits of the inns along the road as if they were the "Trafalgar" or the "Star and Garter." How stale everything grows! If we were to live in a garden of Eden, now, and the gate were open, we should go out, and tramp forward, and push on, and get up early in the morning, and push on again—anything to keep moving, anything to get a change: anything but quiet for the restless children of Cain.

So many thousands of English folks have been at Rougetnoirbourg in this and last seasons, that it is scarcely needful to alter the name of that pretty little gay, wicked place. There were so many British barristers there this year that they called the "Hotel des Quatre Saisons" the "Hotel of Quarter Sessions." There were judges and their wives, serjeants and their ladies, Queen's counsel learned in the law, the Northern circuit and the Western circuit: there were officers of half-pay and full-pay, military officers, naval officers, and sheriffs' officers. There were people of high fashion and rank, and people of no rank at all; there were men and women of reputation, and of the two kinds of reputation; there were English boys playing cricket; English pointers putting up the German partridges, and English guns knocking them down; there were women whose husbands, and men whose wives were at home; there were High Church and Low Church —England turned out for a holiday, in a word. How much farther shall we extend our holiday ground, and where shall we camp next? A winter at Cairo is nothing now. Perhaps ere long we shall be going to Saratoga Springs, and the Americans coming to Margate for the summer.

Apartments befitting her dignity and the number of her family had been secured for Lady Kicklebury by her dutiful son, in the same house in which one of Lankin's friends had secured for us much humbler lodgings. Kicklebury received his mother's advent with a great deal of good humor; and a wonderful figure the good-natured little baronet was when he presented himself to his astonished friends, scarcely recognizable by his own parent and sisters, and the staring retainers of their house.

"Mercy, Kicklebury! have you become a red republican?" his mother asked.

"I can't find a place to kiss you," said Miss Fanny, laughing to her brother; and he gave her pretty cheek such a scrub with his red beard, as made some folks think it would be very pleasant to be Miss Fanny's brother.

In the course of his travels, one of Sir Thomas Kicklebury's chief amusements and cares had been to cultivate this bushy auburn ornament. He said that no man could pronounce German properly without a beard to his jaws; but he did not appear to have got much beyond this preliminary step to learning; and, in spite of his beard, his honest English accent came out, as his jolly English face looked forth from behind that fierce and bristly decoration, perfectly good-humored and unmistakable. We try our best to look like foreigners, but we can't. Every Italian mendicant or Pont Neuf beggar knows his Englishman in spite of blouse, and beard, and slouched hat. "There is a peculiar high-bred grace about us," I whisper to Lady Kicklebury, "an aristocratic je ne scais quoi, which is not to be found in any but Englishmen; and it is that which makes us so immensely liked and admired all over the Continent." Well, this may be truth or joke—this may be a sneer or a simple assertion: our vulgarities and our insolences may, perhaps, make us as remarkable as that high breeding which we assume to possess. It may be that the Continental society ridicules and detests us, as we walk domineering over Europe; but, after all, which of us would denationalize himself? who wouldn't be an Englishman? Come, sir, cosmopolite as you are, passing all your winters at Rome or at Paris; exiled by choice, or poverty, from your own country; preferring easier manners, cheaper pleasures, a simpler life: are you not still proud of your British citizenship? and would you like to be a Frenchman?

Kicklebury has a great acquaintance at Noirbourg, and as he walks into the great concert-room at night, introducing his mother and sisters there, he seemed to look about with a little anxiety, lest all of his acquaintance should recognize him. There are some in that most strange and motley company with whom he had rather not exchange salutations, under present circumstances. Pleasure- seekers from every nation in the world are here, sharpers of both sexes, wearers of the stars and cordons of every court in Europe; Russian princesses, Spanish grandees, Belgian, French, and English nobles, every degree of Briton, from the ambassador, who has his conge, to the London apprentice who has come out for his fortnight's lark. Kicklebury knows them all, and has a good- natured nod for each.

"Who is that lady with the three daughters who saluted you, Kicklebury?" asks his mother.

"That is our Ambassadress at X., ma'am. I saw her yesterday buying a penny toy for one of her little children in Frankfort Fair."

Lady Kicklebury looks towards Lady X.: she makes her excellency an undeveloped curtsy, as it were; she waves her plumed head (Lady K. is got up in great style, in a rich dejeuner toilette, perfectly regardless of expense); she salutes the ambassadress with a sweeping gesture from her chair, and backs before her as before royalty, and turns to her daughters large eyes full of meaning, and spreads out her silks in state.

"And who is that distinguished-looking man who just passed, and who gave you a reserved nod?" asks her ladyship. "Is that Lord X.?"

Kicklebury burst out laughing. "That, ma'am, is Mr. Higmore, of Conduit Street, tailor, draper, and habit-maker: and I owe him a hundred pound."

"The insolence of that sort of people is really intolerable," says Lady Kicklebury. "There MUST be some distinction of classes. They ought not to be allowed to go everywhere. And who is yonder, that lady with the two boys and the—the very high complexion?" Lady Kicklebury asks.

"That is a Russian princess: and one of those little boys, the one who is sucking a piece of barley-sugar, plays, and wins five hundred louis in a night."

"Kicklebury, you do not play? Promise your mother you do not! Swear to me at this moment you do not! Where are the horrid gambling-rooms? There, at that door where the crowd is? Of course, I shall never enter them!"

"Of course not, ma'am," says the affectionate son on duty. "And if you come to the balls here, please don't let Fanny dance with anybody, until you ask me first: you understand. Fanny, you will take care."

"Yes, Tom," says Fanny.

"What, Hicks, how are you, old fellow? How is Platts? Who would have thought of you being here? When did you come?"

"I had the pleasure of travelling with Lady Kicklebury and her daughters in the London boat to Antwerp," says Captain Hicks, making the ladies a bow. Kicklebury introduces Hicks to his mother as his most particular friend—and he whispers Fanny that "he's as good a fellow as ever lived, Hicks is." Fanny says, "He seems very kind and good-natured: and—and Captain Hicks waltzes very well," says Miss Fanny with a blush, "and I hope I may have him for one of my partners."

What a Babel of tongues it is in this splendid hall with gleaming marble pillars: a ceaseless rushing whisper as if the band were playing its music by a waterfall! The British lawyers are all got together, and my friend Lankin, on his arrival, has been carried off by his brother serjeants, and becomes once more a lawyer. "Well, brother Lankin," says old Sir Thomas Minos, with his venerable kind face, "you have got your rule, I see." And they fall into talk about their law matters, as they always do, wherever they are—at a club, in a ball-room, at a dinner-table, at the top of Chimborazo. Some of the young barristers appear as bucks with uncommon splendor, and dance and hang about the ladies. But they have not the easy languid deuce-may-care air of the young bucks of the Hicks and Kicklebury school—they can't put on their clothes with that happy negligence; their neck-cloths sit quite differently on them, somehow: they become very hot when they dance, and yet do not spin round near so quickly as those London youths, who have acquired experience in corpore vili, and learned to dance easily by the practice of a thousand casinos.

Above the Babel tongues and the clang of the music, as you listen in the great saloon, you hear from a neighboring room a certain sharp ringing clatter, and a hard clear voice cries out, "Zero rouge," or " Trente-cinq noir. Impair et passe." And then there is a pause of a couple of minutes, and then the voice says, "Faites le jeu, Messieurs. Le jeu est fait, rien ne va plus"—and the sharp ringing clatter recommences. You know what that room is? That is Hades. That is where the spirited proprietor of the establishment takes his toll, and thither the people go who pay the money which supports the spirited proprietor of this fine palace and gardens. Let us enter Hades, and see what is going on there.

Hades is not an unpleasant place. Most of the people look rather cheerful. You don't see any frantic gamblers gnashing their teeth or dashing down their last stakes. The winners have the most anxious faces; or the poor shabby fellows who have got systems, and are pricking down the alternations of red and black on cards, and don't seem to be playing at all. On fete days the country people come in, men and women, to gamble; and THEY seem to be excited as they put down their hard-earned florins with trembling rough hands, and watch the turn of the wheel. But what you call the good company is very quiet and easy. A man loses his mass of gold, and gets up and walks off, without any particular mark of despair. The only gentleman whom I saw at Noirbourg who seemed really affected was a certain Count de Mustacheff, a Russian of enormous wealth, who clenched his fists, beat his breast, cursed his stars, and absolutely cried with grief: not for losing money, but for neglecting to win and play upon a coup de vingt, a series in which the red was turned up twenty times running: which series, had he but played, it is clear that he might have broken M. Lenoir's bank, and shut up the gambling-house, and doubled his own fortune—when he would have been no happier, and all the balls and music, all the newspaper-rooms and parks, all the feasting and pleasure of this delightful Rougetnoirbourg would have been at an end.

For though he is a wicked gambling prince, Lenoir, he is beloved in all these regions; his establishment gives life to the town, to the lodging-house and hotel-keepers, to the milliners and hackney- coachmen, to the letters of horse-flesh, to the huntsmen and gardes-de-chasse; to all these honest fiddlers and trumpeters who play so delectably. Were Lenoir's bank to break, the whole little city would shut up; and all the Noirbourgers wish him prosperity, and benefit by his good fortune.

Three years since the Noirbourgers underwent a mighty panic. There came, at a time when the chief Lenoir was at Paris, and the reins of government were in the hands of his younger brother, a company of adventurers from Belgium, with a capital of three hundred thousand francs, and an infallible system for playing rouge et noir, and they boldly challenged the bank of Lenoir, and sat down before his croupiers, and defied him. They called themselves in their pride the Contrebanque de Noirbourg: they had their croupiers and punters, even as Lenoir had his: they had their rouleaux of Napoleons, stamped with their Contrebanquish seal:—and they began to play.

As when two mighty giants step out of a host and engage, the armies stand still in expectation, and the puny privates and commonalty remain quiet to witness the combat of the tremendous champions of the war: so it is said that when the Contrebanque arrived, and ranged itself before the officers of Lenoir—rouleau to rouleau, bank-note to bank-note, war for war, controlment for controlment— all the minor punters and gamblers ceased their peddling play, and looked on in silence, round the verdant plain where the great combat was to be decided.

Not used to the vast operations of war, like his elder brother, Lenoir junior, the lieutenant, telegraphed to his absent chief the news of the mighty enemy who had come down upon him, asked for instructions, and in the meanwhile met the foe-man like a man. The Contrebanque of Noirbourg gallantly opened its campaign.

The Lenoir bank was defeated day after day, in numerous savage encounters. The tactics of the Contrebanquist generals were irresistible: their infernal system bore down everything before it, and they marched onwards terrible and victorious as the Macedonian phalanx. Tuesday, a loss of eighteen thousand florins; Wednesday, a loss of twelve thousand florins; Thursday, a loss of forty thousand florins: night after night, the young Lenoir had to chronicle these disasters in melancholy despatches to his chief. What was to be done? Night after night, the Noirbourgers retired home doubtful and disconsolate; the horrid Contrebanquists gathered up their spoils and retired to a victorious supper. How was it to end?

Far away at Paris, the elder Lenoir answered these appeals of his brother by sending reinforcements of money. Chests of gold arrived for the bank. The Prince of Noirbourg bade his beleaguered lieutenant not to lose heart: he himself never for a moment blenched in this trying hour of danger.

The Contrebanquists still went on victorious. Rouleau after rouleau fell into their possession. At last the news came: The Emperor has joined the Grand Army. Lenoir himself had arrived from Paris, and was once more among his children, his people. The daily combats continued: and still, still, though Napoleon was with the Eagles, the abominable Contrebanquists fought and conquered. And far greater than Napoleon, as great as Ney himself under disaster, the bold Lenoir never lost courage, never lost good-humor, was affable, was gentle, was careful of his subjects' pleasures and comforts, and met an adverse fortune with a dauntless smile.

With a devilish forbearance and coolness, the atrocious Contrebanque—like Polyphemus, who only took one of his prisoners out of the cave at a time, and so ate them off at leisure—the horrid Contrebanquists, I say, contented themselves with winning so much before dinner, and so much before supper—say five thousand florins for each meal. They played and won at noon: they played and won at eventide. They of Noirbourg went home sadly every night: the invader was carrying all before him. What must have been the feelings of the great Lenoir? What were those of Washington before Trenton, when it seemed all up with the cause of American Independence; what those of the virgin Elizabeth, when the Armada was signalled; what those of Miltiades, when the multitudinous Persian bore down on Marathon? The people looked on at the combat, and saw their chieftain stricken, bleeding, fallen, fighting still.

At last there came one day when the Contrebanquists had won their allotted sum, and were about to leave the tables which they had swept so often. But pride and lust of gold had seized upon the heart of one of their vainglorious chieftains; and he said, "Do not let us go yet—let us win a thousand florins more!" So they stayed and set the bank yet a thousand florins. The Noirbourgers looked on, and trembled for their prince.

Some three hours afterwards—a shout, a mighty shout was heard around the windows of that palace: the town, the gardens, the hills, the fountains took up and echoed the jubilant acclaim. Hip, hip, hip, hurrah, hurrah, hurrah! People rushed into each other's arms; men, women, and children cried and kissed each other. Croupiers, who never feel, who never tremble, who never care whether black wins or red loses, took snuff from each other's boxes, and laughed for joy; and Lenoir the dauntless, the INVINCIBLE Lenoir, wiped the drops of perspiration from his calm forehead, as he drew the enemy's last rouleau into his till. He had conquered. The Persians were beaten, horse and foot—the Armada had gone down. Since Wellington shut up his telescope at Waterloo, when the Prussians came charging on to the field, and the Guard broke and fled, there had been no such heroic endurance, such utter defeat, such signal and crowning victory. Vive Lenoir! I am a Lenoirite. I have read his newspapers, strolled in his gardens, listened to his music, and rejoice in his victory: I am glad he beat those Contrebanquists. Dissipati sunt. The game is up with them.

The instances of this man's magnanimity are numerous, and worthy of Alexander the Great, or Harry the Fifth, or Robin Hood. Most gentle is he, and thoughtful to the poor, and merciful to the vanquished. When Jeremy Diddler, who had lost twenty pounds at his table, lay in inglorious pawn at his inn—when O'Toole could not leave Noirbourg until he had received his remittances from Ireland— the noble Lenoir paid Diddler's inn bill, advanced O'Toole money upon his well-known signature, franked both of them back to their native country again; and has never, wonderful to state, been paid from that day to this. If you will go play at his table, you may; but nobody forces you. If you lose, pay with a cheerful heart. Dulce est desipere in loco. This is not a treatise of morals. Friar Tuck was not an exemplary ecclesiastic, nor Robin Hood a model man; but he was a jolly outlaw; and I dare say the Sheriff of Nottingham, whose money he took, rather relished his feast at Robin's green table.

And if you lose, worthy friend, as possibly you will, at Lenoir's pretty games, console yourself by thinking that it is much better for you in the end that you should lose, than that you should win. Let me, for my part, make a clean breast of it, and own that your humble servant did, on one occasion, win a score of Napoleons; and beginning with a sum of no less than five shillings. But until I had lost them again I was so feverish, excited, and uneasy, that I had neither delectation in reading the most exciting French novels, nor pleasure in seeing pretty landscapes, nor appetite for dinner. The moment, however, that graceless money was gone, equanimity was restored: Paul Feval and Eugene Sue began to be terrifically interesting again; and the dinners at Noirbourg, though by no means good culinary specimens, were perfectly sufficient for my easy and tranquil mind. Lankin, who played only a lawyer's rubber at whist, marked the salutary change in his friend's condition; and, for my part, I hope and pray that every honest reader of this volume who plays at M. Lenoir's table will lose every shilling of his winnings before he goes away. Where are the gamblers whom we have read of? Where are the card-players whom we can remember in our early days? At one time almost every gentleman played, and there were whist- tables in every lady's drawing-room. But trumps are going out along with numbers of old-world institutions; and, before very long, a blackleg will be as rare an animal as a knight in armor.

There was a little dwarfish, abortive, counter bank set up at Noirbourg this year: but the gentlemen soon disagreed among themselves; and, let us hope, were cut off in detail by the great Lenoir. And there was a Frenchman at our inn who had won two Napoleons per day for the last six weeks, and who had an infallible system, whereof he kindly offered to communicate the secret for the consideration of a hundred louis; but there came one fatal night when the poor Frenchman's system could not make head against fortune, and her wheel went over him, and he disappeared utterly.

With the early morning everybody rises and makes his or her appearance at the Springs, where they partake of water with a wonderful energy and perseverance. They say that people get to be fond of this water at last; as to what tastes cannot men accustom themselves? I drank a couple of glasses of an abominable sort of feeble salts in a state of very gentle effervescence; but, though there was a very pretty girl who served it, the drink was abominable, and it was a marvel to see the various topers, who tossed off glass after glass, which the fair-haired little Hebe delivered sparkling from the well.

Seeing my wry faces, old Captain Carver expostulated, with a jolly twinkle of his eye, as he absorbed the contents of a sparkling crystal beaker. "Pooh! take another glass, sir: you'll like it better and better every day. It refreshes you, sir: it fortifies you: and as for liking it—gad! I remember the time when I didn't like claret. Times are altered now, ha! ha! Mrs. Fantail, madam, I wish you a very good morning. How is Fantail? He don't come to drink the water: so much the worse for him."

To see Mrs. Fantail of an evening is to behold a magnificent sight. She ought to be shown in a room by herself; and, indeed, would occupy a moderate-sized one with her person and adornments. Marie Antoinette's hoop is not bigger than Mrs. Fantail's flounces. Twenty men taking hands (and, indeed, she likes to have at least that number about her) would scarcely encompass her. Her chestnut ringlets spread out in a halo round her face: she must want two or three coiffeurs to arrange that prodigious head-dress; and then, when it is done, how can she endure that extraordinary gown? Her travelling bandboxes must be as large as omnibuses.

But see Mrs. Fantail in the morning, having taken in all sail: the chestnut curls have disappeared, and two limp bands of brown hair border her lean, sallow face; you see before you an ascetic, a nun, a woman worn by mortifications, of a sad yellow aspect, drinking salts at the well: a vision quite different from that rapturous one of the previous night's ball-room. No wonder Fantail does not come out of a morning; he had rather not see such a Rebecca at the well.

Lady Kicklebury came for some mornings pretty regularly, and was very civil to Mr. Leader, and made Miss Fanny drink when his lordship took a cup, and asked Lord Talboys and his tutor to dinner. But the tutor came, and, blushing, brought an excuse from Talboys; and poor Milliken had not a very pleasant evening after Mr. Baring Leader rose to go away.

But though the water was not good the sun was bright, the music cheery, the landscape fresh and pleasant, and it was always amusing to see the vast varieties of our human species that congregated at the Springs, and trudged up and down the green allees. One of the gambling conspirators of the roulette-table it was good to see here, in his private character, drinking down pints of salts like any other sinner, having a homely wife on his arm, and between them a poodle on which they lavished their tenderest affection. You see these people care for other things besides trumps; and are not always thinking about black and red:—as even ogres are represented, in their histories, as of cruel natures, and licentious appetites, and, to be sure, fond of eating men and women; but yet it appears that their wives often respected them, and they had a sincere liking for their own hideous children. And, besides the card-players, there are band-players: every now and then a fiddle from the neighboring orchestra, or a disorganized bassoon, will step down and drink a glass of the water, and jump back into his rank again.

Then come the burly troops of English, the honest lawyers, merchants, and gentlemen, with their wives and buxom daughters, and stout sons, that, almost grown to the height of manhood, are boys still, with rough wide-awake hats and shooting-jackets, full of lark and laughter. A French boy of sixteen has had des passions ere that time, very likely, and is already particular in his dress, an ogler of the women, and preparing to kill. Adolphe says to Alphonse—"La voila cette charmante Miss Fanni, la belle Kickleburi! je te donne ma parole, elle est fraiche comme une rose! la crois-tu riche, Alphonse?" "Je me range, mon ami, vois-tu? La vie de garcon me pese. Ma parole d'honneur! je me range."

And he gives Miss Fanny a killing bow, and a glance which seems to say, "Sweet Anglaise, I know that I have won your heart."

Then besides the young French buck, whom we will willingly suppose harmless, you see specimens of the French raff, who goes aux eaux: gambler, speculator, sentimentalist, duellist, travelling with madame his wife, at whom other raffs nod and wink familiarly. This rogue is much more picturesque and civilized than the similar person in our own country: whose manners betray the stable; who never reads anything but Bell's Life; and who is much more at ease in conversing with a groom than with his employer. Here come Mr. Boucher and Mr. Fowler: better to gamble for a score of nights with honest Monsieur Lenoir, than to sit down in private once with those gentlemen. But we have said that their profession is going down, and the number of Greeks daily diminishes. They are travelling with Mr. Bloundell, who was a gentleman once, and still retains about him some faint odor of that time of bloom; and Bloundell has put himself on young Lord Talboys, and is trying to get some money out of that young nobleman. But the English youth of the present day is a wide-awake youth, and male or female artifices are expended pretty much in vain on our young travelling companion.

Who come yonder? Those two fellows whom we met at the table-d'hote at the "Hotel de Russie" the other day: gentlemen of splendid costume, and yet questionable appearances, the eldest of whom called for the list of wines, and cried out loud enough for all the company to hear, "Lafite, six florins. 'Arry, shall we have some Lafite? You don't mind? No more do I then. I say, waiter, let's 'ave a pint of ordinaire." Truth is stranger than fiction. You good fellow, wherever you are, why did you ask 'Arry to 'ave that pint of ordinaire in the presence of your obedient servant? How could he do otherwise than chronicle the speech?

And see: here is a lady who is doubly desirous to be put into print, who encourages it and invites it. It appears that on Lankin's first arrival at Noirbourg with his travelling companion, a certain sensation was created in the little society by the rumor that an emissary of the famous Mr. Punch had arrived in the place; and, as we were smoking the cigar of peace on the lawn after dinner, looking on at the benevolent, pretty scene, Mrs. Hopkins, Miss Hopkins, and the excellent head of the family, walked many times up and down before us; eyed us severely face to face, and then walking away, shot back fierce glances at us in the Parthian manner; and at length, at the third or fourth turn, and when we could not but overhear so fine a voice, Mrs. Hopkins looks at us steadily, and says, "I'm sure he may put ME in if he likes: I don't mind."

Oh, ma'am! Oh, Mrs. Hopkins! how should a gentleman, who had never seen your face or heard of you before, want to put YOU in? What interest can the British public have in you? But as you wish it, and court publicity, here you are. Good luck go with you, madam. I have forgotten your real name, and should not know you again if I saw you. But why could not you leave a man to take his coffee and smoke his pipe in quiet?

We could never have time to make a catalogue of all the portraits that figure in this motley gallery. Among the travellers in Europe, who are daily multiplying in numbers and increasing in splendor, the United States' dandies must not be omitted. They seem as rich as the Milor of old days; they crowd in European capitals; they have elbowed out people of the old country from many hotels which we used to frequent; they adopt the French fashion of dressing rather than ours, and they grow handsomer beards than English beards: as some plants are found to flourish and shoot up prodigiously when introduced into a new soil. The ladies seem to be as well dressed as Parisians, and as handsome; though somewhat more delicate, perhaps, than the native English roses. They drive the finest carriages, they keep the grandest houses, they frequent the grandest company—and, in a word, the Broadway Swell has now taken his station and asserted his dignity amongst the grandees of Europe. He is fond of asking Count Reineck to dinner, and Grafinn Laura will condescend to look kindly upon a gentleman who has millions of dollars. Here comes a pair of New Yorkers. Behold their elegant curling beards, their velvet coats, their delicate primrose gloves and cambric handkerchiefs, and the aristocratic beauty of their boots. Why, if you had sixteen quarterings, you could not have smaller feet than those; and if you were descended from a line of kings you could not smoke better or bigger cigars.

Lady Kicklebury deigns to think very well of these young men, since she has seen them in the company of grandees and heard how rich they are. "Who is that very stylish-looking woman, to whom Mr. Washington Walker spoke just now?" she asks of Kicklebury.

Kicklebury gives a twinkle of his eye. "Oh, that, mother! that is Madame La Princesse de Mogador—it's a French title."

"She danced last night, and danced exceedingly well; I remarked her. There's a very high-bred grace about the princess."

"Yes, exceedingly. We'd better come on," says Kicklebury, blushing rather as he returns the princess's nod.

It is wonderful how large Kicklebury's acquaintance is. He has a word and a joke, in the best German he can muster, for everybody— for the high well-born lady, as for the German peasant maiden, or the pretty little washerwoman, who comes full sail down the streets, a basket on her head and one of Mrs. Fantail's wonderful gowns swelling on each arm. As we were going to the Schloss-Garten I caught a sight of the rogue's grinning face yesterday, close at little Gretel's ear under her basket; but spying out his mother advancing, he dashed down a bystreet, and when we came up with her, Gretel was alone.

One but seldom sees the English and the holiday visitors in the ancient parts of Noirbourg; they keep to the streets of new buildings and garden villas, which have sprung up under the magic influence of M. Lenoir, under the white towers and gables of the old German town. The Prince of Trente et Quarante has quite overcome the old serene sovereign of Noirbourg, whom one cannot help fancying a prince like a prince in a Christmas pantomime—a burlesque prince with twopence-halfpenny for a revenue, jolly and irascible, a prime-minister-kicking prince, fed upon fabulous plum- puddings and enormous pasteboard joints, by cooks and valets with large heads which never alter their grin. Not that this portrait is from the life. Perhaps he has no life. Perhaps there is no prince in the great white tower, that we see for miles before we enter the little town. Perhaps he has been mediatized, and sold his kingdom to Monsieur Lenoir. Before the palace of Lenoir there is a grove of orange-trees in tubs, which Lenoir bought from another German prince; who went straightway and lost the money, which he had been paid for his wonderful orange-trees, over Lenoir's green tables, at his roulette and trente-et-quarante. A great prince is Lenoir in his way; a generous and magnanimous prince. You may come to his feast and pay nothing, unless you please. You may walk in his gardens, sit in his palace, and read his thousand newspapers. You may go and play at whist in his small drawing-rooms, or dance and hear concerts in his grand saloon—and there is not a penny to pay. His fiddlers and trumpeters begin trumpeting and fiddling for you at the early dawn—they twang and blow for you in the afternoon, they pipe for you at night that you may dance— and there is nothing to pay—Lenoir pays for all. Give him but the chances of the table, and he will do all this and more. It is better to live under Prince Lenoir than a fabulous old German Durchlaucht whose cavalry ride wicker horses with petticoats, and whose prime minister has a great pasteboard head. Vive le Prince Lenoir!

There is a grotesque old carved gate to the palace of the Durchlaucht, from which you could expect none but a pantomime procession to pass. The place looks asleep; the courts are grass- grown and deserted. Is the Sleeping Beauty lying yonder, in the great white tower? What is the little army about? It seems a sham army: a sort of grotesque military. The only charge of infantry was this: one day when passing through the old town, looking for sketches. Perhaps they become croupiers at night. What can such a fabulous prince want with anything but a sham army? My favorite walk was in the ancient quarter of the town—the dear old fabulous quarter, away from the noisy actualities of life and Prince Lenoir's new palace—out of eye and earshot of the dandies and the ladies in their grand best clothes at the promenades—and the rattling whirl of the roulette wheel—and I liked to wander in the glum old gardens under the palace wall, and imagine the Sleeping Beauty within there.

Some one persuaded us one day to break the charm, and see the interior of the palace. I am sorry we did. There was no Sleeping Beauty in any chamber that we saw; nor any fairies, good or malevolent. There was a shabby set of clean old rooms, which looked as if they had belonged to a prince hard put to it for money, and whose tin crown jewels would not fetch more than King Stephen's pantaloons. A fugitive prince, a brave prince struggling with the storms of fate, a prince in exile may be poor; but a prince looking out of his own palace windows with a dressing-gown out at elbows, and dunned by his subject washerwoman—I say this is a painful object. When they get shabby they ought not to be seen. "Don't you think so, Lady Kicklebury?" Lady Kicklebury evidently had calculated the price of the carpets and hangings, and set them justly down at a low figure. "These German princes," she said, "are not to be put on a level with English noblemen." "Indeed," we answer, "there is nothing so perfect as England: nothing so good as our aristocracy; nothing so perfect as our institutions." "Nothing! NOTHING!" says Lady K.

An English princess was once brought to reign here; and almost the whole of the little court was kept upon her dowry. The people still regard her name fondly; and they show, at the Schloss, the rooms which she inhabited. Her old books are still there—her old furniture brought from home; the presents and keepsakes sent by her family are as they were in the princess's lifetime: the very clock has the name of a Windsor maker on its face; and portraits of all her numerous race decorate the homely walls of the now empty chambers. There is the benighted old king, his beard hanging down to the star on his breast; and the first gentleman of Europe—so lavish of his portrait everywhere, and so chary of showing his royal person—all the stalwart brothers of the now all but extinct generation are there; their quarrels and their pleasures, their glories and disgraces, enemies, flatterers, detractors, admirers— all now buried. Is it not curious to think that the King of Trumps now virtually reigns in this place, and has deposed the other dynasty?

Very early one morning, wishing to have a sketch of the White Tower in which our English princess had been imprisoned, I repaired to the gardens, and set about a work, which, when completed, will no doubt have the honor of a place on the line at the Exhibition; and, returning homewards to breakfast, musing upon the strange fortunes and inhabitants of the queer, fantastic, melancholy place, behold, I came suddenly upon a couple of persons, a male and a female; the latter of whom wore a blue hood or "ugly," and blushed very much on seeing me. The man began to laugh behind his moustaches, the which cachinnation was checked by an appealing look from the young lady; and he held out his hand and said, "How d'ye do, Titmarsh? Been out making some cawickachaws, hay?"

I need not say that the youth before me was the heavy dragoon, and that the maiden was Miss Fanny Kicklebury. Or need I repeat that, in the course of my blighted being, I never loved a young gazelle to glad me with its dark blue eye, but when it came to, the usual disappointment, was sure to ensue? There is no necessity why I should allude to my feelings at this most manifest and outrageous case. I gave a withering glance of scorn at the pair, and, with a stately salutation, passed on.

Miss Fanny came tripping after me. She held out her little hand with such a pretty look of deprecation, that I could not but take it; and she said, "Mr. Titmarsh, if you please, I want to speak to you, if you please;" and, choking with emotion, I bade her speak on.

"My brother knows all about it, and, highly approves of Captain Hicks," she said, with her head hanging down; "and oh, he's very good and kind: and I know him MUCH better now, than I did when we were on board the steamer."

I thought how I had mimicked him, and what an ass I had been.

"And you know," she continued, "that you have quite deserted me for the last ten days for your great acquaintances."

"I have been to play chess with Lord Knightsbridge, who has the gout."

"And to drink tea constantly with that American lady; and you have written verses in her album; and in Lavinia's album; and as I saw that you had quite thrown me off, why I—my brother approves of it highly; and—and Captain Hicks likes you very much, and says you amuse him very much—indeed he does," says the arch little wretch. And then she added a postscript, as it were to her letter, which contained, as usual, the point which she wished to urge:—

"You—won't break it to mamma—will you be so kind? My brother will do that"—and I promised her; and she ran away, kissing her hand to me. And I did not say a word to Lady Kicklebury, and not above a thousand people at Noirbourg knew that Miss Kicklebury and Captain Hicks were engaged.

And now let those who are too confident of their virtue listen to the truthful and melancholy story which I have to relate, and humble themselves, and bear in mind that the most perfect among us are occasionally liable to fall. Kicklebury was not perfect,—I do not defend his practice. He spent a great deal more time and money than was good for him at M. Lenoir's gaming-table, and the only thing which the young fellow never lost was his good humor. If Fortune shook her swift wings and fled away from him, he laughed at the retreating pinions, and you saw him dancing and laughing as gayly after losing a rouleau, as if he was made of money, and really had the five thousand a year which his mother said was the amount of the Kicklebury property. But when her ladyship's jointure, and the young ladies' allowances, and the interest of mortgages were paid out of the five thousand a year, I grieve to say that the gallant Kicklebury's income was to be counted by hundreds and not by thousands; so that, for any young lady who wants a carriage (and who can live without one?) our friend the baronet is not a desirable specimen of bachelors. Now, whether it was that the presence of his mamma interrupted his pleasures, or certain of her ways did not please him, or that he had lost all his money at roulette and could afford no more, certain it is, that after about a fortnight's stay at Noirbourg, he went off to shoot with Count Einhorn in Westphalia; he and Hicks parting the dearest of friends, and the baronet going off on a pony which the captain lent to him. Between him and Millikin, his brother-in-law, there was not much sympathy: for he pronounced Mr. Milliken to be what is called a muff; and had never been familiar with his elder sister Lavinia, of whose poems he had a mean opinion, and who used to tease and worry him by teaching him French, and telling tales of him to his mamma, when he was a schoolboy home for the holidays. Whereas, between the baronet and Miss Fanny there seemed to be the closest affection: they walked together every morning to the waters; they joked and laughed with each other as happily as possible. Fanny was almost ready to tell fibs to screen her brother's malpractices from her mamma: she cried when she heard of his mishaps, and that he had lost too much money at the green table; and when Sir Thomas went away, the good little soul brought him five louis; which was all the money she had: for you see she paid her mother handsomely for her board; and when her little gloves and milliner's bills were settled how much was there left out of two hundred a year? And she cried when she

PRELUDE

It happened that the undersigned spent the last Christmas season in a foreign city where there were many English children.

In that city, if you wanted to give a child's party, you could not even get a magic-lantern or buy Twelfth-Night characters—those funny painted pictures of the King, the Queen, the Lover, the Lady, the Dandy, the Captain, and so on—with which our young ones are wont to recreate themselves at this festive time.

My friend Miss Bunch, who was governess of a large family that lived in the Piano Nobile of the house inhabited by myself and my young charges (it was the Palazzo Poniatowski at Rome, and Messrs. Spillmann, two of the best pastry-cooks in Christendom, have their shop on the ground floor): Miss Bunch, I say, begged me to draw a set of Twelfth-Night characters for the amusement of our young people.

She is a lady of great fancy and droll imagination, and having looked at the characters, she and I composed a history about them, which was recited to the little folks at night, and served as our FIRE-SIDE PANTOMIME.

Our juvenile audience was amused by the adventures of Giglio and Bulbo, Rosalba and Angelica. I am bound to say the fate of the Hall Porter created a considerable sensation; and the wrath of Countess Gruffanuff was received with extreme pleasure.

If these children are pleased, thought I, why should not others be amused also? In a few days Dr. Birch's young friends will be expected to reassemble at Rodwell Regis, where they will learn everything that is useful, and under the eyes of careful ushers continue the business of their little lives.

But, in the meanwhile, and for a brief holiday, let us laugh and be as pleasant as we can. And you elder folk—a little joking, and dancing, and fooling will do even you no harm. The author wishes you a merry Christmas, and welcomes you to the Fire-side Pantomime.

M. A. TITMARSH.

December 1854.

I. SHOWS HOW THE ROYAL FAMILY SAT DOWN TO BREAKFAST

This is Valoroso XXIV., King of Paflagonia, seated with his Queen and only child at their royal breakfast-table, and receiving the letter which announces to his Majesty a proposed visit from Prince Bulbo, heir of Padella, reigning King of Crim Tartary. Remark the delight upon the monarch's royal features. He is so absorbed in the perusal of the King of Crim Tartary's letter, that he allows his eggs to get cold, and leaves his august muffins untasted.

"What! that wicked, brave, delightful Prince Bulbo!" cries Princess Angelica; "so handsome, so accomplished, so witty—the conqueror of Rimbombamento, where he slew ten thousand giants!"

"Who told you of him, my dear?" asks his Majesty.

"A little bird," says Angelica.

"Poor Giglio!" says mamma, pouring out the tea.

"Bother Giglio!" cries Angelica, tossing up her head, which rustled with a thousand curl-papers.

"I wish," growls the King—"I wish Giglio was. . ."

"Was better? Yes, dear, he is better," says the Queen. "Angelica's little maid, Betsinda, told me so when she came to my room this morning with my early tea."

"You are always drinking tea," said the monarch, with a scowl.

"It is better than drinking port or brandy-and-water," replies her Majesty.

"Well, well, my dear, I only said you were fond of drinking tea," said the King of Paflagonia, with an effort as if to command his temper. "Angelica! I hope you have plenty of new dresses; your milliners' bills are long enough. My dear Queen, you must see and have some parties. I prefer dinners, but of course you will be for balls. Your everlasting blue velvet quite tires me: and, my love, I should like you to have a new necklace. Order one. Not more than a hundred or a hundred and fifty thousand pounds."

"And Giglio, dear?" says the Queen.

"GIGLIO MAY GO TO THE ——"

"Oh, sir!" screams her Majesty. "Your own nephew! our late King's only son."

"Giglio may go to the tailor's, and order the bills to be sent in to Glumboso to pay. Confound him! I mean bless his dear heart. He need want for nothing; give him a couple of guineas for pocket- money, my dear; and you may as well order yourself bracelets while you are about the necklace, Mrs. V."

Her Majesty, or MRS. V., as the monarch facetiously called her (for even royalty will have its sport, and this august family were very much attached), embraced her husband, and, twining her arm round her daughter's waist, they quitted the breakfast-room in order to make all things ready for the princely stranger.

When they were gone, the smile that had lighted up the eyes of the HUSBAND and FATHER fled—the pride of the KING fled—the MAN was alone. Had I the pen of a G. P. R. James, I would describe Valoroso's torments in the choicest language; in which I would also depict his flashing eye, his distended nostril—his dressing-gown, pocket-handkerchief, and boots. But I need not say I have NOT the pen of that novelist; suffice it to say, Valoroso was alone.

He rushed to the cupboard, seizing from the table one of the many egg-cups with which his princely board was served for the matin meal, drew out a bottle of right Nantz or Cognac, filled and emptied the cup several times, and laid it down with a hoarse "Ha, ha, ha! now Valoroso is a man again!"

"But oh!" he went on (still sipping, I am sorry to say), "ere I was a king, I needed not this intoxicating draught; once I detested the hot brandy wine, and quaffed no other fount but nature's rill. It dashes not more quickly o'er the rocks than I did, as, with blunderbuss in hand, I brushed away the early morning dew, and shot the partridge, snipe, or antlered deer! Ah! well may England's dramatist remark, "Uneasy lies the head that wears a crown!" Why did I steal my nephew's, my young Giglio's—? Steal! said I? no, no, no, not steal, not steal. Let me withdraw that odious expression. I took, and on my manly head I set, the royal crown of Paflagonia; I took, and with my royal arm I wield, the sceptral rod of Paflagonia; I took, and in my outstretched hand I hold, the royal orb of Paflagonia! Could a poor boy, a snivelling, drivelling boy—was in his nurse's arms but yesterday, and cried for sugarplums and puled for pap—bear up the awful weight of crown, orb, sceptre? gird on the sword my royal fathers wore, and meet in fight the tough Crimean foe?"

And then the monarch went on to argue in his own mind (though we need not say that blank verse is not argument) that what he had got it was his duty to keep, and that, if at one time he had entertained ideas of a certain restitution, which shall be nameless, the prospect by a CERTAIN MARRIAGE of uniting two crowns and two nations which had been engaged in bloody and expensive wars, as the Paflagonians and the Crimeans had been, put the idea of Giglio's restoration to the throne out of the question: nay, were his own brother, King Savio, alive, he would certainly will the crown from his own son in order to bring about such a desirable union.

Thus easily do we deceive ourselves! Thus do we fancy what we wish is right! The King took courage, read the papers, finished his muffins and eggs, and rang the bell for his Prime Minister. The Queen, after thinking whether she should go up and see Giglio, who had been sick, thought, "Not now. Business first; pleasure afterwards. I will go and see dear Giglio this afternoon; and now I will drive to the jeweller's, to look for the necklace and bracelets." The Princess went up into her own room, and made Betsinda, her maid, bring out all her dresses; and as for Giglio, they forgot him as much as I forget what I had for dinner last Tuesday twelve-month.

II. HOW KING VALOROSO GOT THE CROWN, AND PRINCE GIGLIO WENT WITHOUT.

Paflagonia, ten or twenty thousand years ago, appears to have been one of those kingdoms where the laws of succession were not settled; for when King Savio died, leaving his brother Regent of the kingdom, and guardian of Savio's orphan infant, this unfaithful regent took no sort of regard of the late monarch's will; had himself proclaimed sovereign of Paflagonia under the title of King Valoroso XXIV., had a most splendid coronation, and ordered all the nobles of the kingdom to pay him homage. So long as Valoroso gave them plenty of balls at Court, plenty of money and lucrative places, the Paflagonian nobility did not care who was king; and as for the people, in those early times, they were equally indifferent. The Prince Giglio, by reason of his tender age at his royal father's death, did not feel the loss of his crown and empire. As long as he had plenty of toys and sweetmeats, a holiday five times a week and a horse and gun to go out shooting when he grew a little older, and, above all, the company of his darling cousin, the King's only child, poor Giglio was perfectly contented; nor did he envy his uncle the royal robes and sceptre, the great hot uncomfortable throne of state, and the enormous cumbersome crown in which that monarch appeared from morning till night. King Valoroso's portrait has been left to us; and I think you will agree with me that he must have been sometimes RATHER TIRED of his velvet, and his diamonds, and his ermine, and his grandeur. I shouldn't like to sit in that stifling robe with such a thing as that on my head.

No doubt, the Queen must have been lovely in her youth; for though she grew rather stout in after life, yet her features, as shown in her portrait, are certainly PLEASING. If she was fond of flattery, scandal, cards, and fine clothes, let us deal gently with her infirmities, which, after all, may be no greater than our own. She was kind to her nephew; and if she had any scruples of conscience about her husband's taking the young Prince's crown, consoled herself by thinking that the King, though a usurper, was a most respectable man, and that at his death Prince Giglio would be restored to his throne, and share it with his cousin, whom he loved so fondly.

The Prime Minister was Glumboso, an old statesman, who most

cheerfully swore fidelity to King Valoroso, and in whose hands the monarch left all the affairs of his kingdom. All Valoroso wanted was plenty of money, plenty of hunting, plenty of flattery, and as little trouble as possible. As long as he had his sport, this monarch cared little how his people paid for it: he engaged in some wars, and of course the Paflagonian newspapers announced that he had gained prodigious victories: he had statues erected to himself in every city of the empire; and of course his pictures placed everywhere, and in all the print-shops: he was Valoroso the Magnanimous, Valoroso the Victorious, Valoroso the Great, and so forth;—for even in these early times courtiers and people knew how to flatter.

This royal pair had one only child, the Princess Angelica, who, you may be sure, was a paragon in the courtiers' eyes, in her parents', and in her own. It was said she had the longest hair, the largest eyes, the slimmest waist, the smallest foot, and the most lovely complexion of any young lady in the Paflagonian dominions. Her accomplishments were announced to be even superior to her beauty; and governesses used to shame their idle pupils by telling them what Princess Angelica could do. She could play the most difficult pieces of music at sight. She could answer any one of "Mangnall's Questions." She knew every date in the history of Paflagonia, and every other country. She knew French, English, Italian, German, Spanish, Hebrew, Greek, Latin, Cappadocian, Samothracian, Aegean, and Crim Tartar. In a word, she was a most accomplished young creature; and her governess and lady-in-waiting was the severe Countess Gruffanuff.

Would you not fancy, from this picture, that Gruffanuff must have been a person of highest birth? She looks so haughty that I should have thought her a princess at the very least, with a pedigree reaching as far back as the Deluge. But this lady was no better born than many other ladies who give themselves airs; and all sensible people laughed at her absurd pretensions. The fact is, she had been maid-servant to the Queen when her Majesty was only Princess, and her husband had been head footman; but after his death or DISAPPEARANCE, of which you shall hear presently, this Mrs. Gruffanuff, by flattering, toadying, and wheedling her royal mistress, became a favorite with the Queen (who was rather a weak woman), and her Majesty gave her a title, and made her nursery governess to the Princess.

And now I must tell you about the Princess's learning and accomplishments, for which she had such a wonderful character. Clever Angelica certainly was, but as IDLE AS POSSIBLE. Play at sight, indeed!

she could play one or two pieces, and pretend that she had never seen them before; she could answer half a dozen "Mangnall's Questions;" but then you must take care to ask the RIGHT ones. As for her languages, she had masters in plenty, but I doubt whether she knew more than a few phrases in each, for all her presence; and as for her embroidery and her drawing, she showed beautiful specimens, it is true, but WHO DID THEM?

This obliges me to tell the truth, and to do so I must go back ever so far, and tell you about the FAIRY BLACKSTICK.

III. TELLS WHO THE FAIRY BLACKSTICK WAS, AND WHO WERE EVER SO MANY

GRAND PERSONAGES BESIDES.

Between the kingdoms of Paflagonia and Crim Tartary, there lived a mysterious personage, who was known in those countries as the Fairy Blackstick, from the ebony wand or crutch which she carried; on which she rode to the moon sometimes, or upon other excursions of business or pleasure, and with which she performed her wonders. When she was young, and had been first taught the art of conjuring by the necromancer, her father, she was always practicing her skill, whizzing about from one kingdom to another upon her black stick, and conferring her fairy favors upon this Prince or that. She had scores of royal godchildren; turned numberless wicked people into beasts, birds, millstones, clocks, pumps, boot jacks, umbrellas, or other absurd shapes; and, in a word, was one of the most active and officious of the whole college of fairies.

But after two or three thousand years of this sport, I suppose Blackstick grew tired of it. Or perhaps she thought, "What good am I doing by sending this Princess to sleep for a hundred years? by fixing a black pudding on to that booby's nose? by causing diamonds and pearls to drop from one little girl's mouth, and vipers and toads from another's? I begin to think I do as much harm as good by my performances. I might as well shut my incantations up, and allow things to take their natural course.

"There were my two young goddaughters, King Savio's wife, and Duke Padella's wife: I gave them each a present, which was to render them charming in the eyes of their husbands, and secure the affection of those gentlemen as long as they lived. What good did my Rose and my Ring do these two women? None on earth. From having all their whims indulged by their husbands, they became capricious, lazy, ill-humored, absurdly vain, and leered and languished, and fancied themselves irresistibly beautiful, when they were really quite old and hideous, the ridiculous creatures! They used actually to patronise me when I went to pay them a visit— ME, the Fairy Blackstick, who knows all the wisdom of the necromancers, and could have turned them into baboons, and all their diamonds into strings of onions, by a single wave of my rod!" So she locked up her books in her cupboard, declined further magical performances, and scarcely used her wand at all except as a cane to walk about with.

So when Duke Padella's lady had a little son (the Duke was at that time only one of the principal noblemen in Crim Tartary), Blackstick, although invited to the christening, would not so much as attend; but merely sent her compliments and a silver papboat for the baby, which was really not worth a couple of guineas. About the same time the Queen of Paflagonia presented his Majesty with a son and heir; and guns were fired, the capital illuminated, and no end of feasts ordained to celebrate the young Prince's birth. It was thought the fairy, who was asked to be his godmother, would at least have presented him with an invisible jacket, a flying horse, a Fortunatus's purse, or some other valuable token of her favor; but instead, Blackstick went up to the cradle of the child Giglio, when everybody was admiring him and complimenting his royal papa and mamma, and said, "My poor child, the best thing I can send you is a little MISFORTUNE;" and this was all she would utter, to the disgust of Giglio's parents, who died very soon after, when Giglio's uncle took the throne, as we read in Chapter I.

In like manner, when CAVOLFIORE, King of Crim Tartary, had a christening of his only child, ROSALBA, the Fairy Blackstick, who had been invited, was not more gracious than in Prince Giglio's case. Whilst everybody was expatiating over the beauty of the darling child, and congratulating its parents, the Fairy Blackstick looked very sadly at the baby and its mother, and said, "My good woman (for the Fairy was very familiar, and no more minded a Queen than a washerwoman)—my good woman, these people who are following you will be the first to turn against you; and as for this little lady, the best thing I can wish her is a LITTLE MISFORTUNE." So she touched Rosalba with her black wand, looked severely at the courtiers, motioned the Queen an adieu with her hand, and sailed slowly up into the air out of the window.

When she was gone, the Court people, who had been awed and silent in her presence, began to speak. "What an odious Fairy she is" (they said)—"a pretty Fairy, indeed! Why, she went to the King of Paflagonia's christening, and pretended to do all sorts of things for that family; and what has happened—the Prince, her godson, has been turned off his throne by his uncle. Would we allow our sweet Princess to be deprived of her rights by any enemy? Never, never, never, never!"

And they all shouted in a chorus, "Never, never, never, never!"

Now, I should like to know, and how did these fine courtiers show their fidelity? One of King Cavolfiore's vassals, the Duke Padella just mentioned, rebelled against the King, who went out to chastise his rebellious subject. "Any one rebel against our beloved and august Monarch!" cried the courtiers; "any one resist HIM? Pooh! He is invincible, irresistible. He will bring home Padella a prisoner, and tie him to a donkey's tail, and drive him round the town, saying, 'This is the way the Great Cavolfiore treats rebels.'"

The King went forth to vanquish Padella; and the poor Queen, who was a very timid, anxious creature, grew so frightened and ill that I am sorry to say she died; leaving injunctions with her ladies to take care of the dear little Rosalba. Of course they said they would. Of course they vowed they would die rather than any harm should happen to the Princess. At first the Crim Tartar Court Journal stated that the King was obtaining great victories over the audacious rebel: then it was announced that the troops of the infamous Padella were in flight: then it was said that the royal army would soon come up with the enemy, and then—then the news came that King Cavolfiore was vanquished and slain by his Majesty, King Padella the First!

At this news, half the courtiers ran off to pay their duty to the conquering chief, and the other half ran away, laying hands on all the best articles in the palace; and poor little Rosalba was left there quite alone— quite alone: she toddled from one room to another, crying, "Countess! Duchess!" (only she said "Tountess, Duttess," not being able to speak plain) "bring me my mutton-sop; my Royal Highness hungy! Tountess! Duttess!" And she went from the private apartments into the throne-room and nobody was there;— and thence into the ballroom and nobody was there;—and thence into the pages' room and nobody was there; —and she toddled down the great staircase into the hall and nobody was there;—and the door was open, and she went into the court, and into the garden, and thence into the wilderness, and thence into the forest where the wild beasts live, and was never heard of any more!

A piece of her torn mantle and one of her shoes were found in the wood in the mouths of two lionesses' cubs whom KING PADELLA and a royal hunting party shot—for he was King now, and reigned over Crim Tartary. "So the poor little Princess is done for," said he; "well, what's done can't be helped. Gentlemen, let us go to luncheon!" And one of the courtiers took up the shoe and put it in his pocket. And there was an end of Rosalba!

IV. HOW BLACKSTICK WAS NOT ASKED TO THE PRINCESS ANGELICA'S CHRISTENING.

When the Princess Angelica was born, her parents not only did not ask the Fairy Blackstick to the christening party, but gave orders to their porter absolutely to refuse her if she called. This porter's name was Gruffanuff, and he had been selected for the post by their Royal Highnesses because he was a very tall fierce man, who could say "Not at home" to a tradesman or an unwelcome visitor with a rudeness which frightened most such persons away. He was the husband of that Countess whose picture we have just seen, and as long as they were together they quarrelled from morning till night. Now this fellow tried his rudeness once too often, as you shall hear. For the Fairy Blackstick coming to call upon the Prince and Princess, who were actually sitting at the open drawing- room window, Gruffanuff not only denied them, but made the most ODIOUS VULGAR SIGN as he was going to slam the door in the Fairy's face! "Git away, hold Blackstick!" said he. "I tell you, Master and Missis ain't at home to you;" and he was, as we have said, GOING to slam the door.

But the Fairy, with her wand, prevented the door being shut; and Gruffanuff came out again in a fury, swearing in the most abominable way, and asking the Fairy "whether she thought he was a-going to stay at that there door hall day?"

"You ARE going to stay at that door all day and all night, and for many a long year," the Fairy said, very majestically; and Gruffanuff, coming out of the door, straddling before it with his great calves, burst out laughing, and cried, "Ha, ha, ha! this IS a good un! Ha—ah—what's this? Let me down—oh—o—h'm!" and then he was dumb!

For, as the Fairy waved her wand over him, he felt himself rising off the ground, and fluttering up against the door, and then, as if a screw ran into his stomach, he felt a dreadful pain there, and was pinned to the door; and then his arms flew up over his head; and his legs, after writhing about wildly, twisted under his body; and he felt cold, cold, growing over him, as if he was turning into metal; and he said, "Oh—o—h'm!" and could say no more, because he was dumb.

He WAS turned into metal! He was, from being BRAZEN, BRASS! He was neither more nor less than a knocker! And there he was, nailed to the door in the blazing summer day, till he burned almost red- hot; and there he was, nailed to the door all the bitter winter nights, till his brass nose was dropping with icicles. And the postman came and rapped at him, and the vulgarest boy with a letter came and hit him up against the door. And the King and Queen (Princess and Prince they were then) coming home from a walk that evening, the King said, "Hullo, my dear! you have had a new knocker put on the door. Why, it's rather like our porter in the face! What has become of that boozy vagabond?" And the housemaid came and scrubbed his nose with sand-paper; and once, when the Princess Angelica's little sister was born, he was tied up in an old kid- glove; and, another night, some LARKING young men tried to wrench him off, and put him to the most excruciating agony with a turn screw. And then the Queen had a fancy to have the color of the door altered; and the painters dabbed him over the mouth and eyes, and nearly choked him, as they painted him pea-green. I warrant he had leisure to repent of having been rude to the Fairy Blackstick!

As for his wife, she did not miss him; and as he was always guzzling beer at the public-house, and notoriously quarrelling with his wife, and in debt to the tradesmen, it was supposed he had run away from all these evils, and emigrated to Australia or America. And when the Prince and Princess chose to become King and Queen, they left their old house, and nobody thought of the porter any more.

V. HOW PRINCESS ANGELICA TOOK A LITTLE MAID.

One day, when the Princess Angelica was quite a little girl, she was walking in the garden of the palace, with Mrs. Gruffanuff, the governess, holding a parasol over her head, to keep her sweet complexion from the freckles, and Angelica was carrying a bun, to feed the swans and ducks in the royal pond.

They had not reached the duck-pond, when there came toddling up to them such a funny little girl! She had a great quantity of hair blowing about her chubby little cheeks, and looked as if she had not been washed or combed for ever so long. She wore a ragged bit of a cloak, and had only one shoe on.

"You little wretch, who let you in here?" asked Mrs. Gruffanuff.

"Div me dat bun," said the little girl, "me vely hungry."

"Hungry! what is that?" asked Princess Angelica, and gave the child the bun.

"Oh, Princess!" says Mrs. Gruffanuff, "how good, how kind, how truly angelical you are! See, Your Majesties," she said to the King and Queen, who now came up, along with their nephew, Prince Giglio, "how kind the Princess is! She met this little dirty wretch in the garden—I can't tell how she came in here, or why the guards did not shoot her dead at the gate!— and the dear darling of a Princess has given her the whole of her bun!"

"I didn't want it," said Angelica.

"But you are a darling little angel all the same," says the governess.

"Yes; I know I am," said Angelica. "Dirty little girl, don't you think I am very pretty?" Indeed, she had on the finest of little dresses and hats; and, as her hair was carefully curled, she really looked very well.

"Oh, pooty, pooty!" says the little girl, capering about, laughing, and dancing, and munching her bun; and as she ate it she began to sing, "O what fun to have a plum bun! how I wis it never was done!" At which, and her funny accent, Angelica, Giglio, and the King and Queen began to laugh very merrily.

"I can dance as well as sing," says the little girl. "I can dance, and I can sing, and I can do all sorts of ting." And she ran to a flower-bed, and pulling a few polyanthuses, rhododendrons, and other flowers, made herself a little wreath, and danced before the King and Queen so drolly and prettily, that everybody was delighted.

"Who was your mother—who were your relations, little girl?" said the Queen.

The little girl said, "Little lion was my brudder; great big lioness my mudder; neber heard of any udder." And she capered away on her one shoe, and everybody was exceedingly diverted.

So Angelica said to the Queen, "Mamma, my parrot flew away yesterday out of its cage, and I don't care any more for any of my toys; and I think this funny little dirty child will amuse me. I will take her home, and give her some of my old frocks—"

"Oh, the generous darling!" says Mrs. Gruffanuff.

"—Which I have worn ever so many times, and am quite tired of," Angelica went on; "and she shall be my little maid. Will you come home with me, little dirty girl?"

The child clapped her hands, and said, "Go home with you—yes! You pooty Princess! Have a nice dinner, and wear a new dress!"

And they all laughed again, and took home the child to the palace, where, when she was washed and combed, and had one of the Princess's frocks given to her, she looked as handsome as Angelica, almost. Not that Angelica ever thought so; for this little lady never imagined that anybody in the world could be as pretty, as good, or as clever as herself. In order that the little girl should not become too proud and conceited, Mrs. Gruffanuff took her old ragged mantle and one shoe, and put them into a glass box, with a card laid upon them, upon which was written, "These were the old clothes in which little BETSINDA was found when the great goodness and admirable kindness of Her Royal Highness the Princess Angelica received this little outcast." And the date was added, and the box locked up.

For a while little Betsinda was a great favorite with the Princess, and she danced, and sang, and made her little rhymes, to amuse her mistress. But then the Princess got a monkey, and afterwards a little dog, and afterwards a doll, and did not care for Betsinda any more, who became very melancholy and quiet, and sang no more funny songs, because nobody cared to hear her. And then, as she grew older, she was made a little lady's-maid to the Princess; and though she had no wages, she worked and mended, and put Angelica's hair in papers, and was never cross when scolded, and was always eager to please her mistress, and was always up early and to bed late, and at hand when wanted, and in fact became a perfect little maid. So the two girls grew up, and, when the Princess came out, Betsinda was never tired of waiting on her; and made her dresses better than the best milliner, and was useful in a hundred ways. Whilst the Princess was having her masters, Betsinda would sit and watch them; and in this way she picked up a great deal of learning; for she was always awake, though her mistress was not, and listened to the wise professors when Angelica was yawning or thinking of the next ball. And when the dancing-master came, Betsinda learned along with Angelica; and when the music-master came, she watched him, and practiced the Princess's pieces when Angelica was away at balls and parties; and when the drawing-master came, she took note of all he said and did; and the same with French, Italian, and all other languages—she learned them from the teacher who came to Angelica. When the Princess was going out of an evening she would say, "My good Betsinda, you may as well finish what I have begun." "Yes, miss," Betsinda would say, and sit down very cheerful, not to FINISH what Angelica began, but to DO it.

For instance, the Princess would begin a head of a warrior, let us say, and when it was begun it was something like this:

But when it was done, the warrior was like this:—(only handsomer still if possible), and the Princess put her name to the drawing; and the Court and King and Queen, and above all poor Giglio, admired the picture of all things, and said, "Was there ever a genius like Angelica?" So, I am sorry to say, was it with the Princess's embroidery and other accomplishments; and Angelica actually believed that she did these things herself, and received all the flattery of the Court as if every word of it was true. Thus she began to think that there was no young woman in all the world equal to herself, and that no young man was good enough for her. As for Betsinda, as she heard none of these praises, she was not puffed up by them, and being a most grateful, good-natured girl, she was only too anxious to do everything which might give her mistress pleasure. Now you begin to perceive that Angelica had faults of her own, and was by no means such a wonder of wonders as people represented Her Royal Highness to be.

VI. HOW PRINCE GIGLIO BEHAVED HIMSELF.

And now let us speak about Prince Giglio, the nephew of the reigning monarch of Paflagonia. It has already been stated, in page seven, that as long as he had a smart coat to wear, a good horse to ride, and money in his pocket, or rather to take out of his pocket, for he was very good-natured, my young Prince did not care for the loss of his crown and sceptre, being a thoughtless youth, not much inclined to politics or any kind of learning. So his tutor had a sinecure. Giglio would not learn classics or mathematics, and the Lord Chancellor of Paflagonia, SQUARETOSO, pulled a very long face because the Prince could not be got to study the Paflagonian laws and constitution; but, on the other hand, the King's gamekeepers and huntsmen found the Prince an apt pupil; the dancing-master pronounced that he was a most elegant and assiduous scholar; the First Lord of the Billiard Table gave the most flattering reports of the Prince's skill; so did the Groom of the Tennis Court; and as for the Captain of the Guard and Fencing- master, the VALIANT and VETERAN Count KUTASOFF HEDZOFF, he avowed that since he ran the General of Crim Tartary, the dreadful Grumbuskin, through the body, he never had encountered so expert a swordsman as Prince Giglio.

I hope you do not imagine that there was any impropriety in the Prince and Princess walking together in the palace garden, and because Giglio kissed Angelica's hand in a polite manner. In the first place they are cousins; next, the Queen is walking in the garden too (you cannot see her, for she happens to be behind that tree), and her Majesty always wished that Angelica and Giglio should marry: so did Giglio: so did Angelica sometimes, for she thought her cousin very handsome, brave, and good-natured: but then you know she was so clever and knew so many things, and poor Giglio knew nothing, and had no conversation. When they looked at the stars, what did Giglio know of the heavenly bodies? Once, when on a sweet night in a balcony where they were standing, Angelica said, "There is the Bear." "Where?" says Giglio. "Don't be afraid, Angelica! if a dozen bears come, I will kill them rather than they shall hurt you." "Oh, you silly creature!" says she; "you are very good, but you are not very wise." When they looked at the flowers, Giglio was utterly unacquainted with botany, and had never heard of Linnaeus. When the butterflies passed, Giglio knew nothing about them, being as ignorant of entomology as I am of algebra. So you see, Angelica, though she liked Giglio pretty well, despised him on account of his ignorance. I think she probably valued HER OWN LEARNING rather too much; but to think too well of one's self is the fault of people of all ages and both sexes. Finally, when nobody else was there, Angelica liked her cousin well enough.

King Valoroso was very delicate in health, and withal so fond of good dinners (which were prepared for him by his French cook Marmitonio), that it was supposed he could not live long. Now the idea of anything happening to the King struck the artful Prime Minister and the designing old lady-in-waiting with terror. For, thought Glumboso and the Countess, "when Prince Giglio marries his cousin and comes to the throne, what a pretty position we shall be in, whom he dislikes, and who have always been unkind to him. We shall lose our places in a trice; Mrs. Gruffanuff will have to give up all the jewels, laces, snuff-boxes, rings, and watches which belonged to the Queen, Giglio's mother; and Glumboso will be forced to refund two hundred and seventeen thousand millions nine hundred and eighty-seven thousand four hundred and thirty-nine pounds, thirteen shillings, and sixpence halfpenny, money left to Prince Giglio by his poor dear father."

So the Lady of Honor and the Prime Minister hated Giglio because they had done him a wrong; and these unprincipled people invented a hundred cruel stories about poor Giglio, in order to influence the King, Queen, and Princess against him; how he was so ignorant that he could not spell the commonest words, and actually wrote Valoroso Valloroso, and spelt Angelica with two l's; how he drank a great deal too much wine at dinner, and was always idling in the stables with the grooms; how he owed ever so much money at the pastry- cook's and the haberdasher's; how he used to go to sleep at church; how he was fond of playing cards with the pages. So did the Queen like playing cards; so did the King go to sleep at church, and eat and drink too much; and, if Giglio owed a trifle for tarts, who owed him two hundred and seventeen thousand millions nine hundred and eighty-seven thousand four hundred and thirty-nine pounds, thirteen shillings, and sixpence halfpenny, I should like to know? Detractors and tale-bearers (in my humble opinion) had much better look at HOME. All this backbiting and slandering had effect upon Princess Angelica, who began to look coldly on her cousin, then to laugh at him and scorn him for being so stupid, then to sneer at him for having vulgar associates; and at Court balls, dinners, and so forth, to treat him so unkindly that poor Giglio became quite ill, took to his bed, and sent for the doctor.

His Majesty King Valoroso, as we have seen, had his own reasons for disliking his nephew; and as for those innocent readers who ask why?—I beg (with the permission of their dear parents) to refer them to Shakespeare's pages, where they will read why King John disliked Prince Arthur. With the Queen, his royal but weak-minded aunt, when Giglio was out of sight he was out of mind. While she had her whist and her evening parties, she cared for little else.

I dare say TWO VILLAINS, who shall be nameless, wished Doctor Pildrafto, the Court Physician, had killed Giglio right out, but he only bled and physicked him so severely that the Prince was kept to his room for several months, and grew as thin as a post.

Whilst he was lying sick in this way, there came to the Court of Paflagonia a famous painter, whose name was Tomaso Lorenzo, and who was Painter in Ordinary to the King of Crim Tartary, Paflagonia's neighbor. Tomaso Lorenzo painted all the Court, who were delighted with his works; for even Countess Gruffanuff looked young and Glumboso good-humored in his pictures. "He flatters very much," some people said. "Nay!" says Princess Angelica, "I am above flattery, and I think he did not make my picture handsome enough. I can't bear to hear a man of genius unjustly cried down, and I hope my dear papa will make Lorenzo a knight of his Order of the Cucumber."

The Princess Angelica, although the courtiers vowed Her Royal Highness could draw so BEAUTIFULLY that the idea of her taking lessons was absurd, yet chose to have Lorenzo for a teacher, and it was wonderful, AS LONG AS SHE PAINTED IN HIS STUDIO, what beautiful pictures she made! Some of the performances were engraved for the "Book of Beauty:" others were sold for enormous sums at Charity Bazaars. She wrote the SIGNATURES under the drawings, no doubt, but I think I know who did the pictures—this artful painter, who had come with other designs on Angelica than merely to teach her to draw.

One day, Lorenzo showed the Princess a portrait of a young man in armor, with fair hair and the loveliest blue eyes, and an expression at once melancholy and interesting.

"Dear Signor Lorenzo, who is this?" asked the Princess. "I never saw anyone so handsome," says Countess Gruffanuff (the old humbug).

"That," said the painter, "that, Madam, is the portrait of my august young master, his Royal Highness Bulbo, Crown Prince of Crim Tartary, Duke of Acroceraunia, Marquis of Poluphloisboio, and Knight Grand Cross of the Order of the Pumpkin. That is the Order of the Pumpkin glittering on his manly breast, and received by His Royal Highness from his august father, his Majesty King PADELLA I., for his gallantry at the battle of Rimbombamento, when he slew with his own princely hand the King of Ograria and two hundred and eleven giants of the two hundred and eighteen who formed the King's bodyguard. The remainder were destroyed by the brave Crim Tartar army after an obstinate combat, in which the Crim Tartars suffered severely."

"What a Prince!" thought Angelica: "so brave—so calm-looking—so young—what a hero!"

"He is as accomplished as he is brave," continued the Court Painter. "He knows all languages perfectly: sings deliciously: plays every instrument: composes operas which have been acted a thousand nights running at the Imperial Theatre of Crim Tartary, and danced in a ballet there before the King and Queen; in which he looked so beautiful, that his cousin, the lovely daughter of the King of Circassia, died for love of him."

"Why did he not marry the poor Princess?" asked Angelica, with a sigh.

"Because they were FIRST COUSINS, Madam, and the clergy forbid these unions," said the Painter. "And, besides, the young Prince had given his royal heart ELSEWHERE."

"And to whom?" asked Her Royal Highness.

"I am not at liberty to mention the Princess's name," answered the Painter.

"But you may tell me the first letter of it," gasped out the Princess.

"That Your Royal Highness is at liberty to guess," said Lorenzo.

"Does it begin with a Z?" asked Angelica.

The Painter said it wasn't a Z; then she tried a Y; then an X; then a W, and went so backwards through almost the whole alphabet.

When she came to D, and it wasn't D, she grew very excited; when she came to C, and it wasn't C, she was still more nervous; when she came to B, AND IT WASN'T B, "Oh dearest Gruffanuff," she said, "lend me your smelling-bottle!" and, hiding her head in the Countess's shoulder, she faintly whispered, "Ah, Signor, can it be A?"

"It was A; and though I may not, by my Royal Master's orders, tell Your

Royal Highness the Princess's name, whom he fondly, madly, devotedly, rapturously loves, I may show you her portrait," says this slyboots: and leading the Princess up to a gilt frame, he drew a curtain which was before it.

O goodness! the frame contained A LOOKING-GLASS! and Angelica saw her own face!

VII. HOW GIGLIO AND ANGELICA HAD A QUARREL.

The Court Painter of his Majesty the King of Crim Tartary returned to that monarch's dominions, carrying away a number of sketches which he had made in the Paflagonian capital (you know, of course, my dears, that the name of that capital is Blombodinga); but the most charming of all his pieces was a portrait of the Princess Angelica, which all the Crim Tartar nobles came to see. With this work the King was so delighted, that he decorated the Painter with his Order of the Pumpkin (sixth class) and the artist became Sir Tomaso Lorenzo, K.P., thenceforth.

King Valoroso also sent Sir Tomaso his Order of the Cucumber, besides a handsome order for money, for he painted the King, Queen, and principal nobility while at Blombodinga, and became all the fashion, to the perfect rage of all the artists in Paflagonia, where the King used to point to the portrait of Prince Bulbo, which Sir Tomaso had left behind him, and say "Which among you can paint a picture like that?"

It hung in the royal parlor over the royal sideboard, and Princess Angelica could always look at it as she sat making the tea. Each day it seemed to grow handsomer and handsomer, and the Princess grew so fond of looking at it, that she would often spill the tea over the cloth, at which her father and mother would wink and wag their heads; and say to each other, "Aha! we see how things are going."

In the meantime poor Giglio lay upstairs very sick in his chamber, though he took all the doctor's horrible medicines like a good young lad: as I hope YOU do, my dears, when you are ill and mamma sends for the medical man. And the only person who visited Giglio (besides his friend the captain of the guard, who was almost always busy or on parade), was little Betsinda the housemaid, who used to do his bedroom and sitting-room out, bring him his gruel, and warm his bed.

When the little housemaid came to him in the morning and evening, Prince Giglio used to say, "Betsinda, Betsinda, how is the Princess Angelica?"

And Betsinda used to answer, "The Princess is very well, thank you, my Lord." And Giglio would heave a sigh, and think, "If Angelica were sick, I am sure I should not be very well."

Then Giglio would say, "Betsinda, has the Princess Angelica asked for me today?" And Betsinda would answer, "No, my Lord, not today"; or, "She was very busy practicing the piano when I saw her"; or, "She was writing invitations for an evening party, and did not speak to me"; or make some excuse or other, not strictly consonant with truth: for Betsinda was such a good-natured creature that she strove to do everything to prevent annoyance to Prince Giglio, and even brought him up roast chicken and jellies from the kitchen (when the Doctor allowed them, and Giglio was getting better), saying, "that the Princess had made the jelly, or the bread-sauce, with her own hands, on purpose for Giglio."

When Giglio heard this he took heart and began to mend immediately; and gobbled up all the jelly, and picked the last bone of the chicken—drumsticks, merry-thought, sides'-bones, back, pope's nose, and all—thanking his dear Angelica; and he felt so much better the next day, that he dressed and went downstairs—where, whom should he meet but Angelica going into the drawing-room? All the covers were off the chairs, the chandeliers taken out of the bags, the damask curtains uncovered, the work and things carried away, and the handsomest albums on the tables. Angelica had her hair in papers: in a word, it was evident there was going to be a party.

"Heavens, Giglio!" cries Angelica: "YOU here in such a dress! What a figure you are!"

"Yes, dear Angelica, I am come downstairs, and feel so well today, thanks to the FOWL and the JELLY."

"What do I know about fowls and jellies, that you allude to them in that rude way?" says Angelica.

"Why, didn't—didn't you send them, Angelica dear?" says Giglio.

"I send them indeed! Angelica dear! No, Giglio dear," says she, mocking him, "I was engaged in getting the rooms ready for His Royal Highness the Prince of Crim Tartary, who is coming to pay my papa's Court a visit."

"The—Prince—of—Crim—Tartary!" Giglio said, aghast.

"Yes, the Prince of Crim Tartary," says Angelica, mocking him. "I dare say you never heard of such a country. What DID you ever hear of? You don't know whether Crim Tartary is on the Red Sea or on the Black Sea, I dare say."

"Yes, I do: it's on the Red Sea," says Giglio; at which the Princess burst out laughing at him, and said, "Oh, you ninny! You are so ignorant, you are really not fit for society! You know nothing but about horses and dogs, and are only fit to dine in a mess-room with my Royal Father's heaviest dragoons. Don't look so surprised at me, sir: go and put your best clothes on to receive the Prince, and let me get the drawing-room ready."

Giglio said, "Oh, Angelica, Angelica, I didn't think this of you. THIS wasn't your language to me when you gave me this ring, and I gave you mine in the garden, and you gave me that k—"

But what k— was we never shall know, for Angelica, in a rage, cried, "Get out, you saucy, rude creature! How dare you to remind me of your rudeness? As for your little trumpery twopenny ring, there, sir—there!" And she flung it out of the window.

"It was my mother's marriage-ring," cried Giglio.

"I don't care whose marriage-ring it was," cries Angelica. "Marry the person who picks it up if she's a woman; you shan't marry ME. And give me back MY ring. I've no patience with people who boast about the things they give away! I know who'll give me much finer things than you ever gave me. A beggarly ring indeed, not worth five shillings!"

Now Angelica little knew that the ring which Giglio had given her was a fairy ring; if a man wore it, it made all the women in love with him; if a woman, all the gentlemen. The Queen, Giglio's mother, quite an ordinary-looking person, was admired immensely whilst she wore this ring, and her husband was frantic when she was ill. But when she called her little Giglio to her, and put the ring on his finger, King Savio did not seem to care for his wife so much any more, but transferred all his love to little Giglio. So did everybody love him as long as he had the ring; but when, as quite a child, he gave it to Angelica, people began to love and admire HER; and Giglio, as the saying is, played only second fiddle.

"Yes," says Angelica, going on in her foolish ungrateful way. "I know who'll give me much finer things than your beggarly little pearl nonsense."

"Very good, miss! You may take back your ring too!" says Giglio, his eyes flashing fire at her, and then, as his eyes had been suddenly opened, he cried out, "Ha! what does this mean? Is THIS the woman I have been in love with all my life? Have I been such a ninny as to throw away my regard upon you? Why—actually—yes—you are a little crooked!"

"Oh, you wretch!" cries Angelica.

"And, upon my conscience, you—you squint a little."

"Eh!" cries Angelica.

"And your hair is red—and you are marked with the smallpox—and what? you have three false teeth—and one leg shorter than the other!"

"You brute, you brute, you!" Angelica screamed out: and as she seized the ring with one hand, she dealt Giglio one, two, three smacks on the face, and would have pulled the hair off his head had he not started laughing, and crying,

"Oh dear me, Angelica, don't pull out MY hair, it hurts! You might remove a great deal of YOUR OWN, as I perceive, without scissors or pulling at all. Oh, ho, ho! ha, ha, ha! he he he!"

And he nearly choked himself with laughing, and she with rage; when, with a low bow, and dressed in his Court habit, Count Gambabella, the first lord-in-waiting, entered and said, "Royal Highnesses! Their Majesties expect you in the Pink Throne-room, where they await the arrival of the Prince of CRIM TARTARY."

VIII. HOW GRUFFANUFF PICKED THE FAIRY RING UP, AND PRINCE BULBO CAME TO COURT.

Prince Bulbo's arrival had set all the court in a flutter: everybody was ordered to put his or her best clothes on: the footmen had their gala liveries; the Lord Chancellor his new wig; the Guards their last new tunics; and Countess Gruffanuff, you may be sure, was glad of an opportunity of decorating HER old person with her finest things. She was walking through the court of the Palace on her way to wait upon their Majesties, when she espied something glittering on the pavement, and bade the boy in buttons who was holding up her train, to go and pick up the article shining yonder. He was an ugly little wretch, in some of the late groom- porter's old clothes cut down, and much too tight for him; and yet, when he had taken up the ring (as it turned out to be), and was carrying it to his mistress, she thought he looked like a little cupid. He gave the ring to her; it was a trumpery little thing enough, but too small for any of her old knuckles, so she put it into her pocket.

"Oh, mum!" says the boy, looking at her "how—how beyoutiful you do look, mum, to-day, mum!"

"And you, too, Jacky," she was going to say; but, looking down at him —no, he was no longer good-looking at all—but only the carroty-haired little Jacky of the morning. However, praise is welcome from the ugliest of men or boys, and Gruffanuff, bidding the boy hold up her train, walked on in high good-humor. The Guards saluted her with peculiar respect. Captain Hedzoff, in the anteroom, said, "My dear madam, you look like an angel today." And so, bowing and smirking, Gruffanuff went in and took her place behind her Royal Master and Mistress, who were in the throne-room, awaiting the Prince of Crim Tartary. Princess Angelica sat at their feet, and behind the King's chair stood Prince Giglio, looking very savage.

The Prince of Crim Tartary made his appearance, attended by Baron Sleibootz, his chamberlain, and followed by a black page carrying the most beautiful crown you ever saw! He was dressed in his travelling costume, and his hair, as you see, was a little in disorder. "I have ridden three hundred miles since breakfast," said he, "so eager was I to behold the Prin—the Court and august family of Paflagonia, and I could not wait one minute before appearing in Your Majesties' presences."

Giglio, from behind the throne, burst out into a roar of contemptuous laughter; but all the Royal party, in fact, were so flurried, that they did not hear this little outbreak. "Your R. H. is welcome in any dress," says the King. "Glumboso, a chair for His Royal Highness."

"Any dress His Royal Highness wears IS a Court-dress," says Princess Angelica, smiling graciously.

"Ah! but you should see my other clothes," said the Prince. "I should have had them on, but that stupid carrier has not brought them. Who's that laughing?"

It was Giglio laughing. "I was laughing," he said, "because you said just now that you were in such a hurry to see the Princess, that you could not wait to change your dress; and now you say you come in those clothes because you have no others."

"And who are you?" says Prince Bulbo, very fiercely.

"My father was King of this country, and I am his only son, Prince!" replies Giglio, with equal haughtiness.

"Ha!" said the King and Glumboso, looking very flurried; but the former, collecting himself, said, "Dear Prince Bulbo, I forgot to introduce to Your Royal Highness my dear nephew, His Royal Highness Prince Giglio! Know each other! Embrace each other! Giglio, give His Royal Highness your hand!" and Giglio, giving his hand, squeezed poor Bulbo's until the tears ran out of his eyes. Glumboso now brought a chair for the Royal visitor, and placed it on the platform on which the King, Queen, and Prince were seated; but the chair was on the edge of the platform, and as Bulbo sat down, it toppled over, and he with it, rolling over and over, and bellowing like a bull. Giglio roared still louder at this disaster, but it was with laughter; so did all the Court when Prince Bulbo got up; for though when he entered the room he appeared not very ridiculous, as he stood up from his fall for a moment he looked so exceedingly plain and foolish, that nobody could help laughing at him. When he had entered the room, he was observed to carry a rose in his hand, which fell out of it as he tumbled.

"My rose! my rose!" cried Bulbo; and his chamberlain dashed forwards and picked it up, and gave it to the Prince, who put it in his waistcoat. Then people wondered why they had laughed; there was nothing particularly ridiculous in him. He was rather short, rather stout, rather red-haired, but, in fine, for a Prince, not so bad.

So they sat and talked, the Royal personages together, the Crim Tartar officers with those of Paflagonia—Giglio very comfortable with Gruffanuff behind the throne. He looked at her with such tender eyes, that her heart was all in a flutter. "Oh, dear Prince," she said, "how could you speak so haughtily in presence of Their Majesties? I protest I thought I should have fainted."

"I should have caught you in my arms," said Giglio, looking raptures.

"Why were you so cruel to Prince Bulbo, dear Prince?" says Gruff.

"Because I hate him," says Gil.

"You are jealous of him, and still love poor Angelica," cries Gruffanuff, putting her handkerchief to her eyes.

"I did, but I love her no more!" Giglio cried. "I despise her! Were she heiress to twenty thousand thrones, I would despise her and scorn her. But why speak of thrones? I have lost mine. I am too weak to recover it—I am alone, and have no friend."

"Oh, say not so, dear Prince!" says Gruffanuff.

"Besides," says he, "I am so happy here BEHIND THE THRONE, that I would not change my place, no, not for the throne of the world!"

"What are you two people chattering about there?" says the Queen, who was rather good-natured, though not over-burthened with wisdom. "It is time to dress for dinner. Giglio, show Prince Bulbo to his room. Prince, if your clothes have not come, we shall be very happy to see you as you are." But when Prince Bulbo got to his bedroom, his luggage was there and unpacked; and the hairdresser coming in, cut and curled him entirely to his own satisfaction; and when the dinner-bell rang, the Royal company had not to wait above five-and-twenty minutes until Bulbo appeared, during which time the King, who could not bear to wait, grew as sulky as possible. As for Giglio, he never left Madam Gruffanuff all this time, but stood with her in the embrasure of a window, paying her compliments. At length the Groom of the Chambers announced His Royal Highness the Prince of Crim Tartary! and the noble company went into the royal dining-room. It was quite a small party; only the King and Queen, the Princess, whom Bulbo took out, the two Princes, Countess Gruffanuff, Glumboso the Prime Minister, and Prince Bulbo's chamberlain. You may be sure they had a very good dinner—let every boy or girl think of what he or she likes best, and fancy it on the table.*

    * Here a very pretty game may be played by all the children saying

what they like best for dinner.

The Princess talked incessantly all dinner-time to the Prince of Crimea, who ate an immense deal too much, and never took his eyes off his plate, except when Giglio, who was carving a goose, sent a quantity of stuffing and onion sauce into one of them. Giglio only burst out a-laughing as the Crimean Prince wiped his shirt-front and face with his scented pocket-handkerchief. He did not make Prince Bulbo any apology. When the Prince looked at him, Giglio would not look that way. When Prince Bulbo said, "Prince Giglio, may I have the honor of taking a glass of wine with you?" Giglio WOULDN'T answer. All his talk and his eyes were for Countess Gruffanuff, who you may be sure was pleased with Giglio's attentions—the vain old creature! When he was not complimenting her, he was making fun of Prince Bulbo, so loud that Gruffanuff was always tapping him with her fan, and saying, "Oh, you satirical Prince! Oh, fie, the Prince will hear!" "Well, I don't mind," says Giglio, louder still. The King and Queen luckily did not hear; for her Majesty was a little deaf, and the King thought so much about his own dinner, and, besides, made such a dreadful noise, hob-gobbling in eating it, that he heard nothing else. After dinner, his Majesty and the Queen went to sleep in their arm- chairs.

This was the time when Giglio began his tricks with Prince Bulbo, plying that young gentleman with port, sherry, madeira, champagne, marsala, cherry-brandy, and pale ale, of all of which Master Bulbo drank without stint. But in plying his guest, Giglio was obliged to drink himself, and, I am sorry to say, took more than was good for him, so that the young men were very noisy, rude, and foolish when they joined the ladies after dinner; and dearly did they pay for that imprudence, as now, my darlings, you shall hear!

Bulbo went and sat by the piano, where Angelica was playing and singing, and he sang out of tune, and he upset the coffee when the footman brought it, and he laughed out of place, and talked absurdly, and fell asleep and snored horridly. Booh, the nasty pig! But as he lay there stretched on the pink satin sofa, Angelica still persisted in thinking him the most beautiful of human beings. No doubt the magic rose which Bulbo wore caused this infatuation on Angelica's part; but is she the first young woman who has thought a silly fellow charming?

Giglio must go and sit by Gruffanuff, whose old face he, too, every moment began to find more lovely. He paid the most outrageous compliments to her:—There never was such a darling. Older than he was? —Fiddle-de-dee! He would marry her—he would, have nothing but her!

To marry the heir to the throne! Here was a chance! The artful hussy actually got a sheet of paper, and wrote upon it, "This is to give notice that I, Giglio, only son of Savio, King of Paflagonia, hereby promise to marry the charming and virtuous Barbara Griselda Countess Gruffanuff, and widow of the late Jenkins Gruffanuff, Esq."

"What is it you are writing, you charming Gruffy?" says Giglio, who was lolling on the sofa, by the writing-table.

"Only an order for you to sign, dear Prince, for giving coals and blankets to the poor, this cold weather. Look! the King and Queen are both asleep, and your Royal Highness's order will do."

So Giglio, who was very good-natured, as Gruffy well knew, signed the order immediately; and, when she had it in her pocket, you may fancy what airs she gave herself. She was ready to flounce out of the room before the Queen herself, as now she was the wife of the RIGHTFUL King of Paflagonia! She would not speak to Glumboso, whom she thought a brute, for depriving her DEAR HUSBAND of the crown! And when candles came, and she had helped to undress the Queen and Princess, she went into her own room, and actually practiced on a sheet of paper, "Griselda Paflagonia," "Barbara Regina," "Griselda Barbara, Paf. Reg.," and I don't know what signatures besides, against the day when she should be Queen forsooth!

IX. HOW BETSINDA GOT THE WARMING PAN.

Little Betsinda came in to put Gruffanuff's hair in papers; and the Countess was so pleased, that, for a wonder, she complimented Betsinda. "Betsinda!" she said, "you dressed my hair very nicely today; I promised you a little present. Here are five sh—no, here is a pretty little ring, that I picked—that I have had some time." And she gave Betsinda the ring she had picked up in the court. It fitted Betsinda exactly.

"It's like the ring the Princess used to wear," says the maid.

"No such thing," says Gruffanuff, "I have had it this ever so long. There, tuck me up quite comfortable; and now, as it's a very cold night (the snow was beating in at the window), you may go and warm dear Prince Giglio's bed, like a good girl, and then you may unrip my green silk, and then you can just do me up a little cap for the morning, and then you can mend that hole in my silk stocking, and then you can go to bed, Betsinda. Mind I shall want my cup of tea at five o'clock in the morning."

"I suppose I had best warm both the young gentlemen's beds, Ma'am," says Betsinda.

Gruffanuff, for reply, said, "Hau-au-ho!—Grau-haw-hoo!—Hong-hrho!" In fact, she was snoring sound asleep.

Her room, you know, is next to the King and Queen, and the Princess is next to them. So pretty Betsinda went away for the coals to the kitchen, and filled the royal warming-pan.

Now, she was a very kind, merry, civil, pretty girl; but there must have been something very captivating about her this evening, for all the women in the servants' hall began to scold and abuse her. The housekeeper said she was a pert, stuck-up thing: the upper- housemaid asked, how dare she wear such ringlets and ribbons, it was quite improper! The cook (for there was a woman-cook as well as a man-cook) said to the kitchen-maid that SHE never could see anything in that creetur: but as for the men, every one of them, Coachman, John, Buttons, the page, and Monsieur, the Prince of Crim Tartary's valet, started up, and said—

"My eyes! } "O mussey! } what a pretty girl Betsinda is!" "O jemmany! } "O ciel! }

"Hands off; none of your impertinence, you vulgar, low people!" says

Betsinda, walking off with her pan of coals. She heard the young gentlemen playing at billiards as she went upstairs: first to Prince Giglio's bed, which she warmed, and then to Prince Bulbo's room.

He came in just as she had done; and as soon as he saw her, "O! O! O! O! O! O! what a beyou—oo—ootiful creature you are! You angel— you Peri—you rosebud, let me be thy bulbul—thy Bulbo, too! Fly to the desert, fly with me! I never saw a young gazelle to glad me with its dark blue eye that had eyes like thine. Thou nymph of beauty, take, take this young heart. A truer never did itself sustain within a soldier's waistcoat. Be mine! Be mine! Be Princess of Crim Tartary! My Royal father will approve our union; and, as for that little carroty-haired Angelica, I do not care a fig for her any more."

"Go away, Your Royal Highness, and go to bed, please," said Betsinda, with the warming-pan.

But Bulbo said, "No, never, till thou swearest to be mine, thou lovely, blushing chambermaid divine! Here, at thy feet, the Royal Bulbo lies, the trembling captive of Betsinda's eyes."

And he went on, making himself SO ABSURD AND RIDICULOUS, that Betsinda, who was full of fun, gave him a touch with the warming- pan, which, I promise you, made him cry "O-o-o-o!" in a very different manner.

Prince Bulbo made such a noise that Prince Giglio, who heard him from the next room, came in to see what was the matter. As soon as he saw what was taking place, Giglio, in a fury, rushed on Bulbo, kicked him in the rudest manner up to the ceiling, and went on kicking him till his hair was quite out of curl.

Poor Betsinda did not know whether to laugh or to cry; the kicking certainly must hurt the Prince, but then he looked so droll! When Giglio had done knocking him up and down to the ground, and whilst he went into a corner rubbing himself, what do you think Giglio does? He goes down on his own knees to Betsinda, takes her hand, begs her to accept his heart, and offers to marry her that moment. Fancy Betsinda's condition, who had been in love with the Prince ever since she first saw him in the palace garden, when she was quite a little child.

"Oh, divine Betsinda!" says the Prince, "how have I lived fifteen years in thy company without seeing thy perfections? What woman in all Europe, Asia, Africa, and America, nay, in Australia, only it is not yet discovered, can presume to be thy equal? Angelica? Pish! Gruffanuff? Phoo! The

Queen? Ha, ha! Thou art my Queen. Thou art the real Angelica, because thou art really angelic."

"Oh, Prince! I am but a poor chambermaid," says Betsinda, looking, however, very much pleased.

"Didst thou not tend me in my sickness, when all forsook me?" continues Giglio. "Did not thy gentle hand smooth my pillow, and bring me jelly and roast chicken?"

"Yes, dear Prince, I did," says Betsinda, "and I sewed Your Royal Highness's shirt-buttons on too, if you please, Your Royal Highness," cries this artless maiden.

When poor Prince Bulbo, who was now madly in love with Betsinda, heard this declaration, when he saw the unmistakable glances which she flung upon Giglio, Bulbo began to cry bitterly, and tore quantities of hair out of his head, till it all covered the room like so much tow.

Betsinda had left the warming-pan on the floor while the princes were going on with their conversation, and as they began now to quarrel and be very fierce with one another, she thought proper to run away.

"You great big blubbering booby, tearing your hair in the corner there; of course you will give me satisfaction for insulting Betsinda. YOU dare to kneel down at Princess Giglio's knees and kiss her hand!"

"She's not Princess Giglio!" roars out Bulbo. "She shall be Princess Bulbo, no other shall be Princess Bulbo."

"You are engaged to my cousin!" bellows out Giglio.

"I hate your cousin," says Bulbo.

"You shall give me satisfaction for insulting her!" cries Giglio in a fury.

"I'll have your life."

"I'll run you through."

"I'll cut your throat."

"I'll blow your brains out."

"I'll knock your head off."

"I'll send a friend to you in the morning."

'I'll send a bullet into you in the afternoon."

"We'll meet again," says Giglio, shaking his fist in Bulbo's face; and seizing up the warming-pan, he kissed it, because, forsooth, Betsinda had carried it, and rushed downstairs. What should he see on the landing but his Majesty talking to Betsinda, whom he called by all sorts of fond names. His Majesty had heard a row in the building, so he stated, and smelling something burning, had come out to see what the matter was.

"It's the young gentlemen smoking, perhaps, sir," says Betsinda.

"Charming chambermaid," says the King (like all the rest of them), "never mind the young men! Turn thy eyes on a middle-aged autocrat, who has been considered not ill-looking in his time."

"Oh, sir! what will her Majesty say?" cries Betsinda.

"Her Majesty!" laughs the monarch. "Her Majesty be hanged. Am I not Autocrat of Paflagonia? Have I not blocks, ropes, axes, hangmen—ha? Runs not a river by my palace wall? Have I not sacks to sew up wives withal? Say but the word, that thou wilt be mine own,—your mistress straightway in a sack is sewn, and thou the sharer of my heart and throne."

When Giglio heard these atrocious sentiments, he forgot the respect usually paid to Royalty, lifted up the warming-pan, and knocked down the King as flat as a pancake; after which, Master Giglio took to his heels and ran away, and Betsinda went off screaming, and the Queen, Gruffanuff, and the Princess, all came out of their rooms. Fancy their feelings on beholding their husband, father, sovereign, in this posture!

X. HOW KING VALOROSO WAS IN A DREADFUL PASSION.

As soon as the coals began to burn him, the King came to himself and stood up. "Ho! my captain of the guards!" his Majesty exclaimed, stamping his royal feet with rage. O piteous spectacle! the King's nose was bent quite crooked by the blow of Prince Giglio! His Majesty ground his teeth with rage. "Hedzoff," he said, taking a death-warrant out of his dressing-gown pocket, "Hedzoff, good Hedzoff, seize upon the Prince. Thou'lt find him in his chamber two pair up. But now he dared, with sacrilegious hand, to strike the sacred night-cap of a king—Hedzoff, and floor me with a warming-pan! Away, no more demur, the villain dies! See it be done, or else,—h'm—ha!—h'm! mind thine own eyes!" And followed by the ladies, and lifting up the tails of his dressing- gown, the King entered his own apartment.

Captain Hedzoff was very much affected, having a sincere love for Giglio. "Poor, poor Giglio!" he said, the tears rolling over his manly face, and dripping down his moustachios; "my noble young Prince, is it my hand must lead thee to death?"

"Lead him to fiddlestick, Hedzoff," said a female voice. It was Gruffanuff, who had come out in her dressing-gown when she heard the noise. "The King said you were to hang the Prince. Well, hang the Prince."

"I don't understand you," says Hedzoff, who was not a very clever man.

"You Gaby! he didn't say WHICH Prince," says Gruffanuff.

"No; he didn't say which, certainly," said Hedzoff.

"Well then, take Bulbo, and hang HIM!"

When Captain Hedzoff heard this, he began to dance about for joy. "Obedience is a soldier's honor," says he. "Prince Bulbo's head will do capitally;" and he went to arrest the Prince the very first thing next morning.

He knocked at the door. "Who's there?" says Bulbo. "Captain Hedzoff? Step in, pray, my good Captain; I'm delighted to see you; I have been expecting you."

"Have you?" says Hedzoff.

"Sleibootz, my Chamberlain, will act for me," says the Prince.

"I beg Your Royal Highness's pardon, but you will have to act for yourself, and it's a pity to wake Baron Sleibootz."

The Prince Bulbo still seemed to take the matter very coolly. "Of course, Captain," says he, "you are come about that affair with Prince Giglio?"

"Precisely," says Hedzoff, "that affair of Prince Giglio."

"Is it to be pistols, or swords, Captain?" asks Bulbo. "I'm a pretty good hand with both, and I'll do for Prince Giglio as sure as my name is My Royal Highness Prince Bulbo."

"There's some mistake, my Lord," says the Captain. "The business is done with AXES among us."

"Axes? That's sharp work," says Bulbo. "Call my Chamberlain, he'll be my second, and in ten minutes, I flatter myself, you'll see Master Giglio's head off his impertinent shoulders. I'm hungry for his blood Hoo-oo—aw!" and he looked as savage as an ogre.

"I beg your pardon, sir, but by this warrant I am to take you prisoner, and hand you over to—to the executioner."

"Pooh, pooh, my good man!—Stop, I say,—ho!—hulloa!" was all that this luckless Prince was enabled to say: for Hedzoff's guards seizing him, tied a handkerchief over his mouth and face, and carried him to the place of execution.

The King, who happened to be talking to Glumboso, saw him pass, and took a pinch of snuff and said, "So much for Giglio. Now let's go to breakfast."

The Captain of the Guard handed over his prisoner to the Sheriff, with the fatal order,

"AT SIGHT CUT OFF THE BEARER'S HEAD.
"VALOROSO XXIV."

"It's a mistake," says Bulbo, who did not seem to understand the business in the least.

"Poo—poo—pooh," says the Sheriff. "Fetch Jack Ketch instantly. Jack Ketch!"

And poor Bulbo was led to the scaffold, where an executioner with a block and a tremendous axe was always ready in case he should be wanted.

But we must now revert to Giglio and Betsinda.

XI. WHAT GRUFFANUFF DID TO GIGLIO AND BETSINDA.

Gruffanuff, who had seen what had happened with the King, and knew that Giglio must come to grief, got up very early the next morning, and went to devise some plans for rescuing her darling husband, as the silly old thing insisted on calling him. She found him walking up and down the garden, thinking of a rhyme for Betsinda (TINDER and WINDA were all he could find), and indeed having forgotten all about the past evening, except that Betsinda was the most lovely of beings.

"Well, dear Giglio," says Gruff.

"Well, dear Gruffy," says Giglio, only HE was quite satirical.

"I have been thinking, darling, what you must do in this scrape. You must fly the country for a while."

"What scrape?—fly the country? Never without her I love, Countess," says Giglio.

"No, she will accompany you, dear Prince," she says, in her most coaxing accents. "First, we must get the jewels belonging to our royal parents, and those of her and his present Majesty. Here is the key, duck; they are all yours, you know, by right, for you are the rightful King of Paflagonia, and your wife will be the rightful Queen."

"Will she?" says Giglio.

"Yes; and having got the jewels, go to Glumboso's apartment, where, under his bed, you will find sacks containing money to the amount of L217,000,000,987,439, 13s. 6-1/2d., all belonging to you, for he took it out of your royal father's room on the day of his death. With this we will fly."

"WE will fly?" says Giglio.

"Yes, you and your bride—your affianced love—your Gruffy!" says the Countess, with a languishing leer.

"YOU my bride!" says Giglio. "You, you hideous old woman!"

"Oh, you—you wretch! didn't you give me this paper promising marriage?" cries Gruff.

"Get away, you old goose! I love Betsinda, and Betsinda only!" And in a fit of terror he ran from her as quickly as he could.

"He! he! he!" shrieks out Gruff; "a promise is a promise if there are laws in Paflagonia! And as for that monster, that wretch, that fiend, that ugly little vixen—as for that upstart, that ingrate, that beast, Betsinda, Master Giglio will have no little difficulty in discovering her whereabouts. He may look very long before finding HER, I warrant. He little knows that Miss Betsinda is—"

Is—what? Now, you shall hear. Poor Betsinda got up at five in winter's morning to bring her cruel mistress her tea; and instead of finding her in a good humor, found Gruffy as cross as two sticks. The Countess boxed Betsinda's ears half a dozen times whilst she was dressing; but as poor little Betsinda was used to this kind of treatment, she did not feel any special alarm. "And now," says she, "when her Majesty rings her bell twice, I'll trouble you, miss, to attend."

So when the Queen's bell rang twice, Betsinda came to her Majesty and made a pretty little curtsey. The Queen, the Princess, and Gruffanuff were all three in the room. As soon as they saw her they began,

"You wretch!" says the Queen.

"You little vulgar thing!" says the Princess.

"You beast!" says Gruffanuff.

"Get out of my sight!" says the Queen.

"Go away with you, do!" says the Princess.

"Quit the premises!" says Gruffanuff.

"Alas! and woe is me!" very lamentable events had occurred to Betsinda that morning, and all in consequence of that fatal warming-pan business of the previous night. The King had offered to marry her; of course her Majesty the Queen was jealous: Bulbo had fallen in love with her; of course Angelica was furious: Giglio was in love with her, and oh, what a fury Gruffy was in!

{ cap } "Take off that {petticoat} I gave you," they said, all at once, { gown }

and began tearing the clothes off poor Betsinda.


```
                          {  the King?"    }
"How dare you flirt with {Prince Bulbo?" } cried the Queen, the
                          {Prince Giglio?"}    Princess, and
Countess.
```

"Give her the rags she wore when she came into the house, and turn her out of it!" cries the Queen.

"Mind she does not go with MY shoes on, which I lent her so kindly," says the Princess; and indeed the Princess's shoes were a great deal too big for Betsinda.

"Come with me, you filthy hussy!" and taking up the Queen's poker, the cruel Gruffanuff drove Betsinda into her room.

The Countess went to the glass box in which she had kept Betsinda's old cloak and shoe this ever so long, and said, "Take those rags, you little beggar creature, and strip off everything belonging to honest people, and go about your business"; and she actually tore off the poor little delicate thing's back almost all her things, and told her to be off out of the house.

Poor Betsinda huddled the cloak round her back, on which were embroidered the letters PRIN. . . . ROSAL . . and then came a great rent.

As for the shoe, what was she to do with one poor little tootsey sandal? The string was still to it, so she hung it round her neck.

"Won't you give me a pair of shoes to go out in the snow, mum, if you please, mum?" cried the poor child.

"No, you wicked beast!" says Gruffanuff, driving her along with the poker—driving her down the cold stairs—driving her through the cold hall —flinging her out into the cold street, so that the knocker itself shed tears to see her!

But a kind fairy made the soft snow warm for her little feet, and she wrapped herself up in the ermine of her mantle, and was gone!

"And now let us think about breakfast," says the greedy Queen.

"What dress shall I put on, mamma? the pink or the pea-green?" says Angelica. "Which do you think the dear Prince will like best?"

"Mrs. V.!" sings out the King from his dressing-room, "let us have sausages for breakfast! Remember we have Prince Bulbo staying with us!"

And they all went to get ready.

Nine o'clock came, and they were all in the breakfast-room, and no Prince Bulbo as yet. The urn was hissing and humming: the muffins were smoking—such a heap of muffins! the eggs were done, there was a pot of raspberry jam, and coffee, and a beautiful chicken and tongue on the side-table. Marmitonio the cook brought in the sausages. Oh, how nice they smelt!

"Where is Bulbo?" said the King. "John, where is His Royal Highness?"

John said he had a took hup His Roilighnessesses shaving-water, and his clothes and things, and he wasn't in his room, which he sposed His

Royliness was just stepped hout.

"Stepped out before breakfast in the snow! Impossible!" says the King, sticking his fork into a sausage. "My dear, take one. Angelica, won't you have a saveloy?" The Princess took one, being very fond of them; and at this moment Glumboso entered with Captain Hedzoff, both looking very much disturbed.

"I am afraid Your Majesty—" cries Glumboso.

"No business before breakfast, Glum!" says the King." Breakfast first, business next. Mrs. V., some more sugar!"

"Sire, I am afraid if we wait till after breakfast it will be too late," says Glumboso. "He—he—he'll be hanged at half-past nine."

"Don't talk about hanging and spoil my breakfast, you unkind, vulgar man you," cries the Princess. "John, some mustard. Pray who is to be hanged?"

"Sire, it is the Prince," whispers Glumboso to the King.

"Talk about business after breakfast, I tell you!" says his Majesty, quite sulky.

"We shall have a war, Sire, depend on it," says the Minister. "His father, King Padella. . . ."

"His father, King WHO?" says the King. "King Padella is not Giglio's father. My brother, King Savio, was Giglio's father."

"It's Prince Bulbo they are hanging, Sire, not Prince Giglio," says the Prime Minister.

"You told me to hang the Prince, and I took the ugly one," says Hedzoff. "I didn't, of course, think Your Majesty intended to murder your own flesh and blood!"

The King for all reply flung the plate of sausages at Hedzoff's head. The Princess cried out "Hee-karee-karee!" and fell down in a fainting fit.

"Turn the cock of the urn upon Her Royal Highness," said the King, and the boiling water gradually revived her. His Majesty looked at his watch, compared it by the clock in the parlor, and by that of the church in the square opposite; then he wound it up; then he looked at it again. "The great question is," says he, "am I fast or am I slow? If I'm slow, we may as well go on with breakfast. If I'm fast, why, there is just the possibility of saving Prince Bulbo. It's a doosid awkward mistake, and upon my word, Hedzoff, I have the greatest mind to have you hanged too."

"Sire, I did but my duty: a soldier has but his orders. I didn't expect after forty-seven years of faithful service, that my sovereign would think of putting me to a felon's death!"

"A hundred thousand plagues upon you! Can't you see that while you are talking my Bulbo is being hung?" screamed the Princess.

"By Jove! she's always right, that girl, and I'm so absent," says the King, looking at his watch again. "Ha! there go the drums! What a doosid awkward thing though!"

"O, papa, you goose! Write the reprieve, and let me run with it," cries the Princess—and she got a sheet of paper, and pen and ink, and laid them before the King.

"Confound it! Where are my spectacles?" the Monarch exclaimed. "Angelica! Go up into my bedroom, look under my pillow, not your mamma's; there you'll see my keys. Bring them down to me, and— Well, well! what impetuous things these girls are!" Angelica was gone, and had run up panting to the bedroom, and found the keys, and was back again before the King had finished a muffin. "Now, love," says he, "you must go all the way back for my desk, in which my spectacles are. If you would but have heard me out. . . . Be hanged to her! There she is off again. Angelica! ANGELICA!" When his Majesty called in his LOUD voice, she knew she must obey, and came back.

"My dear, when you go out of a room, how often have I told you, SHUT THE DOOR. That's a darling. That's all." At last the keys and the desk and the spectacles were got, and the King mended his pen, and signed his name to a reprieve, and Angelica ran with it as swift as the wind. "You'd better stay, my love, and finish the muffins. There's no use going. Be sure it's too late. Hand me over that raspberry jam, please," said the Monarch. "Bong! Bawong! There goes the half-hour. I knew it was."

Angelica ran, and ran, and ran, and ran. She ran up Fore Street, and down High Street, and through the Market-place, and down to the left, and over the bridge, and up the blind alley, and back again, and round by the Castle, and so along by the Haberdasher's on the right, opposite the lamp-post, and round the square, and she came— she came to the EXECUTION PLACE, where she saw Bulbo laying his head on the block!!! The executioner raised his axe, but at that moment the Princess came panting up and cried Reprieve! "Reprieve!" screamed the Princess. "Reprieve!" shouted all the people. Up the scaffold stairs she sprang, with the agility of a lighter of lamps; and flinging herself in Bulbo's arms, regardless of all ceremony, she cried out, "Oh, my Prince! my lord! my love! my Bulbo! Thine Angelica has been in time to save thy precious existence, sweet rosebud; to prevent thy being nipped in thy young bloom! Had aught befallen thee, Angelica too had died, and welcomed death that joined her to her Bulbo."

"H'm! there's no accounting for tastes," said Bulbo, looking so very much puzzled and uncomfortable that the Princess, in tones of tenderest strain, asked the cause of his disquiet.

"I tell you what it is, Angelica," said he, "since I came here yesterday, there has been such a row, and disturbance, and quarrelling, and fighting, and chopping of heads off, and the deuce to pay, that I am inclined to go back to Crim Tartary."

"But with me as thy bride, my Bulbo! Though wherever thou art is Crim Tartary to me, my bold, my beautiful, my Bulbo!"

"Well, well, I suppose we must be married," says Bulbo. "Doctor, you came to read the Funeral Service—read the Marriage Service, will you? What must be, must. That will satisfy Angelica, and then, in the name of peace and quietness, do let us go back to breakfast."

Bulbo had carried a rose in his mouth all the time of the dismal ceremony. It was a fairy rose, and he was told by his mother that he ought never to part with it. So he had kept it between his teeth, even when he laid his poor head upon the block, hoping vaguely that some chance would turn up in his favor. As he began to speak to Angelica, he forgot about the rose, and of course it dropped out of his mouth. The romantic Princess instantly stooped and seized it. "Sweet rose!" she exclaimed, "that bloomed upon my Bulbo's lip, never, never will I part from thee!" and she placed it in her bosom. And you know Bulbo COULDN'T ask her to give the rose back again. And they went to breakfast; and as they walked, it appeared to Bulbo that Angelica became more exquisitely lovely every moment.

He was frantic until they were married; and now, strange to say, it was Angelica who didn't care about him! He knelt down, he kissed her hand, he prayed and begged; he cried with admiration; while she for her part said she really thought they might wait; it seemed to her he was not handsome any more—no, not at all, quite the reverse; and not clever, no, very stupid; and not well bred, like Giglio; no, on the contrary, dreadfully vul—

XII. HOW BETSINDA FLED, AND WHAT BECAME OF HER.

Betsinda wandered on and on, till she passed through the town gates, and so on the great Crim Tartary road, the very way on which Giglio too was going. "Ah!" thought she, as the diligence passed her, of which the conductor was blowing a delightful tune on his horn, "how I should like to be on that coach!" But the coach and the jingling horses were very soon gone. She little knew who was in it, though very likely she was thinking of him all the time.

Then came an empty cart, returning from market; and the driver being a kind man, and seeing such a very pretty girl trudging along the road with bare feet, most good-naturedly gave her a seat. He said he lived on the confines of the forest, where his old father was a woodman, and, if she liked, he would take her so far on her road. All roads were the same to little Betsinda, so she very thankfully took this one.

And the carter put a cloth round her bare feet, and gave her some bread and cold bacon, and was very kind to her. For all that she was very cold and melancholy. When after travelling on and on, evening came, and all the black pines were bending with snow, and there, at last, was the comfortable light beaming in the woodman's windows; and so they arrived, and went into his cottage. He was an old man, and had a number of children, who were just at supper, with nice hot bread-and-milk, when their elder brother arrived with the cart. And they jumped and clapped their hands; for they were good children; and he had brought them toys from the town. And when they saw the pretty stranger, they ran to her, and brought her to the fire, and rubbed her poor little feet, and brought her bread and milk.

"Look, father!" they said to the old woodman, "look at this poor girl, and see what pretty cold feet she has. They are as white as our milk! And look and see what an odd cloak she has, just like the bit of velvet that hangs up in our cupboard, and which you found that day the little cubs were killed by King Padella, in the forest! And look, why, bless us all! she has got round her neck just such another little shoe as that you brought home, and have shown us so often—a little blue velvet shoe!"

"What," said the old woodman, "what is all this about a shoe and a cloak?"

And Betsinda explained that she had been left, when quite a little child, at the town with this cloak and this shoe. And the persons who had taken care of her had—had been angry with her, for no fault, she hoped, of her own. And they had sent her away with her old clothes—and here, in fact, she was. She remembered having been in a forest—and perhaps it was a dream—it was so very odd and strange—having lived in a cave with lions there; and, before that, having lived in a very, very fine house, as fine as the King's, in the town.

When the woodman heard this, he was so astonished, it was quite curious to see how astonished he was. He went to his cupboard, and took out of a stocking a five-shilling piece of King Cavolfiore, and vowed it was exactly like the young woman. And then he produced the shoe and piece of velvet which he had kept so long, and compared them with the things which Betsinda wore. In Betsinda's little shoe was written, "Hopkins, maker to the Royal Family"; so in the other shoe was written, "Hopkins, maker to the Royal Family." In the inside of Betsinda's piece of cloak was embroidered, "PRIN ROSAL"; in the other piece of cloak was embroidered "CESS BA. NO. 246." So that when put together you read, "PRINCESS ROSALBA. NO. 246."

On seeing this, the dear old woodman fell down on his knee, saying, "O my Princess, O my gracious royal lady, O my rightful Queen of Crim Tartary,—I hail thee—I acknowledge thee—I do thee homage!" And in token of his fealty, he rubbed his venerable nose three times on the ground, and put the Princess's foot on his head.

"Why," said she, "my good woodman, you must be a nobleman of my royal father's Court!" For in her lowly retreat, and under the name of Betsinda, HER MAJESTY, ROSALBA, Queen of Crim Tartary, had read of the customs of all foreign courts and nations.

"Marry, indeed, am I, my gracious liege—the poor Lord Spinachi once —the humble woodman these fifteen years syne—ever since the tyrant Padella (may ruin overtake the treacherous knave!) dismissed me from my post of First Lord."

"First Lord of the Toothpick and Joint Keeper of the Snuffbox? I mind me! Thou heldest these posts under our royal Sire. They are restored to thee, Lord Spinachi! I make thee knight of the second class of our Order of the Pumpkin (the first class being reserved for crowned heads alone). Rise,

Marquis of Spinachi!" And with indescribable majesty, the Queen, who had no sword handy, waved the pewter spoon with which she had been taking her bread-and-milk, over the bald head of the old nobleman, whose tears absolutely made a puddle on the ground, and whose dear children went to bed that night Lords and Ladies Bartolomeo, Ubaldo, Catarina, and Ottavia degli Spinachi!

The acquaintance HER MAJESTY showed with the history, and NOBLE FAMILIES of her empire, was wonderful. "The House of Broccoli should remain faithful to us," she said; "they were ever welcome at our Court. Have the Articiocchi, as was their wont, turned to the Rising Sun? The family of Sauerkraut must sure be with us—they were ever welcome in the halls of King Cavolfiore." And so she went on enumerating quite a list of the nobility and gentry of Crim Tartary, so admirably had her Majesty profited by her studies while in exile.

The old Marquis of Spinachi said he could answer for them all; that the whole country groaned under Padella's tyranny, and longed to return to its rightful sovereign; and late as it was, he sent his children, who knew the forest well, to summon this nobleman and that; and when his eldest son, who had been rubbing the horse down and giving him his supper, came into the house for his own, the Marquis told him to put his boots on, and a saddle on the mare, and ride hither and thither to such and such people.

When the young man heard who his companion in the cart had been, he too knelt down and put her royal foot on his head; he too bedewed the ground with his tears; he was frantically in love with her, as everybody now was who saw her: so were the young Lords Bartolomeo and Ubaldo, who punched each other's little heads out of jealousy: and so, when they came from east and west at the summons of the Marquis degli Spinachi, were the Crim Tartar Lords who still remained faithful to the House of Cavolfiore. They were such very old gentlemen for the most part that her Majesty never suspected their absurd passion, and went among them quite unaware of the havoc her beauty was causing, until an old blind Lord who had joined her party told her what the truth was; after which, for fear of making the people too much in love with her, she always wore a veil. She went about privately, from one nobleman's castle to another; and they visited among themselves again, and had meetings, and composed proclamations and counter-proclamations, and distributed all the best places of the kingdom amongst one another, and selected who of the opposition party should be executed when the Queen came to her own. And so in about a year they were ready to move.

The party of Fidelity was in truth composed of very feeble old fogies for the most part; they went about the country waving their old swords and flags, and calling "God save the Queen!" and King Padella happening to be absent upon an invasion, they had their own way for a little, and to be sure the people were very enthusiastic whenever they saw the Queen; otherwise the vulgar took matters very quietly, for they said, as far as they could recollect, they were pretty well as much taxed in Cavolfiore's time, as now in Padella's.

XIII. HOW QUEEN ROSALBA CAME TO THE CASTLE OF THE BOLD COUNT HOGGINARMO.

Her Majesty, having indeed nothing else to give, made all her followers Knights of the Pumpkin, and Marquises, Earls, and Baronets; and they had a little court for her, and made her a little crown of gilt paper, and a robe of cotton velvet; and they quarrelled about the places to be given away in her court, and about rank and precedence and dignities;—you can't think how they quarrelled! The poor Queen was very tired of her honors before she had had them a month, and I dare say sighed sometimes even to be a lady's-maid again. But we must all do our duty in our respective stations, so the Queen resigned herself to perform hers.

We have said how it happened that none of the Usurper's troops came out to oppose this Army of Fidelity: it pottered along as nimbly as the gout of the principal commanders allowed: it consisted of twice as many officers as soldiers: and at length passed near the estates of one of the most powerful noblemen of the country, who had not declared for the Queen, but of whom her party had hopes, as he was always quarrelling with King Padella.

When they came close to his park gates, this nobleman sent to say he would wait upon her Majesty: he was a most powerful warrior, and his name was Count Hogginarmo, whose helmet it took two strong negroes to carry. He knelt down before her and said, "Madam and liege lady! it becomes the great nobles of the Crimean realm to show every outward sign of respect to the wearer of the Crown, whoever that may be. We testify to our own nobility in acknowledging yours. The bold Hogginarmo bends the knee to the first of the aristocracy of his country."

Rosalba said the bold Count of Hogginarmo was uncommonly kind; but she felt afraid of him, even while he was kneeling, and his eyes scowled at her from between his whiskers, which grew up to them.

"The first Count of the Empire, madam," he went on, "salutes the Sovereign. The Prince addresses himself to the not more noble lady! Madam, my hand is free, and I offer it, and my heart and my sword to your service! My three wives lie buried in my ancestral vaults. The third perished but a year since; and this heart pines for a consort! Deign to be mine, and I swear to bring to your bridal table the head of King Padella, the eyes and nose of his son Prince Bulbo, the right hand and ears of the usurping Sovereign of Paflagonia, which country shall thenceforth be an appanage to your— to OUR Crown! Say yes; Hogginarmo is not accustomed to be denied. Indeed I cannot contemplate the possibility of a refusal; for frightful will be the result; dreadful the murders; furious the devastations; horrible the tyranny; tremendous the tortures, misery, taxation, which the people of this realm will endure, if Hogginarmo's wrath be aroused! I see consent in Your Majesty's lovely eyes—their glances fill my soul with rapture!"

"Oh, sir!" Rosalba said, withdrawing her hand in great fright. "Your Lordship is exceedingly kind; but I am sorry to tell you that I have a prior attachment to a young gentleman by the name of— Prince Giglio—and never—never can marry any one but him."

Who can describe Hogginarmo's wrath at this remark? Rising up from the ground, he ground his teeth so that fire flashed out of his mouth, from which at the same time issued remarks and language, so LOUD, VIOLENT, AND IMPROPER, that this pen shall never repeat them! "R-r-r-r-r— Rejected! Fiends and perdition! The bold Hogginarmo rejected! All the world shall hear of my rage; and you, madam, you above all shall rue it!" And kicking the two negroes before him, he rushed away, his whiskers streaming in the wind.

Her Majesty's Privy Council was in a dreadful panic when they saw Hogginarmo issue from the royal presence in such a towering rage, making footballs of the poor negroes—a panic which the events justified. They marched off from Hogginarmo's park very crest- fallen; and in another half-hour they were met by that rapacious chieftain with a few of his followers, who cut, slashed, charged, whacked, banged, and pommelled amongst them, took the Queen prisoner, and drove the Army of Fidelity to I don't know where.

Poor Queen! Hogginarmo, her conqueror, would not condescend to see her. "Get a horse-van!" he said to his grooms, "clap the hussy into it, and send her, with my compliments, to his Majesty King Padella."

Along with his lovely prisoner, Hogginarmo sent a letter full of servile compliments and loathsome flatteries to King Padella, for whose life, and that of his royal family, the HYPOCRITICAL HUMBUG pretended to offer the most fulsome prayers. And Hogginarmo promised speedily to pay his humble homage at his august master's throne, of which he begged leave to be counted the most loyal and constant defender. Such a WARY old BIRD as King Padella was not to be caught by Master Hogginarmo's CHAFF and we shall hear presently how the tyrant treated his upstart vassal. No, no; depend on't, two such rogues do not trust one another.

So this poor Queen was laid in the straw like Margery Daw, and driven along in the dark ever so many miles to the Court, where King Padella had now arrived, having vanquished all his enemies, murdered most of them, and brought some of the richest into captivity with him for the purpose of torturing them and finding out where they had hidden their money.

Rosalba heard their shrieks and groans in the dungeon in which she was thrust; a most awful black hole, full of bats, rats, mice, toads, frogs, mosquitoes, bugs, fleas, serpents, and every kind of horror. No light was let into it, otherwise the gaolers might have seen her and fallen in love with her, as an owl that lived up in the roof of the tower did, and a cat, you know, who can see in the dark, and having set its green eyes on Rosalba, never would be got to go back to the turnkey's wife to whom it belonged. And the toads in the dungeon came and kissed her feet, and the vipers wound round her neck and arms, and never hurt her, so charming was this poor Princess in the midst of her misfortunes.

At last, after she had been kept in this place EVER SO LONG, the door of the dungeon opened, and the terrible KING PADELLA came in.

But what he said and did must be reserved for another chapter, as we must now back to Prince Giglio.

XIV. WHAT BECAME OF GIGLIO.

The idea of marrying such an old creature as Gruffanuff frightened Prince Giglio so, that he ran up to his room, packed his trunks, fetched in a couple of porters, and was off to the diligence office in a twinkling.

It was well that he was so quick in his operations, did not dawdle over his luggage, and took the early coach: for as soon as the mistake about Prince Bulbo was found out, that cruel Glumboso sent up a couple of policemen to Prince Giglio's room, with orders that he should be carried to Newgate, and his head taken off before twelve o'clock. But the coach was out of the Paflagonian dominions before two o'clock; and I dare say the express that was sent after Prince Giglio did not ride very quick, for many people in Paflagonia had a regard for Giglio, as the son of their old sovereign; a Prince who, with all his weaknesses, was very much better than his brother, the usurping, lazy, careless, passionate, tyrannical, reigning monarch. That Prince busied himself with the balls, fetes, masquerades, hunting-parties, and so forth, which he thought proper to give on occasion of his daughter's marriage to Prince Bulbo; and let us trust was not sorry in his own heart that his brother's son had escaped the scaffold.

It was very cold weather, and the snow was on the ground, and Giglio, who gave his name as simple Mr. Giles, was very glad to get a comfortable place in the coupe of the diligence, where he sat with the conductor and another gentleman. At the first stage from Blombodinga, as they stopped to change horses, there came up to the diligence a very ordinary, vulgar-looking woman, with a bag under her arm, who asked for a place. All the inside places were taken, and the young woman was informed that if she wished to travel, she must go upon the roof; and the passenger inside with Giglio (a rude person, I should think), put his head out of the window, and said, "Nice weather for travelling outside! I wish you a pleasant journey, my dear." The poor woman coughed very much, and Giglio pitied her. "I will give up my place to her," says he, "rather than she should travel in the cold air with that horrid cough." On which the vulgar traveller said, "YOU'D keep her warm, I am sure, if it's a MUFF she wants." On which Giglio pulled his nose, boxed his ears, hit him in the eye, and gave this vulgar person a warning never to call him MUFF again.

Then he sprang up gaily on to the roof of the diligence, and made himself very comfortable in the straw. The vulgar traveller got down only at the next station, and Giglio took his place again, and talked to the person next to him. She appeared to be a most agreeable, well-informed, and entertaining female. They travelled together till night, and she gave Giglio all sorts of things out of the bag which she carried, and which indeed seemed to contain the most wonderful collection of articles. He was thirsty —out there came a pint bottle of Bass's pale ale, and a silver mug! Hungry — she took out a cold fowl, some slices of ham, bread, salt, and a most delicious piece of cold plum-pudding, and a little glass of brandy afterwards.

As they travelled, this plain-looking, queer woman talked to Giglio on a variety of subjects, in which the poor Prince showed his ignorance as much as she did her capacity. He owned, with many blushes, how ignorant he was; on which the lady said, "My dear Gigl—my good Mr. Giles, you are a young man, and have plenty of time before you. You have nothing to do but to improve yourself. Who knows but that you may find use for your knowledge some day? When—when you may be wanted at home, as some people may be."

"Good heavens, madam!" says he, "do you know me?"

"I know a number of funny things," says the lady. "I have been at some people's christenings, and turned away from other folks' doors. I have seen some people spoilt by good fortune, and others, as I hope, improved by hardship. I advise you to stay at the town where the coach stops for the night. Stay there and study, and remember your old friend to whom you were kind."

"And who is my old friend?" asked Giglio.

"When you want anything," says the lady, "look in this bag, which I leave to you as a present, and be grateful to—"

"To whom, madam?" says he.

"To the Fairy Blackstick," says the lady, flying out of the window. And then Giglio asked the conductor if he knew where the lady was?

"What lady?" says the man; "there has been no lady in this coach, except the old woman, who got out at the last stage." And Giglio thought he had been dreaming. But there was the bag which Blackstick had given him lying on his lap; and when he came to the town he took it in his hand and went into the inn.

They gave him a very bad bedroom, and Giglio, when he woke in the morning, fancying himself in the Royal Palace at home, called, "John, Charles, Thomas! My chocolate—my dressing-gown—my slippers;" but nobody came. There was no bell, so he went and bawled out for water on the top of the stairs.

The landlady came up, looking—looking like this—

"What are you a-hollering and a-bellaring for here, young man?" says she.

"There's no warm water—no servants; my boots are not even cleaned."

"He, he! Clean 'em yourself," says the landlady. "You young students give yourselves pretty airs. I never heard such impudence."

"I'll quit the house this instant," says Giglio.

"The sooner the better, young man. Pay your bill and be off. All my rooms is wanted for gentlefolks, and not for such as you."

"You may well keep the Bear Inn," said Giglio. "You should have yourself painted as the sign."

The landlady of the Bear went away GROWLING. And Giglio returned to his room, where the first thing he saw was the fairy bag lying on the table, which seemed to give a little hop as he came in. "I hope it has some breakfast in it," says Giglio, "for I have only a very little money left." But on opening the bag, what do you think was there? A blacking brush and a pot of Warren's jet, and on the pot was written,

```
"Poor young men their boots must black:
  Use me and cork me and put me back."
```

So Giglio laughed and blacked his boots, and put back the brush and the bottle into the bag.

When he had done dressing himself, the bag gave another little hop, and he went to it and took out—

1. A tablecloth and a napkin.

2. A sugar-basin full of the best loaf-sugar.

4, 6, 8, 10. Two forks, two teaspoons, two knives, and a pair of sugar-tongs, and a butter-knife all marked G.

11, 12, 13. A teacup, saucer, and slop-basin.

14. A jug full of delicious cream.

15. A canister with black tea and green.

16. A large tea-urn and boiling water.

17. A saucepan, containing three eggs nicely done.

18. A quarter of a pound of best Epping butter.

19. A brown loaf.

And if he hadn't enough now for a good breakfast, I should like to know who ever had one?

Giglio, having had his breakfast, popped all the things back into the bag, and went out looking for lodgings. I forgot to say that this celebrated university town was called Bosforo.

He took a modest lodging opposite the Schools, paid his bill at the inn, and went to his apartment with his trunk, carpet-bag, and not forgetting, we may be sure, his OTHER bag.

When he opened his trunk, which the day before he had filled with his best clothes, he found it contained only books. And in the first of them which he opened there was written—

```
"Clothes for the back, books for the head:
 Read, and remember them when they are read."
```

And in his bag, when Giglio looked in it, he found a student's cap and gown, a writing-book full of paper, an inkstand, pens, and a Johnson's dictionary, which was very useful to him, as his spelling had been sadly neglected.

So he sat down and worked away, very, very hard for a whole year, during which "Mr. Giles" was quite an example to all the students in the University of Bosforo. He never got into any riots or disturbances. The Professors all spoke well of him, and the students liked him too; so that, when at examination, he took all the prizes, viz.:—

```
{The Spelling Prize        {The French Prize
{The Writing Prize         {The Arithmetic Prize
{The History Prize         {The Latin Prize
{The Catechism Prize       {The Good Conduct Prize,
```

all his fellow-students said, "Hurrah! Hurray for Giles! Giles is the boy —the student's joy! Hurray for Giles!" And he brought quite a quantity of medals, crowns, books, and tokens of distinction home to his lodgings.

One day after the Examinations, as he was diverting himself at a coffee-house with two friends—(Did I tell you that in his bag, every Saturday night, he found just enough to pay his bills, with a guinea over, for pocket-money? Didn't I tell you? Well, he did, as sure as twice twenty makes forty-five)—he chanced to look in the Bosforo Chronicle, and read off, quite easily (for he could spell, read, and write the longest words now), the following:—

"ROMANTIC CIRCUMSTANCE.—One of the most extraordinary adventures that we have ever heard has set the neighboring country of Crim Tartary in a state of great excitement.

"It will be remembered that when the present revered sovereign of Crim Tartary, his Majesty King PADELLA, took possession of the throne, after having vanquished, in the terrific battle of Blunderbusco, the late King CAVOLFIORE, that Prince's only child, the Princess Rosalba, was not found in the royal palace, of which King Padella took possession, and, it was said, had strayed into the forest (being abandoned by all her attendants) where she had been eaten up by those ferocious lions, the last pair of which were captured some time since, and brought to the Tower, after killing several hundred persons.

"His Majesty King Padella, who has the kindest heart in the world, was grieved at the accident which had occurred to the harmless little Princess, for whom his Majesty's known benevolence would certainly have provided a fitting establishment. But her death seemed to be certain. The mangled remains of a cloak, and a little shoe, were found in the forest, during a hunting-party, in which the intrepid sovereign of Crim Tartary slew two of the lions' cubs with his own spear. And these interesting relics of an innocent little creature were carried home and kept by their finder, the Baron Spinachi, formerly an officer in Cavolfiore's household. The Baron was disgraced in consequence of his known legitimist opinions, and has lived for some time in the humble capacity of a wood-cutter, in a forest on the outskirts of the Kingdom of Crim Tartary.

"Last Tuesday week Baron Spinachi and a number of gentlemen, attached to the former dynasty, appeared in arms, crying, "God save Rosalba, the first Queen of Crim Tartary!" and surrounding a lady whom report describes as "BEAUTIFUL EXCEEDINGLY." Her history MAY be authentic, IS certainly most romantic.

"The personage calling herself Rosalba states that she was brought out of the forest, fifteen years since, by a lady in a car drawn by dragons (this account is certainly IMPROBABLE), that she was left in the Palace Garden of Blombodinga, where Her Royal Highness the Princess Angelica, now married to His Royal Highness Bulbo, Crown Prince of Crim Tartary, found the child, and, with THAT ELEGANT BENEVOLENCE which has always distinguished the heiress of the throne of Paflagonia, gave the little outcast a SHELTER AND A HOME! Her parentage not being known, and her garb very humble, the foundling was educated in the Palace in a menial capacity, under the name of BETSINDA.

"She did not give satisfaction, and was dismissed, carrying with her, certainly, part of a mantle and a shoe, which she had on when first found. According to her statement she quitted Blombodinga about a year ago, since which time she has been with the Spinachi family. On the very same morning the Prince Giglio, nephew to the King of Paflagonia, a young Prince whose character for TALENT and ORDER were, to say truth, NONE OF THE HIGHEST, also quitted Blombodinga, and has not been since heard of!"

"What an extraordinary story!" said Smith and Jones, two young students, Giglio's especial friends.

"Ha! what is this?" Giglio went on, reading:—

"SECOND EDITION, EXPRESS.—We hear that the troop under Baron Spinachi has been surrounded, and utterly routed, by General Count Hogginarmo, and the soi-disant Princess is sent a prisoner to the capital.

"UNIVERSITY NEWS.—Yesterday, at the Schools, the distinguished young student, Mr. Giles, read a Latin oration, and was complimented by the Chancellor of Bosforo, Dr. Prugnaro, with the highest University honor —the wooden spoon."

"Never mind that stuff," says GILES, greatly disturbed. "Come home with me, my friends. Gallant Smith! intrepid Jones! friends of my studies— partakers of my academic toils—I have that to tell which shall astonish your honest minds."

"Go it, old boy!" cries the impetuous Smith.

"Talk away, my buck!" says Jones, a lively fellow.

With an air of indescribable dignity, Giglio checked their natural, but no more seemly, familiarity. "Jones, Smith, my good friends," said the PRINCE, "disguise is henceforth useless; I am no more the humble student Giles, I am the descendant of a royal line."

"Atavis edite regibus. I know, old co—" cried Jones. He was going to say old cock, but a flash from THE ROYAL EYE again awed him.

"Friends," continued the Prince, "I am that Giglio: I am, in fact, Paflagonia. Rise, Smith, and kneel not in the public street. Jones, thou true heart! My faithless uncle, when I was a baby, filched from me that brave crown my father left me, bred me, all young and careless of my rights, like unto hapless Hamlet, Prince of Denmark; and had I any thoughts about my wrongs, soothed me with promises of near redress. I should espouse his daughter, young Angelica; we two indeed should reign in Paflagonia. His words were false—false as Angelica's heart!—false as Angelica's hair, color, front teeth! She looked with her skew eyes upon young Bulbo, Crim Tartary's stupid heir, and she preferred him." Twas then I turned my eyes upon Betsinda—Rosalba, as she now is. And I saw in her the blushing sum of all perfection; the pink of maiden modesty; the nymph that my fond heart had ever woo'd in dreams,"

(I don't give this speech, which was very fine, but very long; and though Smith and Jones knew nothing about the circumstances, my dear reader does, so I go on.)

The Prince and his young friends hastened home to his apartment, highly excited by the intelligence, as no doubt by the ROYAL NARRATOR'S admirable manner of recounting it, and they ran up to his room where he had worked so hard at his books.

On his writing-table was his bag, grown so long that the Prince could not help remarking it. He went to it, opened it, and what do you think he found in it?

A splendid long, gold-handled, red-velvet-scabbarded, cut-and- thrust sword, and on the sheath was embroidered "ROSALBA FOR EVER!"

He drew out the sword, which flashed and illuminated the whole room, and called out "Rosalba for ever!" Smith and Jones following him, but quite respectfully this time, and taking the time from His Royal Highness.

And now his trunk opened with a sudden pong, and out there came three ostrich feathers in a gold crown, surrounding a beautiful shining steel helmet, a cuirass, a pair of spurs, finally a complete suit of armor.

The books on Giglio's shelves were all gone. Where there had been some great dictionaries, Giglio's friends found two pairs of jack- boots labelled, "Lieutenant Smith," "—— Jones, Esq.," which fitted them to a nicety. Besides, there were helmets, back and breast plates, swords, just like in Mr. G. P. R. James's novels; and that evening three cavaliers might have been seen issuing from the gates of Bosforo, in whom the porters, proctors, never thought of recognising the young Prince and his friends.

They got horses at a livery stable-keeper's, and never drew bridle until they reached the last town on the frontier before you come to Crim Tartary. Here, as their animals were tired, and the cavaliers hungry, they stopped and refreshed at an hostel. I could make a chapter of this if I were like some writers, but I like to cram my measure tight down, you see, and give you a great deal for your money, and, in a word, they had some bread and cheese and ale upstairs on the balcony of the inn. As they were drinking, drums and trumpets sounded nearer and nearer, the marketplace was filled with soldiers, and His Royal Highness looking forth, recognised the Paflagonian banners, and the Paflagonian national air which the bands were playing.

The troops all made for the tavern at once, and as they came up Giglio exclaimed, on beholding their leader, "Whom do I see? Yes!— no! It is, it is!—Phoo!—No, it can't be! Yes! it is my friend, my gallant faithful veteran, Captain Hedzoff! Ho, Hedzoff! Knowest thou not thy Prince, thy Giglio? Good Corporal, methinks we once were friends. Ha, Sergeant, an my memory serves me right, we have had many a bout at singlestick."

"I' faith, we have, a many, good my Lord," says the Sergeant.

"Tell me, what means this mighty armament," continued His Royal Highness from the balcony, "and whither march my Paflagonians?"

Hedzoff's head fell. "My Lord," he said, "we march as the allies of great Padella, Crim Tartary's monarch."

"Crim Tartary's usurper, gallant Hedzoff! Crim Tartary's grim tyrant, honest Hedzoff!" said the Prince, on the balcony, quite sarcastically.

"A soldier, Prince, must needs obey his orders: mine are to help his Majesty Padella. And also (though alack that I should say it!) to seize wherever I should light upon him—"

"First catch your hare! ha, Hedzoff!" exclaimed His Royal Highness.

"—On the body of GIGLIO, whilome Prince of Paflagonia' Hedzoff went on, with indescribable emotion. "My Prince, give up your sword without ado. Look! we are thirty thousand men to one!"

"Give up my sword! Giglio give up his sword!" cried the Prince; and stepping well forward on to the balcony, the royal youth, WITHOUT PREPARATION, delivered a speech so magnificent, that no report can do justice to it. It was all in blank verse (in which, from this time, he invariably spoke, as more becoming his majestic station). It lasted for three days and three nights, during which not a single person who heard him was tired, or remarked the difference between daylight and dark. The soldiers only cheering tremendously, when occasionally, once in nine hours, the Prince paused to suck an orange, which Jones took out of the bag. He explained, in terms which we say we shall not attempt to convey, the whole history of the previous transaction, and his determination not only not to give up his sword, but to assume his rightful crown; and at the end of this extraordinary, this truly GIGANTIC effort, Captain Hedzoff flung up his helmet, and cried, "Hurray! Hurray! Long live King Giglio!"

Such were the consequences of having employed his time well at College!

When the excitement had ceased, beer was ordered out for the army, and their Sovereign himself did not disdain a little! And now it was with some alarm that Captain Hedzoff told him his division was only the advanced guard of the Paflagonian contingent, hastening to King Padella's aid; the main force being a day's march in the rear under His Royal Highness Prince Bulbo.

"We will wait here, good friend, to beat the Prince," his Majesty said, "and THEN will make his royal father wince."

XV. WE RETURN TO ROSALBA.

King Padella made very similar proposals to Rosalba to those which she had received from the various princes who, as we have seen, had fallen in love with her. His Majesty was a widower, and offered to marry his fair captive that instant, but she declined his invitation in her usual polite gentle manner, stating that Prince Giglio was her love, and that any other union was out of the question. Having tried tears and supplications in vain, this violent-tempered monarch menaced her with threats and tortures; but she declared she would rather suffer all these than accept the hand of her father's murderer, who left her finally, uttering the most awful imprecations, and bidding her prepare for death on the following morning.

All night long the King spent in advising how he should get rid of this obdurate young creature. Cutting off her head was much too easy a death for her; hanging was so common in his Majesty's dominions that it no longer afforded him any sport; finally, he bethought himself of a pair of fierce lions which had lately been sent to him as presents, and he determined, with these ferocious brutes, to hunt poor Rosalba down. Adjoining his castle was an amphitheatre where the Prince indulged in bull-baiting, rat- hunting, and other ferocious sports. The two lions were kept in a cage under this place; their roaring might be heard over the whole city, the inhabitants of which, I am sorry to say, thronged in numbers to see a poor young lady gobbled up by two wild beasts.

The King took his place in the royal box, having the officers of his Court around and the Count Hogginarmo by his side, upon whom his Majesty was observed to look very fiercely: the fact is, royal spies had told the monarch of Hogginarmo's behavior, his proposals to Rosalba, and his offer to fight for the crown. Black as thunder looked King Padella at this proud noble, as they sat in the front seats of the theatre waiting to see the tragedy whereof poor Rosalba was to be the heroine.

At length that Princess was brought out in her nightgown, with all her beautiful hair falling down her back, and looking so pretty that even the beef-eaters and keepers of the wild animals wept plentifully at seeing her. And she walked with her poor little feet (only luckily the arena was covered with sawdust), and went and leaned up against a great stone in the centre of the amphitheatre, round which the Court and the people were seated in boxes, with bars before them, for fear of the great, fierce, red- maned, black-throated, long-tailed, roaring, bellowing, rushing lions.

And now the gates were opened, and with a "Wurrawarrurawarar!" two great lean, hungry, roaring lions rushed out of their den, where they had been kept for three weeks on nothing but a little toast- and-water, and dashed straight up to the stone where poor Rosalba was waiting. Commend her to your patron saints, all you kind people, for she is in a dreadful state!

There was a hum and a buzz all through the circus, and the fierce King Padella even felt a little compassion. But Count Hogginarmo, seated by his Majesty, roared out "Hurray! Now for it! Soo-soo- soo!" that nobleman being uncommonly angry still at Rosalba's refusal of him.

But, O strange event! O remarkable circumstance! O extraordinary coincidence, which I am sure none of you could BY ANY POSSIBILITY have divined! When the lions came to Rosalba, instead of devouring her with their great teeth, it was with kisses they gobbled her up! They licked her pretty feet, they nuzzled their noses in her lap, they moo'd, they seemed to say, "Dear, dear sister don't you recollect your brothers in the forest?" And she put her pretty white arms round their tawny necks, and kissed them.

King Padella was immensely astonished. The Count Hogginarmo was extremely disgusted. "Pooh!" the Count cried. "Gammon!" exclaimed his Lordship. "These lions are tame beasts come from Wombwell's or Astley's. It is a shame to put people off in this way. I believe they are little boys dressed up in door-mats. They are no lions at all."

"Ha!" said the King, "you dare to say 'Gammon!' to your Sovereign, do you? These lions are no lions at all, aren't they? Ho! my beef-eaters! Ho! my bodyguard! Take this Count Hogginarmo and fling him into the circus! Give him a sword and buckler, let him keep his armor on, and his weather-eye out, and fight these lions."

The haughty Hogginarmo laid down his opera-glass, and looked scowling round at the King and his attendants. "Touch me not, dogs!" he said, "or by St. Nicholas the Elder, I will gore you! Your Majesty thinks Hogginarmo is afraid? No, not of a hundred thousand lions! Follow me down into the circus, King Padella, and match thyself against one of yon brutes. Thou darest not. Let them both come on, then!" And opening a grating of the box, he jumped lightly down into the circus.

<pre>
WURRA WURRA WURRA WUR-AW-AW-AW!!!
        In about two minutes
       The Count Hogginarmo was
             GOBBLED UP
                  by
             those lions,
         bones, boots, and all,
                 and
            There was an
             End of him.
</pre>

At this, the King said, "Serve him right, the rebellious ruffian! And now, as those lions won't eat that young woman—"

"Let her off!—let her off!" cried the crowd.

"NO!" roared the King. "Let the beef-eaters go down and chop her into small pieces. If the lions defend her, let the archers shoot them to death. That hussy shall die in tortures!"

"A-a-ah!" cried the crowd. "Shame! shame!"

"Who dares cry out 'Shame?'" cried the furious potentate (so little can tyrants command their passions). "Fling any scoundrel who says a word down among the lions!" I warrant you there was a dead silence then, which was broken by a "Pang arang pang pangkarangpang!" and a Knight and a Herald rode in at the further end of the circus; the Knight, in full armor, with his vizor up, and bearing a letter on the point of his lance.

"Ha!" exclaimed the King, "by my fay, 'tis Elephant and Castle, pursuivant of my brother of Paflagonia; and the Knight, an my memory serves me, is the gallant Captain Hedzoff! What news from Paflagonia, gallant Hedzoff? Elephant and Castle, beshrew me, thy trumpeting must have made thee thirsty. What will my trusty herald like to drink?"

"Bespeaking first safe conduct from your Lordship," said Captain Hedzoff, "before we take a drink of anything, permit us to deliver our King's message."

"My Lordship, ha!" said Crim Tartary, frowning terrifically. "That title soundeth strange in the anointed ears of a crowned King. Straightway speak out your message, Knight and Herald!"

Reining up his charger in a most elegant manner close under the King's balcony, Hedzoff turned to the Herald, and bade him begin.

Elephant and Castle, dropping his trumpet over his shoulder, took a large sheet of paper out of his hat, and began to read:—

"O Yes! O Yes! O Yes! Know all men by these presents, that we, Giglio, King of Paflagonia, Grand Duke of Cappadocia, Sovereign Prince of Turkey and the Sausage Islands, having assumed our rightful throne and title, long time falsely borne by our usurping Uncle, styling himself King of Paflagonia—"

"Ha!" growled Padella.

"Hereby summon the false traitor, Padella, calling himself King of Crim Tartary—"

The King's curses were dreadful. "Go on, Elephant and Castle!" said the intrepid Hedzoff.

"—To release from cowardly imprisonment his liege lady and rightful Sovereign, ROSALBA, Queen of Crim Tartary, and restore her to her royal throne: in default of which, I, Giglio, proclaim the said Padella sneak, traitor, humbug, usurper, and coward. I challenge him to meet me, with fists or with pistols, with battle- axe or sword, with blunderbuss or single-stick, alone or at the head of his army, on foot or on horseback; and will prove my words upon his wicked ugly body!"

"God save the King!" said Captain Hedzoff, executing a demivolte, two semilunes, and three caracols.

"Is that all?" said Padella, with the terrific calm of concentrated fury.

"That, sir, is all my royal master's message. Here is his Majesty's letter in autograph, and here is his glove, and if any gentleman of Crim Tartary chooses to find fault with his Majesty's expressions, I, Kustasoff Hedzoff, Captain of the Guard, am very much at his service," and he waved his lance, and looked at the assembly all round.

"And what says my good brother of Paflagonia, my dear son's father- in- law, to this rubbish?" asked the King.

"The King's uncle hath been deprived of the crown he unjustly wore," said Hedzoff gravely. "He and his ex-minister, Glumboso, are now in prison waiting the sentence of my royal master. After the battle of Bombardaro—"

"Of what?" asked the surprised Padella.

"—Of Bombardaro, where my liege, his present Majesty, would have performed prodigies of valor, but that the whole of his uncle's army came over to our side, with the exception of Prince Bulbo—"

"Ah! my boy, my boy, my Bulbo was no traitor!" cried Padella.

"Prince Bulbo, far from coming over to us, ran away, sir; but I caught him. The Prince is a prisoner in our army, and the most terrific tortures await him if a hair of the Princess Rosalba's head is injured."

"Do they?" exclaimed the furious Padella, who was now perfectly LIVID with rage. "Do they indeed? So much the worse for Bulbo. I've twenty sons as lovely each as Bulbo. Not one but is as fit to reign as Bulbo. Whip, whack, flog, starve, rack, punish, torture Bulbo—break all his bones —roast him or flay him alive—pull all his pretty teeth out one by one! But justly dear as Bulbo is to me,—joy of my eyes, fond treasure of my soul!— Ha, ha, ha, ha! revenge is dearer still. Ho! tortures, rack-men, executioners — light up the fires and make the pincers hot! get lots of boiling lead!— Bring out ROSALBA!"

XVI. HOW HEDZOFF RODE BACK AGAIN TO KING GIGLIO.

Captain Hedzoff rode away when King Padella uttered this cruel command, having done his duty in delivering the message with which his royal master had entrusted him. Of course he was very sorry for Rosalba, but what could he do?

So he returned to King Giglio's camp, and found the young monarch in a disturbed state of mind, smoking cigars in the royal tent. His Majesty's agitation was not appeased by the news that was brought by his ambassador. "The brutal, ruthless ruffian royal wretch!" Giglio exclaimed. "As England's poesy has well remarked, 'The man that lays his hand upon a woman, save in the way of kindness, is a villain.' Ha, Hedzoff!"

"That he is, your Majesty," said the attendant.

"And didst thou see her flung into the oil? and didn't the soothing oil—the emollient oil, refuse to boil, good Hedzoff—and to spoil the fairest lady ever eyes did look on?"

"'Faith, good my liege, I had no heart to look and see a beauteous lady boiling down; I took your royal message to Padella, and bore his back to you. I told him you would hold Prince Bulbo answerable. He only said that he had twenty sons as good as Bulbo, and forthwith he bade the ruthless executioners proceed."

"O cruel father—O unhappy son!" cried the King. "Go, some of you, and bring Prince Bulbo hither."

Bulbo was brought in chains, looking very uncomfortable. Though a prisoner, he had been tolerably happy, perhaps because his mind was at rest, and all the fighting was over, and he was playing at marbles with his guards when the King sent for him.

"Oh, my poor Bulbo," said his Majesty, with looks of infinite compassion, "hast thou heard the news?" (for you see Giglio wanted to break the thing gently to the Prince), "thy brutal father has condemned Rosalba—p-p-p-ut her to death, P-p-p-prince Bulbo!"

"What, killed Betsinda! Boo-hoo-hoo," cried out Bulbo. "Betsinda! pretty Betsinda! dear Betsinda! She was the dearest little girl in the world. I love her better twenty thousand times even than Angelica." And he went on expressing his grief in so hearty and unaffected a manner that the King was quite touched by it, and said, shaking Bulbo's hand, that he wished he had known Bulbo sooner.

Bulbo, quite unconsciously, and meaning for the best, offered to come and sit with his Majesty, and smoke a cigar with him, and console him. The ROYAL KINDNESS supplied Bulbo with a cigar; he had not had one, he said, since he was taken prisoner.

And now think what must have been the feelings of the most MERCIFUL OF MONARCHS, when he informed his prisoner that, in consequence of King Padella's CRUEL AND DASTARDLY BEHAVIOR to Rosalba, Prince Bulbo must instantly be executed! The noble Giglio could not restrain his tears, nor could the Grenadiers, nor the officers, nor could Bulbo himself, when the matter was explained to him, and he was brought to understand that his Majesty's promise, of course, was ABOVE EVERYTHING, and Bulbo must submit. So poor Bulbo was led out, Hedzoff trying to console him, by pointing out that if he had won the battle of Bombardaro, he might have hanged Prince Giglio. "Yes! But that is no comfort to me now!" said poor Bulbo; nor indeed was it, poor fellow!

He was told the business would be done the next morning at eight, and was taken back to his dungeon, where every attention was paid to him. The gaoler's wife sent him tea, and the turnkey's daughter begged him to write his name in her album, where a many gentlemen had written it on like occasions! "Bother your album!" says Bulbo. The Undertaker came and measured him for the handsomest coffin which money could buy: even this didn't console Bulbo. The Cook brought him dishes which he once used to like; but he wouldn't touch them: he sat down and began writing an adieu to Angelica, as the clock kept always ticking, and the hands drawing nearer to next morning. The Barber came in at night, and offered to shave him for the next day. Prince Bulbo kicked him away, and went on writing a few words to Princess Angelica, as the clock kept always ticking, and the hands hopping nearer and nearer to next morning. He got up on the top of a hatbox, on the top of a chair, on the top of his bed, on the top of his table, and looked out to see whether he might escape as the clock kept always ticking and the hands drawing nearer, and nearer, and nearer.

But looking out of the window was one thing, and jumping another: and the town clock struck seven. So he got into bed for a little sleep, but the gaoler came and woke him, and said, "Git up, your Royal Ighness, if you please, it's TEN MINUTES TO EIGHT!"

So poor Bulbo got up: he had gone to bed in his clothes (the lazy boy), and he shook himself, and said he didn't mind about dressing, or having any breakfast, thank you; and he saw the soldiers who had come for him. "Lead on!" he said; and they led the way, deeply affected; and they came into the courtyard, and out into the square, and there was King Giglio come to take leave of him, and his Majesty most kindly shook hands with him, and the GLOOMY PROCESSION marched on:—when hark!

"Haw—wurraw—wurraw—aworr!"

A roar of wild beasts was heard. And who should come riding into the town, frightening away the boys, and even the beadle and policeman, but ROSALBA!

The fact is, that when Captain Hedzoff entered into the court of Snapdragon Castle, and was discoursing with King Padella, the Lions made a dash at the open gate, gobbled up the six beef-eaters in a jiffy, and away they went with Rosalba on the back of one of them, and they carried her, turn and turn about, till they came to the city where Prince Giglio's army was encamped.

When the KING heard of the QUEEN'S arrival, you may think how he rushed out of his breakfast-room to hand her Majesty off her Lion! The Lions were grown as fat as pigs now, having had Hogginarmo and all those beef-eaters, and were so tame, anybody might pat them.

While Giglio knelt (most gracefully) and helped the Princess, Bulbo, for his part, rushed up and kissed the Lion. He flung his arms round the forest monarch; he hugged him, and laughed and cried for joy. "Oh, you darling old beast—oh, how glad I am to see you, and the dear, dear Bets—that is, Rosalba."

"What, is it you, poor Bulbo?" said the Queen. "Oh, how glad I am to see you," and she gave him her hand to kiss. King Giglio slapped him most kindly on the back, and said, "Bulbo, my boy, I am delighted, for your sake, that her Majesty has arrived."

"So am I," said Bulbo; "and YOU KNOW WHY." Captain Hedzoff here came up. "Sire, it is half-past eight: shall we proceed with the execution? "

"Execution! what for?" asked Bulbo.

"An officer only knows his orders," replied Captain Hedzoff, showing his warrant: on which his Majesty King Giglio smilingly said Prince Bulbo was reprieved this time, and most graciously invited him to breakfast.

XVII. HOW A TREMENDOUS BATTLE TOOK PLACE,
AND WHO WON IT.

As soon as King Padella heard—what we know already—that his victim, the lovely Rosalba, had escaped him, his Majesty's fury knew no bounds, and he pitched the Lord Chancellor, Lord Chamberlain, and every officer of the Crown whom he could set eyes on, into the cauldron of boiling oil prepared for the Princess. Then he ordered out his whole army, horse, foot, and artillery; and set forth at the head of an innumerable host, and I should think twenty thousand drummers, trumpeters, and fifers.

King Giglio's advance guard, you may be sure, kept that monarch acquainted with the enemy's dealings, and he was in nowise disconcerted. He was much too polite to alarm the Princess, his lovely guest, with any unnecessary rumors of battles impending; on the contrary, he did everything to amuse and divert her; gave her a most elegant breakfast, dinner, lunch, and got up a ball for her that evening, when he danced with her every single dance.

Poor Bulbo was taken into favor again, and allowed to go quite free now. He had new clothes given him, was called "My good cousin" by his Majesty, and was treated with the greatest distinction by everybody. But it was easy to see he was very melancholy. The fact is, the sight of Betsinda, who looked perfectly lovely in an elegant new dress, set poor Bulbo frantic in love with her again. And he never thought about Angelica, now Princess Bulbo, whom he had left at home, and who, as we know, did not care much about him.

The King, dancing the twenty-fifth polka with Rosalba, remarked with wonder the ring she wore; and then Rosalba told him how she had got it from Gruffanuff, who no doubt had picked it up when Angelica flung it away.

"Yes," says the Fairy Blackstick, who had come to see the young people, and who had very likely certain plans regarding them—"that ring I gave the Queen, Giglio's mother, who was not, saving your presence, a very wise woman: it is enchanted, and whoever wears it looks beautiful in the eyes of the world. I made poor Prince Bulbo, when he was christened, the present of a rose which made him look handsome while he had it; but he gave it to Angelica, who instantly looked beautiful again, whilst Bulbo relapsed into his natural plainness."

"Rosalba needs no ring, I am sure," says Giglio, with a low bow. "She is beautiful enough, in my eyes, without any enchanted aid."

"Oh, sir!" said Rosalba.

"Take off the ring and try," said the King, and resolutely drew the ring off her finger. In HIS eyes she looked just as handsome as before!

The King was thinking of throwing the ring away, as it was so dangerous and made all the people so mad about Rosalba; but being a Prince of great humor, and good humor too, he cast eyes upon a poor youth who happened to be looking on very disconsolately, and said—

"Bulbo, my poor lad! come and try on this ring. The Princess Rosalba makes it a present to you." The magic properties of this ring were uncommonly strong, for no sooner had Bulbo put it on, but lo and behold, he appeared a personable, agreeable young Prince enough—with a fine complexion, fair hair, rather stout, and with bandy legs; but these were encased in such a beautiful pair of yellow morocco boots that nobody remarked them. And Bulbo's spirits rose up almost immediately after he had looked in the glass, and he talked to their Majesties in the most lively, agreeable manner, and danced opposite the Queen with one of the prettiest maids of honor, and after looking at her Majesty, could not help saying, "How very odd! she is very pretty, but not so EXTRAORDINARILY handsome." "Oh no, by no means!" says the Maid of Honor.

"But what care I, dear sir," says the Queen, who overheard them, "if YOU think I am good-looking enough?"

His Majesty's glance in reply to this affectionate speech was such that no painter could draw it. And the Fairy Blackstick said, "Bless you, my darling children! Now you are united and happy; and now you see what I said from the first, that a little misfortune has done you both good. YOU, Giglio, had you been bred in prosperity, would scarcely have learned to read or write—you would have been idle and extravagant, and could not have been a good King as now you will be. You, Rosalba, would have been so flattered, that your little head might have been turned like Angelica's, who thought herself too good for Giglio."

"As if anybody could be good enough for HIM," cried Rosalba.

"Oh, you, you darling!" says Giglio. And so she was; and he was just holding out his arms in order to give her a hug before the whole company, when a messenger came rushing in, and said, "My Lord, the enemy!"

"To arms!" cries Giglio.

"Oh, mercy!" says Rosalba, and fainted of course. He snatched one kiss from her lips, and rushed FORTH TO THE FIELD of battle!

The Fairy had provided King Giglio with a suit of armor, which was not only embroidered all over with jewels, and blinding to your eyes to look at, but was water-proof, gun-proof, and sword-proof; so that in the midst of the very hottest battles his Majesty rode about as calmly as if he had been a British Grenadier at Alma. Were I engaged in fighting for my country, I should like such a suit of armor as Prince Giglio wore; but, you know, he was a Prince of a fairy tale, and they always have these wonderful things.

Besides the fairy armor, the Prince had a fairy horse, which would gallop at any pace you pleased; and a fairy sword, which would lengthen and run through a whole regiment of enemies at once. With such a weapon at command, I wonder, for my part, he thought of ordering his army out; but forth they all came, in magnificent new uniforms, Hedzoff and the Prince's two college friends each commanding a division, and his Majesty prancing in person at the head of them all.

Ah! if I had the pen of a Sir Archibald Alison, my dear friends, would I not now entertain you with the account of a most tremendous shindy? Should not fine blows be struck? dreadful wounds be delivered? arrows darken the air? cannon balls crash through the battalions? cavalry charge infantry? infantry pitch into cavalry? bugles blow; drums beat; horses neigh; fifes sing; soldiers roar, swear, hurray; officers shout out, "Forward, my men!" "This way, lads!" "Give it 'em, boys!" "Fight for King Giglio, and the cause of right!" "King Padella for ever!" Would I not describe all this, I say, and in the very finest language too? But this humble pen does not possess the skill necessary for the description of combats. In a word, the overthrow of King Padella's army was so complete, that if they had been Russians you could not have wished them to be more utterly smashed and confounded.

As for that usurping monarch, having performed acts of valor much more considerable than could be expected of a royal ruffian and usurper, who had such a bad cause, and who was so cruel to women,— as for King Padella, I say, when his army ran away, the King ran away too, kicking his first general, Prince Punchikoff, from his saddle, and galloping away on the Prince's horse, having, indeed, had twenty-five or twenty-six of his own shot under him. Hedzoff coming up, and finding Punchikoff down, as you may imagine, very speedily disposed of HIM. Meanwhile King Padella was scampering off as hard as his horse could lay legs to ground. Fast as he scampered, I promise you somebody else galloped faster; and that individual, as no doubt you are aware, was the Royal Giglio, who kept bawling out, "Stay, traitor! Turn, miscreant, and defend thyself! Stand, tyrant, coward, ruffian, royal wretch, till I cut thy ugly head from thy usurping shoulders!" And, with his fairy sword, which elongated itself at will, his Majesty kept poking and prodding Padella in the back, until that wicked monarch roared with anguish.

When he was fairly brought to bay, Padella turned and dealt Prince Giglio a prodigious crack over the sconce with his battle-axe, a most enormous weapon, which had cut down I don't know how many regiments in the course of the afternoon. But, law bless you! though the blow fell right down on his Majesty's helmet, it made no more impression than if Padella had struck him with a pat of butter: his battle-axe crumpled up in Padella's hand, and the Royal Giglio laughed for very scorn at the impotent efforts of that atrocious usurper.

At the ill success of his blow the Crim Tartar monarch was justly irritated. "If," says he to Giglio, "you ride a fairy horse, and wear fairy armor, what on earth is the use of my hitting you? I may as well give myself up a prisoner at once. Your Majesty won't, I suppose, be so mean as to strike a poor fellow who can't strike again?"

The justice of Padella's remark struck the magnanimous Giglio. "Do you yield yourself a prisoner, Padella?" says he.

"Of course I do," says Padella.

"Do you acknowledge Rosalba as your rightful Queen, and give up the crown and all your treasures to your rightful mistress?"

"If I must, I must," says Padella, who was naturally very sulky.

By this time King Giglio's aides-de-camp had come up, whom his Majesty ordered to bind the prisoner. And they tied his hands behind him, and bound his legs tight under his horse, having set him with his face to the tail; and in this fashion he was led back to King Giglio's quarters, and thrust into the very dungeon where young Bulbo had been confined.

Padella (who was a very different person in the depth of his distress, to Padella, the proud wearer of the Crim Tartar crown), now most affectionately and earnestly asked to see his son—his dear eldest boy—his darling Bulbo; and that good-natured young man never once reproached his haughty parent for his unkind conduct the day before, when he would have left Bulbo to be shot without any pity, but came to see his father, and spoke to him through the grating of the door, beyond which he was not allowed to go; and brought him some sandwiches from the grand supper which his Majesty was giving above stairs, in honor of the brilliant victory which had just been achieved.

"I cannot stay with you long, sir," says Bulbo, who was in his best ball dress, as he handed his father in the prog. "I am engaged to dance the next quadrille with her Majesty Queen Rosalba, and I hear the fiddles playing at this very moment."

So Bulbo went back to the ball-room and the wretched Padella ate his solitary supper in silence and tears.

All was now joy in King Giglio's circle. Dancing, feasting, fun, illuminations, and jollifications of all sorts ensued. The people through whose villages they passed were ordered to illuminate their cottages at night, and scatter flowers on the roads during the day. They were requested —and I promise you they did not like to refuse— to serve the troops liberally with eatables and wine; besides, the army was enriched by the immense quantity of plunder which was found in King Padella's camp, and taken from his soldiers; who (after they had given up everything) were allowed to fraternize with the conquerors; and the united forces marched back by easy stages towards King Giglio's capital, his royal banner and that of Queen Rosalba being carried in front of the troops. Hedzoff was made a Duke and a Field Marshal. Smith and Jones were promoted to be Earls; the Crim Tartar Order of the Pumpkin and the Paflagonian decoration of the Cucumber were freely distributed by their Majesties to the army. Queen Rosalba wore the Paflagonian Ribbon of the Cucumber across her riding-habit, whilst King Giglio never appeared without the grand Cordon of the Pumpkin. How the people cheered them as they rode along side by side! They were pronounced to be the handsomest couple ever seen: that was a matter of course; but they really WERE very handsome, and, had they been otherwise, would have looked so, they were so happy! Their Majesties were never separated during the whole day, but breakfasted, dined, and supped together always, and rode side by side, interchanging elegant compliments, and indulging in the most delightful conversation. At night, her Majesty's ladies of honor (who had all rallied round her the day after King Padella's defeat) came and conducted her to the apartments prepared for her; whilst King Giglio, surrounded by his gentlemen, withdrew to his own Royal quarters. It was agreed they should be married as soon as they reached the capital, and orders were dispatched to the Archbishop of Blombodinga, to hold himself in readiness to perform the interesting ceremony. Duke Hedzoff carried the message, and gave instructions to have the Royal Castle splendidly refurnished and painted afresh. The Duke seized Glumboso, the Ex-Prime Minister, and made him refund that considerable sum of money which the old scoundrel had secreted out of the late King's treasure. He also clapped Valoroso into prison (who, by the way, had been dethroned for some considerable period past), and when the ex-monarch weakly remonstrated, Hedzoff said, "A soldier, sir, knows but his duty; my orders are to lock you up along with the ex-King Padella, whom I have brought hither a prisoner under guard." So these two ex-Royal personages were sent for a year to the House of Correction, and thereafter were obliged to become monks of the severest Order of Flagellants, in which state, by fasting, by vigils, by flogging (which they administered to one another, humbly but resolutely), no doubt they exhibited a repentance for their past misdeeds, usurpations, and private and public crimes.

As for Glumboso, that rogue was sent to the galleys, and never had an opportunity to steal any more.

XVIII. HOW THEY ALL JOURNEYED BACK TO THE CAPITAL.

The Fairy Blackstick, by whose means this young King and Queen had certainly won their respective crowns back, would come not unfrequently, to pay them a little visit—as they were riding in their triumphal progress towards Giglio's capital—change her wand into a pony, and travel by their Majesties' side, giving them the very best advice. I am not sure that King Giglio did not think the Fairy and her advice rather a bore, fancying it was his own valor and merits which had put him on his throne, and conquered Padella: and, in fine, I fear he rather gave himself airs towards his best friend and patroness. She exhorted him to deal justly by his subjects, to draw mildly on the taxes, never to break his promise when he had once given it—and in all respects to be a good King.

"A good King, my dear Fairy!" cries Rosalba. "Of course he will. Break his promise! can you fancy my Giglio would ever do anything so improper, so unlike him? No! never!" And she looked fondly towards Giglio, whom she thought a pattern of perfection.

"Why is Fairy Blackstick always advising me, and telling me how to manage my government, and warning me to keep my word? Does she suppose that I am not a man of sense, and a man of honor?" asks Giglio testily. "Methinks she rather presumes upon her position."

"Hush! dear Giglio," says Rosalba. "You know Blackstick has been very kind to us, and we must not offend her." But the Fairy was not listening to Giglio's testy observations, she had fallen back, and was trotting on her pony now, by Master Bulbo's side, who rode a donkey, and made himself generally beloved in the army by his cheerfulness, kindness, and good-humor to everybody. He was eager to see his darling Angelica. He thought there never was such a charming being. Blackstick did not tell him it was the possession of the magic rose that made Angelica so lovely in his eyes. She brought him the very best accounts of his little wife, whose misfortunes and humiliations had indeed very greatly improved her; and, you see, she could whisk off on her wand a hundred miles in a minute, and be back in no time, and so carry polite messages from Bulbo to Angelica, and from Angelica to Bulbo, and comfort that young man upon his journey.

When the Royal party arrived at the last stage before you reach Blombodinga, who should be in waiting, in her carriage there with her lady of honor by her side, but the Princess Angelica? She rushed into her husband's arms, scarcely stopping to make a passing curtsey to the King and Queen. She had no eyes but for Bulbo, who appeared perfectly lovely to her on account of the fairy ring which he wore; whilst she herself, wearing the magic rose in her bonnet, seemed entirely beautiful to the enraptured Bulbo.

A splendid luncheon was served to the Royal party, of which the Archbishop, the Chancellor, Duke Hedzoff, Countess Gruffanuff, and all our friends partook, the Fairy Blackstick being seated on the left of King Giglio, with Bulbo and Angelica beside her. You could hear the joy-bells ringing in the capital, and the guns which the citizens were firing off in honor of their Majesties.

"What can have induced that hideous old Gruffanuff to dress herself up in such an absurd way? Did you ask her to be your bridesmaid, my dear?" says Giglio to Rosalba. "What a figure of fun Gruffy is!"

Gruffy was seated opposite their Majesties, between the Archbishop and the Lord Chancellor, and a figure of fun she certainly was, for she was dressed in a low white silk dress, with lace over, a wreath of white roses on her wig, a splendid lace veil, and her yellow old neck was covered with diamonds. She ogled the King in such a manner that his Majesty burst out laughing.

"Eleven o'clock!" cries Giglio, as the great Cathedral bell of Blombodinga tolled that hour. "Gentlemen and ladies, we must be starting. Archbishop, you must be at church, I think, before twelve?"

"We must be at church before twelve," sighs out Gruffanuff in a languishing voice, hiding her old face behind her fan.

"And then I shall be the happiest man in my dominions," cries Giglio, with an elegant bow to the blushing Rosalba.

"Oh, my Giglio! Oh, my dear Majesty!" exclaims Gruffanuff; "and can it be that this happy moment at length has arrived—"

"Of course it has arrived," says the King.

"—and that I am about to become the enraptured bride of my adored Giglio!" continues Gruffanuff. "Lend me a smelling-bottle, somebody. I certainly shall faint with joy."

"YOU my bride?" roars out Giglio.

"YOU marry my Prince?" cried poor little Rosalba.

"Pooh! Nonsense! The woman's mad!" exclaims the King. And all the courtiers exhibited by their countenances and expressions, marks of surprise, or ridicule, or incredulity, or wonder.

"I should like to know who else is going to be married, if I am not?" shrieks out Gruffanuff. "I should like to know if King Giglio is a gentleman, and if there is such a thing as justice in Paflagonia? Lord Chancellor! my Lord Archbishop! will your Lordships sit by and see a poor, fond, confiding, tender creature put upon? Has not Prince Giglio promised to marry his Barbara? Is not this Giglio's signature? Does not this paper declare that he is mine, and only mine?" And she handed to his Grace the Archbishop the document which the Prince signed that evening when she wore the magic ring, and Giglio drank so much champagne. And the old Archbishop, taking out his eyeglasses, read—"This is to give notice, that I, Giglio, only son of Savio, King of Paflagonia, hereby promise to marry the charming Barbara Griselda Countess Gruffanuff, and widow of the late Jenkins Gruffanuff, Esq."

"H'm," says the Archbishop, "the document is certainly a—a document."

"Phoo!" says the Lord Chancellor, "the signature is not in his Majesty's handwriting." Indeed, since his studies at Bosforo, Giglio had made an immense improvement in caligraphy.

"Is it your handwriting, Giglio?" cries the Fairy Blackstick, with an awful severity of countenance.

"Y—y—y—es," poor Giglio gasps out, "I had quite forgotten the confounded paper: she can't mean to hold me by it. You old wretch, what will you take to let me off? Help the Queen, some one—her Majesty has fainted."

"Chop her head off!" } exclaim the impetuous Hedzoff, "Smother the old witch!" } the ardent Smith, and the "Pitch her into the river!"} faithful Jones.

But Gruffanuff flung her arms round the Archbishop's neck, and bellowed out, "Justice, justice, my Lord Chancellor!" so loudly, that her piercing shrieks caused everybody to pause. As for Rosalba, she was borne away lifeless by her ladies; and you may imagine the look of agony which Giglio cast towards that lovely being, as his hope, his joy, his darling, his all in all, was thus removed, and in her place the horrid old Gruffanuff rushed up to his side, and once more shrieked out, "Justice, justice!"

"Won't you take that sum of money which Glumboso hid?" says Giglio; "two hundred and eighteen thousand millions, or thereabouts. It's a handsome sum."

"I will have that and you too!" says Gruffanuff.

"Let us throw the crown jewels into the bargain," gasps out Giglio.

"I will wear them by my Giglio's side!" says Gruffanuff.

"Will half, three-quarters, five-sixths, nineteen-twentieths, of my kingdom do, Countess?" asks the trembling monarch.

"What were all Europe to me without YOU, my Giglio?" cries Gruff, kissing his hand.

"I won't, I can't, I shan't,—I'll resign the crown first," shouts Giglio, tearing away his hand; but Gruff clung to it.

"I have a competency, my love," she says, "and with thee and a cottage thy Barbara will be happy."

Giglio was half mad with rage by this time. "I will not marry her," says he. "Oh, Fairy, Fairy, give me counsel?" And as he spoke he looked wildly round at the severe face of the Fairy Blackstick.

"'Why is Fairy Blackstick always advising me, and warning me to keep my word? Does she suppose that I am not a man of honor?'" said the Fairy, quoting Giglio's own haughty words. He quailed under the brightness of her eyes; he felt that there was no escape for him from that awful inquisition.

"Well, Archbishop," said he in a dreadful voice, that made his Grace start, "since this Fairy has led me to the height of happiness but to dash me down into the depths of despair, since I am to lose Rosalba, let me at least keep my honor. Get up, Countess, and let us be married; I can keep my word, but I can die afterwards."

"Oh, dear Giglio," cries Gruffanuff, skipping up, "I knew, I knew I could trust thee—I knew that my Prince was the soul of honor. Jump into your carriages, ladies and gentlemen, and let us go to church at once; and as for dying, dear Giglio, no, no:—thou wilt forget that insignificant little chambermaid of a Queen—thou wilt live to be consoled by thy Barbara! She wishes to be a Queen, and not a Queen Dowager, my gracious Lord!" And hanging upon poor Giglio's arm, and leering and grinning in his face in the most disgusting manner, this old wretch tripped off in her white satin shoes, and jumped into the very carriage which had been got ready to convey Giglio and Rosalba to church. The cannons roared again, the bells pealed triple-bobmajors, the people came out flinging flowers upon the path

of the royal bride and bridegroom, and Gruff looked out of the gilt coach
window and bowed and grinned to them. Phoo! the horrid old wretch!

XIX. AND NOW WE COME TO THE LAST SCENE IN THE PANTOMIME.

The many ups and downs of her life had given the Princess Rosalba prodigious strength of mind, and that highly principled young woman presently recovered from her fainting-fit, out of which Fairy Blackstick, by a precious essence which the Fairy always carried in her pocket, awakened her. Instead of tearing her hair, crying, and bemoaning herself, and fainting again, as many young women would have done, Rosalba remembered that she owed an example of firmness to her subjects; and though she loved Giglio more than her life, was determined, as she told the Fairy, not to interfere between him and justice, or to cause him to break his royal word.

"I cannot marry him, but I shall love him always," says she to Blackstick; "I will go and be present at his marriage with the Countess, and sign the book, and wish them happy with all my heart. I will see, when I get home, whether I cannot make the new Queen some handsome presents. The Crim Tartary crown diamonds are uncommonly fine, and I shall never have any use for them. I will live and die unmarried like Queen Elizabeth, and, of course, I shall leave my crown to Giglio when I quit this world. Let us go and see them married, my dear Fairy, let me say one last farewell to him; and then, if you please, I will return to my own dominions."

So the Fairy kissed Rosalba with peculiar tenderness, and at once changed her wand into a very comfortable coach-and-four, with a steady coachman, and two respectable footmen behind, and the Fairy and Rosalba got into the coach, which Angelica and Bulbo entered after them. As for honest Bulbo, he was blubbering in the most pathetic manner, quite overcome by Rosalba's misfortune. She was touched by the honest fellow's sympathy, promised to restore to him the confiscated estates of Duke Padella his father, and created him, as he sat there in the coach, Prince, Highness, and First Grandee of the Crim Tartar Empire. The coach moved on, and, being a fairy coach, soon came up with the bridal procession.

Before the ceremony at church it was the custom in Paflagonia, as it is in other countries, for the bride and bridegroom to sign the Contract of Marriage, which was to be witnessed by the Chancellor, Minister, Lord Mayor, and principal officers of state. Now, as the royal palace was being painted and furnished anew, it was not ready for the reception of the King and his bride, who proposed at first to take up their residence at the Prince's palace, that one which Valoroso occupied when Angelica was born, and before he usurped the throne.

So the marriage party drove up to the palace: the dignitaries got out of their carriages and stood aside: poor Rosalba stepped out of her coach, supported by Bulbo, and stood almost fainting up against the railings so as to have a last look of her dear Giglio. As for Blackstick, she, according to her custom, had flown out of the coach window in some inscrutable manner, and was now standing at the palace door.

Giglio came up the steps with his horrible bride on his arm, looking as pale as if he was going to execution. He only frowned at the Fairy Blackstick—he was angry with her, and thought she came to insult his misery.

"Get out of the way, pray," says Gruffanuff haughtily. "I wonder why you are always poking your nose into other people's affairs?"

"Are you determined to make this poor young man unhappy?" says Blackstick.

"To marry him, yes! What business is it of yours? Pray, madam, don't say 'you' to a Queen," cries Gruffanuff.

"You won't take the money he offered you?"

"No."

"You won't let him off his bargain, though you know you cheated him when you made him sign the paper?"

"Impudence! Policemen, remove this woman!" cries Gruffanuff. And the policemen were rushing forward, but with a wave of her wand the Fairy struck them all like so many statues in their places.

"You won't take anything in exchange for your bond, Mrs. Gruffanuff," cries the Fairy, with awful severity. "I speak for the last time."

"No!" shrieks Gruffanuff, stamping with her foot. "I'll have my husband, my husband, my husband!"

"YOU SHALL HAVE YOUR HUSBAND!" the Fairy Blackstick cried; and advancing a step, laid her hand upon the nose of the KNOCKER.

As she touched it, the brass nose seemed to elongate, the open mouth opened still wider, and uttered a roar which made everybody start. The eyes rolled wildly; the arms and legs uncurled themselves, writhed about, and seemed to lengthen with each twist; the knocker expanded into a figure in yellow livery, six feet high; the screws by which it was fixed to the door unloosed themselves, and JENKINS GRUFFANUFF once more trod the threshold off which he had been lifted more than twenty years ago!

"Master's not at home," says Jenkins, just in his old voice; and Mrs. Jenkins, giving a dreadful YOUP, fell down in a fit, in which nobody minded her.

For everybody was shouting, "Huzzay! huzzay!" "Hip, hip, hurray!" "Long live the King and Queen!" "Were such things ever seen?" "No, never, never, never!" "The Fairy Blackstick for ever!"

The bells were ringing double peals, the guns roaring and banging most prodigiously. Bulbo was embracing everybody; the Lord Chancellor was flinging up his wig and shouting like a madman; Hedzoff had got the Archbishop round the waist, and they were dancing a jig for joy; and as for Giglio, I leave you to imagine what HE was doing, and if he kissed Rosalba once, twice—twenty thousand times, I'm sure I don't think he was wrong.

So Gruffanuff opened the hall door with a low bow, just as he had been accustomed to do, and they all went in and signed the book, and then they went to church and were married, and the Fairy Blackstick sailed away on her cane, and was never more heard of in Paflagonia.